THE RIGHT KIND OF WOMAN

D1607832

VOSS PORTER

The Right Kind of Woman

Copyright © 2015, Voss Porter

Published by Dark Hollows Press

To my wife,

Who will always fix what is broken.

In the Beginning

Andrea Marie Martin had been setting her alarm clock for 8a.m. every morning for the past ten years, weekends included. She had been an early riser almost as long as she had been known simply as 'Dre,' almost as long as she had been close-cutting her unruly black hair and almost as long as she had been renting refurbished industrial apartments in the aptly nicknamed 'Lesbian Capital of the World,' geographically known as South Waterton, Massachusetts.

As a web page designer who primarily worked from home, she supposed it wouldn't really matter what time she chose to rise and greet the day. She could sleep all day long if she wanted to. Statistically speaking, though, those who rose before nine were more likely to accomplish every task they had previously laid out, and she was one of those people who laid out what they were to do the upcoming morning during the evening of the night before (preferably while she took her second shower of the day). Plus, she told herself, Buddy was used to going to the bathroom by 8:15 a.m. He was far too old to change that now. He was far too set in his dog ways.

"Right?" she asked, looking down at the giant behemoth of a Labrador sprawled out on a plaid blanket on the floor beside her queen-sized bed.

The frameless Labrador on the floor raised an eye in response, and swiped his giant, floppy tail back and forth over the polished hardwoods. Long and lanky, with oddly soft chestnut brown hair, Buddy, was God only knew how old. She had been telling people he was only four for the past eight years. Time really seemed to fly once she had rescued him from the shelter. All lesbians had dogs, she knew full well. Or at least that was what the world told her. All lesbians had dogs and wore plaid and built things and sported men's haircuts and Converse sneakers.

For her part, Dre hated Converse sneakers. No arch support. But the rest, she supposed, was true enough if websites were substituted for woodshop projects.

At 8:03 a.m., she crawled out of bed, washed her face and pulled a pair of heather grey sweatpants over her boxer briefs. The last thing she needed was Old Miss Wentner, one of the only heteros in the entire complex, making more comments about her wardrobe, not that it upset her, really. Already in her eighties, Dre figured the geriatric, a Kentucky transplant, was having a hard enough time reconciling her men's haircut with the predetermined feminine ideal of the *Mad Men* era. Maybe there weren't any gay people in whatever hovel she crawled out of. Maybe it was just passed time for Lolly to grab ahold of the change. Regardless, theirs was a laughable pairing, as a misunderstanding of the gay community, as a whole, in an enclave that boasted more drum circles, street markets, and PFLAG chapters than any other city in the continental U.S. was ironic. Even the street signs were decorated with rainbows.

"I am not a woman prone to judgment," she was fond of saying, if ever she ran into Dre and Buddy in the elevator or on the stairwell (which was unavoidably regularly). "But a girl like you ought to have found a man by now, someone you can really settle down with."

Ha! The closest Dre had come to settling down in the past twenty-eight years was going Dutch on a coffee table from Brimfield with a librarian named Stephanie with whom cohabitating had never really felt like the greatest of plans. Reserved, emotionally needy and severe, Steph had three cats, all bearing the names of tertiary R.R. Martin characters. Cat people and dog people never really meshed well. When the whole thing ended, Buddy was more than relieved.

That had been a year ago.

Andrea had been single for a year.

"Come on," she snapped at the dog, even though he never did anything wrong and waited patiently by the door, leash in mouth, as she poured her first coffee of the day—black with only two teaspoons of sugar.

Standing around, reminding herself that she was in the singular did not make for the most pleasant of mornings, not that being alone was bothersome. She was uniquely self-sufficient; it was the main reason her career as a freelancer had been so successful. She was intrinsically motivated, quiet by nature, and, as it turned out, rather in demand. Two months after she had received her Bachelor's, she was offered a position with Corso, Inc., one of the largest web design firms in the country. They paid extremely well, never needed to converse, and alleviated any need to cold-call potential clients in order to market her abilities. When she was needed, they sent her specs and she churned out the product. Her schedule was set by her, so long as fulfilled her deadlines, and she could work while Buddy slept on her feet in the safety of her own space, a tidy one bedroom with brick facades and a wrought iron Juliet balcony that looked out over the public square in which the aforementioned drum circles and public markets occurred. One MacBook, one flat screen television, one iPhone… It was an ideal setup.

"It's not an ideal setup," she sighed, as she made her way down three flights of stairs to the commons area in the back, dotted with potted trees in varying shapes.

The Right Kind of Woman

The truth was, South Waterton had recently begun to smother her. That which blossomed from her collegiate dreams of lesbian equality had become some malicious, flat-lined contest, some rivalry of righteousness in which factions of the LGBTQ community waged war against one another by way of insults and failed stereotypes. Bras were out, shaving was out, fried food was out, pink was out… There were a litany of choices that supported the misogynistic expectations of the heterosexual community, there were at least a hundred different gay pride flags, entire closets were burned, and somehow, everything was the same. All of the people were the same. Having taken the impression of functioning carbon copies of one another with soy tea and sustainable agriculture, and urban farming and organic, paleo, gender-neutral beef, they were an assembly line of backwards vanilla progress, a parody of what was intended.

Buddy sauntered over to his favorite potty spot, just beside a metal bench, and Dre leaned back against a half-wall made of stone that, in England, would have appeared innately British.

The slow burn in her chest had grown to inordinate depths over the course of the past weeks. How could she expect a different outcome while living in the same place? How could she seek a different future while remaining in the same place, carved from stone? And what the hell would a future, away from where she stood, even look like? South Waterton was all she knew. It was all she had ever known, as an adult. South Waterton was home, whatever home was anymore. South Waterton was predictable, even in its attempts to push the purple envelopes of parenting and society and masculine femininity.

She could go back to Boston. Boston was nice. Boston was her childhood home. In Boston, she had attended grammar school and college, explored museums and absorbed the history of one of the most influential areas in the nation, both in terms of baseball and civilization. Boston had everything she could ever want, really. Except her family, or what billed itself as her family, was no longer in Boston, and had not been for quite some time, unless she identified her mother's grave as a member of the family. Jesus, it had been so long since she'd last seen it, she probably couldn't even remember where the cemetery was anymore.

A woman in her mid-twenties jogged past, with a small child succored in an ergonomic baby-wearing device—one of the strap-on contraptions that her friend, Sam, wore constantly, and nursed unabashedly in, even when they went to Target. Her hair was piled high up on her head, the back of her neck exposed. That was Dre's favorite spot, the back of the neck. But it had been a hundred years since she felt any inclination in that area, which led her to the increasingly likely conclusion that her bits were broken.

"You're not broken," Sam and her partner (they said *partner*, not *wife* or *girlfriend* or *love*, which was still popular, it seemed), Tris, often said. "You just haven't found the right woman yet."

No. She hadn't found the right woman in all of South Waterton, which was another reason she thought she might be due for a change. How could she strike out in a place like South Waterton, where more than ninety percent of the population would address that euphemism as relating to softball? And if she was unlucky in the Lesbian Capital of the Free Fucking World, didn't she need to confront the possibility that she just needed to move on with her disastrously unlucky life? Buddy could use a warmer climate, one in which he wouldn't need to pee in three feet of snow, and, theoretically, she could fulfill the requirements of her job from anywhere with a Wi-Fi connection which was nearly all of the world, or at least all of the parts that she would ever want to go without a pineapple filled with liquor.

Seattle? Seattle wasn't necessarily *warmer* than Massachusetts, but there were houseboats in Seattle.

Or California? Everyone in California was happy, if common television programs were to be believed.

Buddy barked once and sat down on his haunches beside her, his fur wet with the early spring dew and frost that coated the nearly desolate communal space. He did not seem to want to commune much at 8ish a.m.

"You done?" Dre asked him.

He seemed to nod, so she trekked back to the complex she shared with about a dozen other lesbians, in various stages of maturation, all lumped together like plants in an incubator. There were two couples on the ground floor, the cheapest studio apartments, who were all of twenty-one, at their most grownup, and prone to loud, banjo-picking parties in the dead of winter. Their balconies, which were street-level and so close to the nearby restaurants that you could, hypothetically, order an appetizer and have it handed over the banister, were routinely covered in cigarette butts and empty liquor bottles from the discount shelf. Above them, a sundry of college students rented a series of larger apartments, splitting the astronomical rents three or four ways as college students were wont to do. One of them, Cassie or Cassidy or Cassandra-Cassanova something, worked for her campus radio station and winked at Dre when they were stuck together in the elevator. She was buxom, to say the least, with highlights she pretended were natural and cut-off shorts that she never seemed to fit into well enough to wear. Sam was convinced she was A Rouse, a faux-lesbian who went where the attention was, man, woman, or toad.

The Right Kind of Woman

"No real lesbian has long fingernails," was her rationale. "And no real lesbian dyes her hair like Dolly Parton."

That last part seemed like a stretch, but that was Sam: a stretch. She spent her days wearing her daughter, Willow, while mixing frappucinos at a lesbian-owned coffee shop downtown, which everyone knew was lesbian-owned because they put a sticker on the front door, as if to distinguish themselves from the seventy thousand other lesbian-owned SW businesses. In this environment, Sam also found her true calling: organizing rallies for a gay pride group with an incredibly long acronym that Dre could never get right. She wore her long, blonde hair (natural, not dyed) unkempt and plain, and had not shaved her legs in about fifteen years, though she never exposed them.

"I won't feed into any feminine ideal fabricated and perpetuated by the misogynistic entertainment goliaths in Hollywood," she declared. "I haven't touched a Bic since I had sex with a woman for the first time."

There were many occasions when Dre wondered if Sam's partner, Tristan, had any complaints about that area of the jungle. Much more methodical/Type A, and funny in the dry way that only a Type-A woman can be funny, Tris was as level-headed as they came, working full-time as an English teacher in a school district thirty miles away, driving a Subaru and shopping at Wal-Mart on the sly. She had close-cut dirty blonde hair and freckles that made her thirty-one years look more youthful than most. It was widely accepted that without her stern financial influence, Samantha would have been practically homeless, albeit happily so, probably growing vegetables in her back window and eating tofu hotdogs grilled on the radiator. When they decided to raise a child together, members of their close-knit community were noticeably shocked. "Lesbihonest," they all

7

seemed to say with their eyes, "we never saw these two really making it in the long run."

Squashing the haters on the daily, they lived one floor up from Dre, in a much-coveted three bedroom unit with a large, winding balcony and a storage closet where they hid their festive winter tree, the one Sam refused to call a Christmas tree, and three boxes of miscellaneous sexual accoutrements that Dre had been dying to open for years. What the hell had they been into? What treasures did these secret brown bins hold?

Hefting Buddy up the additional floor, she resisted the urge to peek, as she came up to their main door and knocked briefly before walking in as if she owned the place. It was Sunday and on Sundays, she and Buddy had breakfast with Tris and Sam and Willow, who was more often than not called Will and dressed in neutral colors and allowed to do pretty much whatever she wanted to do.

"Morning," she called out, swallowing the last of her coffee as Buddy leaped up onto the pristine cream sofa in the main living area. He would leave a pound of reddish mattes behind that Tris would dust bust away, but he was her family and she never seemed to mind much. "What's cooking?"

Sam poked her head through the kitchen, wearing a long brown skirt and plain white tee, and smiled. "A frittata. Soy bacon and mushrooms."

"Soy bacon and mushrooms? Sounds delicious." Dre lied, as she continued through the sprawling space, stepping over Will(ow), who was sucking on wooden blocks while lying on the artificial fur rug.

Soy bacon and mushrooms did not sound delicious.

One room over, not that the open concept gave way to rooms, Tris was seated at an antique dining table looking out over a full view of South Waterton, courtesy of floor-to-ceiling plate glass windows. She had a newspaper in her hand and a textbook opened before her bearing a stack of test papers sans grades.

"Working on a Sunday?" Dre asked, pouring herself another cup of coffee from the carafe on the whitewashed turquoise bar behind her.

"Hashtag teacher life," Tris half-laughed. "We can't all work when we choose." That had been her motto since college, having dedicated her life to educating the young while her best friend opted for a more creative, and vastly more lucrative, tech career.

"Yeah, yeah," Dre smiled.

"Oh, Dre!" Sam squealed, as she was the kind of woman who could squeal and still claim to be a feminist. "I met someone who's perfect for you!"

Tris rolled her green eyes. "Not Gina," she muttered, holding out the sports section.

"Yes, Gina!" Sam corrected. "*Professor* Gina Laudsdale."

She pronounced professor like it was an achievement, but in a place like South Waterton, a sleeper cell for local universities, professors were literally a dime a dozen. And they were all professors of subjects like Gender Studies or Women's Liberation, never Biology or Chemical Engineering.

"She's wonderful. She's a volunteer down at the center." Sam had gone back to her post in the kitchen, though she was very clear she only cooked because she was better at it, she was very seriously not falling into a gender role.

"So she's militant?" Dre rubbed her temple while skimming for any interesting sports highlights.

"They prefer the term militarized," Tris quipped, without looking up.

"She's brilliant and compassionate and you'd love her," Sam replied, ignoring their sarcasm as she skillfully chopped a green pepper, the sound of her knife hitting the butcher block cutting board a quiet thud behind the plea of her words. "She's so good with the LGBTQ youth. It's very inspiring to see."

"Babe," Tris said too-sweetly, "Gina's pretentious."

"She's not pretentious," there was no anger in her words, but Dre could sense it was something of a point of contention between her friends, who were so wildly different it was no wonder they could not see eye-to-eye on Dr. G. "She's outspoken. She considers herself a voice for people who don't have one."

It wasn't the first time that Sam had attempted to play match-maker. She was the Queen of "I Found Someone and She's PERFECT For You!" Only, they never were. She had been responsible for Cat Lady Stephanie, and for three ill-fated blind dates before that, one of whom had confessed to being more into men, but not so much since her ex-husband had split with their babysitter.

Handing over the Business section of the South Waterton Times, Tris continued, with no malice in her words, only patient insistence. "Her Facebook is pretentious."

Sam slapped a spatula down. "Everyone's Facebook is pretentious. The concept of Facebook is pretentious."

They were separated by a thin wall bearing a geodesic patter constructed using framed leaf rubbings and Dre was incredibly grateful that Samantha's face was obscured from view. There were times it was awkward to be so close to them both and she had no desire to add fuel to their marital dispute.

"Actually, I think I'm done with dating for a while," she interrupted, coyly changing the subject. "I'm thinking of making a bigger change."

Out of the corner of her eye, she watched Sam sprinkle a garnish on their frittata. "What kind of a change?"

Dre shrugged. "I don't know. Just…something."

"Something? That's vague," Tris postulated, looked up at her then. "What exactly are you getting at?

Again, Dre shrugged. "I don't know," she said, because that was not a lie. "There's something I miss, something I don't have."

"A woman," both Tristan and Samantha said, simultaneously.

"No, not a woman. Something bigger." At least, Andrea felt like it was something bigger. Direction, perhaps. A home?

"I don't like this," Sam used a pizza cutter to divide the egg pie. "I don't like where this is coming from." And that was a fair statement. Dre was not even certain where it was coming from. It was just there, this snaking desire to shake things up, move, travel, live. She was done waiting, done trying to fit in SW. South Waterton did not suit her anymore, and she had no real strings tying her down. Her father was gone, her grandparents were dead, there were no aunts, no uncles, and no siblings. She was the only child of only children. She had a dog and a laptop.

"I think you're just lonely," Tris prophesied in an unassuming tone. "It's been a long time since Stephanie."

"I'm not lonely." Dre cut her off.

She was totally lonely. But the loneliness was not the inspiration for her change, whatever this change was or would be. The loneliness was simply an ever-present part of her life, a contributing factor to the rigid structure she imposed on herself. Maybe she had always been lonely. All of her friends were lesbians, but she was alone. She had internet colleagues, but she was alone. She had neighbors, but she was alone.

She took a long sip of fair trade java and met Tris's eyes. Tris was studying her, the same way she always did, her eyes narrowed, brows furrowed. She had an assumption, that was as clear as day, but she wouldn't voice her hypothesis. In the same way her partner was loud and pushy and rarely, if ever, held her tongue, Tris would rarely speak her piece. She preferred to mull.

"I just…I feel like I'm drowning," Dre released with a sigh, setting down the newspaper. "Almost as if I'm swimming in stereotypes and I can't break free."

On the floor, Will(ow) made tiny baby cooing sounds, surrounded by alphabet blocks and soft toys, wearing mud brown leggings and a mud brown striped shirt.

"What stereotypes?" Tristan queried, in genuine interest rather than the feigned compassion of any modern semblance of friendship. Still, Andrea struggled with her answer, or any sort of explanation.

I am gay. I love women. I love waking up to a woman. I love the smell of a woman, the soft curves and rough edges of a woman's body. I love living somewhere I am free to love a woman, but I don't' feel gay enough for South Waterton. Like I'm missing something, some integral part of the physiological makeup of this society. God help her, she laughed at most of what Sam ranted about. She did not fancy herself a card-carrying member of the HRC. She did not shave her head to downplay identifiable traits of womanhood. She did not want to raise gender-neutral babies dressed like little turds.

"I feel like…" she began a thought and stopped, abruptly, as Sam came into the dining area, bearing plates. Accepting hers as graciously as she could, given the lackluster ingredients, her friends looked at her as if to say *CONTINUE.* "I feel like I don't fit in."

She had always felt that way, to some extent. She had always felt as if she were on the outside, staring in at the *real* cool kids. She had been too gay to be "one of the girls" in high school, too girly to be "one of the dykes" in college. She never wore makeup, but she certainly did not hate women who did. She did not dye her hair, but when it went grey, she would probably go for it. She favored pants, but enjoyed a good set of legs in a skirt.

When had things gotten so fucking complicated? When did being gay become so hard?

"That's just what they want you to think," Sam piped up, as she took her place by her mate's side, her small, teal plate steeped in gooey, brownish-green frittata that seemed the opposite of appetizing to the other two women in her company. "They want you to feel fractured and alone?"

Tristan spread a napkin over her lap and rubbed her tongue across the inside of her lip. After so much time spent in the company of a woman politely considered a left-wing nut job, she had developed quite a skill in honing her critical interjections to almost simplistic perfection, especially where the topic of homosexuality was concerned.

Leaning forward a little, she pursed her lips before asking, "Who is this omnipotent *they*, babe?"

There seemed to be no real reason to waste words in the shadow of such a politically charged chatterbox, a woman who could be found, seven days a week, donating food, time, and whatever money she made in her stumbling career as a barista down at the Center for Female Equality and LGBTQ Rights where she filed documents, printed petitions and held a microphone, all while wearing her child strapped to her chest in a festive, Mayan print.

Lifting Will(ow) off of the floor, Samantha rolled her eyes. "You wouldn't understand," she bit out, bouncing her daughter on her knee while forming a bite of ooze on her fork.

"Why?" Tris countered. "Because I'm not as gay as you are? Because I don't eat, sleep, and breathe *the movement*?"

Her partner smiled in forced politeness, visibly reminding herself that she had selected the Devil's Advocate to her right to nest with, even though they sat on polar opposites of the social spectrum. "You're gay alright," she retorted, and winked at her friend.

"Just not a real gay's gay," said Dre, swinging her arm for emphasis. "Not a banner-bearing gay, like Sam."

Samantha sighed, sarcastically. "Oh, come on," she tried to laugh. "Is this beat up on Sam day?"

Dre shook her head, and pushed her food around on her plate. "Of course not!"

"There is no clique," Tris chuckled, trying a forkful and talking through her discomfort. "We are a completely unified front."

Of course she was joking. There were unaddressed tiers of acceptable gay behavior in towns like South Waterton, places where the 'lifestyle' was not so much tolerated as encouraged, or required. There was an expectation that a woman's identity would be defined by that sexual preference, or lack thereof, though the entirety of the term 'preference' was a misnomer, given that it was nothing that could really be chosen.

Cocking her head, Samantha let her long hair fall in Will(ow)'s face and rubbed her lips over her daughter's forehead as her tubby hands fingered the safety of the strands. "Are you insinuating that we ostracize women who don't meet a gay standard?"

"Yes," the other two women said, in unison.

"Who's running up the rainbow the fastest?" Tris contributed, spearing more sustenance.

"Who holds the rainbow flag the highest?" Dre giggled, pushing more leaky clumps of frittata, casually. "I'm not in high school. I'm not trying to fit in with the cool kids. I was born a part of this. I'm gay. That should be enough."

"It *is* enough," Sam held her hand up, obviously annoyed with the banter.

"Oh, for the basic membership, sure," Tristan's voice was collected, "but for the premiere membership, you'll need to stop eating all meat and refer to yourself as an *it*."

"Tristan, be serious," snapped Samantha. "There is no *enough*, Dre. We're all in this together." Clutching her offspring in her arm, draped in flowing cloth, hair all askew, she seemed the consummate Earth Mother; calm, open-hearted, and doe-eyed, staring out at the world, waiting for someone to save.

"But that's what you don't see." Andrea refused to let it die, more out of a need to be heard and understood than a desire to rock the boat of their familial relationship. "We're only together so long as we agree. Step out of line, miss a Pride meeting, visit a Chic-Fil-A, buy a deep fryer, vote Republican—you'll see how quickly '*enough*' fades away."

As a silence bloomed between them, Dre felt it fill only by the untapped anger that had begun to take up residence in her heart, festering in the locked down corners that should be full of hope and love. She was tired of the stares. They were bad enough coming from the hetero nation.

15

She did not need them from her own people, and that was ironic given that two members of the LESBO NATION were staring at her now.

"Andrea," Samantha whispered, covering Will(ow)'s ears with her delicate hands. "Are you a Republican?"

Unable to contain herself, Tristan cracked up. "And where can we get a deep fryer?"

In that moment, Dre was incalculably thankful that she had taken the empty seat beside twenty-something Tristan way back at Northeastern, freshman year. They had enrolled in Intro to Lit or Intro to Women's Lit, something liberal and absolutely unnecessary in the great realm of her tech degree, but necessary in term of English credit hours. In addition, having only recently come to terms with her attraction for women, it played right into a grand theme of trolling for loose, emo chicks. By grand cosmic chance, Tristan was none of that and had never been her type, as subjective as that type was. Tris was realistic in the same vein Dre found herself bleeding from. She would need a more imaginative balance in order to float toward happiness, ideally someone who did not also wear boxers and watch copious amounts of Food Network for fun on a Friday night. In every relationship, there should be an anchor, or a pragmatic problem-solver, and a balloon, or a dreamer. That was the love advice Dre's father had given her, at the tender age of ten. Two anchors would never get off of the ground. Two dreamers would simply float away.

Trista was an anchor, Samantha was a dreamer. Dre was an anchor, but Stephanie had been one, too. So had Ann Marie, who had been the only other real adult relationship that Dre had been a part of. Stephanie was politely boring. Ann Marie was domineering in the worst way (talk about an abysmal five years).

16

Bringing her back to reality, Tris gobbled up the last three bites of her frittata in quick succession, hoping against all hope that if she ate it fast enough, she would no longer taste the mushrooms. "So what kind of a change are we talking? A gay cruise?"

Was that even a thing?

Sam rolled her eyes at Tris and plucked a piece of ice from her water for Will(ow) to nibble on. "A vacation?"

"I don't know." Corso didn't give a shit where she went; they only wanted a percentage of her revenue, which was nearly $150,000 in the last year alone. Her lease was up in a month. She even had a car, though she never used it. It probably still ran.

"The world is my oyster, I guess," she stated, and immediately felt corny and also a bit like a failure for her inability to stomach the soy bacon. "I'm not even sure why I've stayed here this long."

Balking, Sam helped herself to a large chunk of frittata. "This is your home, Andrea."

"But I have no family here." Dre turned her attention to her coffee, which she could stomach. "My dad left years ago." Four years ago in May, to be exact, following his new wife's sandy footsteps all the way down to Saint Augustine, Florida, disappointingly far from Disney World.

"We're your family," Samantha told her. "We've always been your family."

"You are," Dre assured her over Will(ow)'s gurgle. "But you are your own family as well, and I'm on the outside."

She scrunched her nose up, playfully staring at the child that she considered a niece. The child she spent Christmas with and Thanksgiving with and Halloween with. The child she rocked late into the night when her parents needed a day off. And she found herself wondering if she would go

on to have her own children, and wondering what that future would look
like?

Dre the housewife.

Dre the partner.

Funny, she never considered it before.

"You could visit your dad," Tris suggested, pushing her plate to the
side. "It's been a few years."

"And he's in the Keys!" Sam's eyes lit up.

"He's in Saint Augustine," Andrea corrected.

"Same thing."

It wasn't the same thing at all, but for people up North and covered in
snow, all of Florida had a tendency to blend together into one giant
peninsula of sunshine-swathed perfection.

"Have you ever even been down there?" Tristan wondered.

No. No she had not. Not because she was avoiding him or anything.
She just…hadn't gone. Florida was a long way off.

"You've never even seen your brothers." For someone like Tristan,
with four older brothers and one younger sister, that must have seemed
strange. For a woman who had been an only child for twenty-two years, it
seemed quite normal.

Rising with Will(ow) in one arm, Samantha moved to clear the table
one-handed. "Tristan," she *tsk*ed, while sweeping things off into the
kitchen, "we don't even know if they like us in Florida."

"Samantha Jean, they love gay people in Florida. South Beach,
Disney World—"

Throwing a plate into the sink, Sam glared. "I hate Disney. Their
obsession with an inane and prehistoric feminine ideal…" Her rant

continued as she clanged things together. "And the idiotic notion that helplessness should be used as a plot device…"

"You love Frozen," Tris said, unabashedly, spearing a piece of charred soy bacon from her plate before it was carted away by Mr. Clean's Equal She-Devil partner. "You listen to it all the time. I don't blame you. It's catchy—"

"It's disturbing!" Civil Rights Sandy shrieked before toting her child into a back bedroom to nurse or change or escape the realization that she was a secret princess fanatic.

Dre smiled and surrendered her dish, having eaten nothing but constructed a convincing diorama of masticated breakfast casserole.

"Do what makes you happy, Dre. Go where you want. You have our blessing," her oldest friend conferred.

"Aw, thanks, Mom."

Playfully slapping her arm, Tristan went back to the stack of papers she'd shoved to the side in favor of eating whatever slop her woman served her. "But brush your hair before you go. You never know who you'll run into."

"And water your plants!" Sam hollered. "The last time I saw them, they looked sad as hell. I'll come and take care of them while you're in Florida."

I have plants? "I'm not going to Florida," Dre insisted.

"Oh, you're totally going to Florida," her friends opposed.

"I really am not."

* * *

"I'm so glad you're coming to Florida!" her father bellowed, heartily, when she called him two hours later.

Somehow Tris's suggestion had taken on quite a life of its own. Even Buddy was excited. He looked up at her, expectantly, as Dre sat, ankles crossed, at her minimalistic work desk, cell in hand, computer open and running as she tinkered with the logo for a Sock-of-the-Month start up.

"Are you sure? I don't want to impose…"

"Impose?" Michael Aaron Martin was sixty-six, larger than life and full of piss and bravado, a trait that both worked to his advantage and worked against him. During the early nineties, he had run off every other bakery owner within twenty miles of his one man show. There was little doubt he was continuing the trend in Florida. "Are you kidding me, kid? We've been waiting fucking years for this!"

The *we* in his declaration being his new wife, Ami, who was twenty-six years his junior, and his twin sons (late in life surprises) Michael Junior and Christian, who were six and all consumed with Legos and baseball.

"I just stopped asking after a while, figured you needed to deal with your shit."

Also, Michael had never been one to mince words. At all.

Dre tapped the very edge of the succulent growing in the ceramic pod nestled in the windowsill. Sam had been wholly accurate in her description of the faltering vegetation she insisted on bringing into the apartment. Everything Dre touched wilted, even the plants that needed little to no water.

"I didn't have any shit, Dad."

"Yeah, you did," he professed. It was late enough in the day for him to be drinking, having surrendered a lot of the physical labor at the bakery, relying on much younger employees. "You had that girl, what was her name? The boring one?"

"Stephanie."

"You had Stephanie. God, what a waste."

"The shit I needed to deal with was Stephanie?"

"Well, you put her out, didn't you?"

"Technically, she put herself out." Technically, they weren't really living together, either, but spending every night together watching HGTV was probably the same thing.

"And now you're coming to see me?"

"Now I'm coming to see you."

"So you dealt with your shit and now you're coming to Florida." He shouted, in the background, "Ames, Dre's coming to Florida!"

She heard, "That's great!" in response. Her stepmother was probably doing yoga. Ami loved yoga.

"You like Ami, don't you?"

"I like Ami, Dad. She's close to my age." Forty and twenty-eight weren't the same age, but her relationship with her father was thus that she felt comfortable making jokes at his expense. "Maybe we can go shopping."

Throughout her childhood, Michael had been her constant—a stalwart and dutiful father. Having lost her mother at three, he was all she had ever really known, as far as parents went. He had taken her to Girl Scouts and sleepovers, he had gotten her that first bra from JC Penney, and he had listened as she poured her heart out, sophomore year of high school, bubbling over with her confession about all of the romantic feelings she had developed toward other girls, even though she was reasonably certain she should be feeling them toward boys and that was evidence that she had a brain tumor, wasn't it?

Taking her roughly by the shoulders, he had explained that was gay and then told her, without apology, "All your mother and I ever wanted was for you to be happy, kid. You do what you want."

For having the capacity to house that reaction, she had never begrudged him his flings over the years. Daisy, the line dance instructor. Sarah Beth, the cocktail waitress from Moe's Bar, where he managed to spend one night a week, communing with other men and pretending he didn't know how to French braid. Elisa, the kindergarten teacher he met in a parent-teacher conference for his own daughter. Penny, the aspiring fashion designer. Ami, the yoga instructor. He must have felt dreadfully abandoned, the lone father in the carpool line. The marriage part was a bit off putting, as were the subsequent children and the move, but he genuinely seemed like he was in a good place. What almost-seventy-year-old wouldn't want a matched pair of first graders?

"If you're almost forty, I've missed a lot of damn time, and if you go shopping, I've missed the second coming of the Christ. When are you coming?"

"I haven't decided yet." Buddy rose on his rickety back legs and ambled into the living room where Dre knew he wanted to lounge about on the Spartan, white furniture that she would not allow him to sleep on.

"See you tomorrow."

"I'm not coming tomorrow, Dad. I have a job."

"You have a laptop and a car. I have Wi-Fi. See you in twenty-four hours."

"I need a couple of days to finish up this project and I'll head your way."

She needed a couple of days to figure out if she was really doing this and to finish the Sock-of-the-Month gig. None of her designs seemed to be working. Nothing screamed, "Buy these socks!"

"Are you seeing anyone?" His question was one of parental concern. It had been a while.

"No," she gave him an honest answer. Lying required more effort than she wanted to put into this conversation and her brain was a laundry mat of bad sock ideas.

"Do you want to see anyone?"

She thought that over for a moment. "I don't know, honestly. I feel like I've tried. It just never seems to work out."

And, embarrassingly, she missed sex. A lot. Not enough to hook up with random strangers in nightclub bathrooms, but enough to spend an inordinate amount of time thinking it over and pretending she would be brave enough to go for it with an illicit can-can dancer should the situation arise. Not that any of that would be a conversation she would entertain with her father. Ever.

"You're young yet," he told her. "There's no rush. Unless you've got some biological clock I don't know about."

"Ew, Dad."

"You brought it up."

"No, I didn't. You did."

She stood and stretched for a moment. Staring at her computer screen wouldn't make her work faster and it wouldn't make her work any better than it was.

"The sunlight will be good for you, I think, kid," Michael foretold. "Lie on a beach, get to know your brothers…"

Lay on a beach sounded nice. *Get to know your brothers* felt weird. For two decades, Dre had been part one of one, never to be replicated. Now, she was part one of three, like there were subsequent volumes of her family that were one part big, hair Italian man and one part tiny, fit yoga instructor who rarely ate processed food.

Am I really going to Florida?

She stewed over that question for two days, second-guessing the trip that was laid out before her. She stewed in the grocery store, buying food for Buddy, and at dinner with Tris and Sam. She stewed at Jiffy Lube when she drove on town over to have the oil changed in the Ford she haphazardly owned. She did not think she wanted this trip, but she somehow knew she needed it. This trip, this adventure, this vacation, this...whatever it was. It would be good for her. It had to be. It had to be something. There had to be something more in her life than a computer screen, numbers, html code, Food Network reruns, and the same boring people drinking Mimosas at brunch and pretending they all bought recycled toilet paper. There had to be somewhere in the world where she would feel like she fit in—not romantically, but socially. Where whatever she was, was enough. A yearning had taken root in her soul, a desire to be part of something bigger, something that felt like a more cosmic sense of family. A home.

"And you think you'll solve this by seeing you actual family?" Tris quizzed her, as they walked Buddy through the common area out back of the apartment.

Her clothes were packed. Her route was planned. The Ford was out front on the curb, luggage and dog blankets crammed inside.

"I'm not sure," Dre acquiesced, not wanting to compromise the feelings of her closest friend by insinuating that her support through the years had meant nothing in the grand scheme of life. "I know you'll always be here."

Sticking her hands in her pockets, Tris shrugged. "But you need more. I get it. That's how I felt before I met Sam. Like I was alone, adrift…spare."

Funny, Dre thought, Tristan had never seemed to be any of those things. Motivated, determined, organized, but never adrift or unworthy.

"I met her when I expected it the very least. I didn't even want it, you remember." She relented. "I wanted a coffee." Luck forced her to stumble into the wrong coffee shop for *just* a coffee.

"And what you ended up with was a wife—"

"Partner," Tris amended.

"Right, partner…and a kid."

"Two kids."

Andrea stopped moving, dropping Buddy's leash. "Two kids?" Surely she misheard. Tristan did nothing but mope about how broke they were with only one baby and one decent, reliable salary. Two babies? Tristan did not want a second baby.

"Sam's pregnant again. Same donor."

"And you wanted this?"

Tris sighed, heavily. "I want…what Sam wants. And what Sam wants is for Will to have a sibling, so a sibling she shall have, I guess. She wanted to keep it a secret until we were certain it was viable." *Viable* made it seem like a plant, taking root. "But you happen to be leaving forever, so I wanted you to know before you got on the road. It seemed like a weird thing to send in a text message."

"It would be weirder if *you* were pregnant."

"Fuck you," Tristan grinned, and they hugged.

As she loaded Buddy up into the backseat of the navy Explorer (the ostentatious cast-off of Ami's when Michael had loaded up his new family to head for brighter, sunnier pastures), Dre couldn't help but marvel at what a complicated thing love truly was.

It was far better that she was alone.

Far, far better.

A Beginning of a Different Sort

The twilight sun rolled over the pastures of the Holloway farm property in just such a way that inspired hunger, Win Holloway mused, as he mounted a dilapidated ladder propped up against the back wall of his parents' now shuttered home, cigarette hanging from his lips. Hunger never failed him when he came out to the old homestead. He disembarked from the truck and the moment his boots touched down on the native soil (approximately two acres from his own backyard soil), he hankered over the buttermilk biscuits and sweet potato pie of his childhood.

It was a shame his parents were gone. Their absence just made the whole place feel deserted, despite the fact that the four Holloway offspring all lived in adjacent buildings on the rambling acres that stretched like fingers into the Piedmont, and the animals were just as populous as ever. One of his sister's dogs, Grey Baby, a rangy heeler in hues of grey and black and white, was even perched dutifully at the base of the ladder, growling low in her throat at his approach, threatening to hang from the torn hem of his jeans as he scaled up.

Hell, that dog was ninety percent of the reason he had been able to find her so quickly.

"Sister!" he shouted, spilling ash down the front of his worn, Jimmy Buffet t-shirt. "Come down here and make me a pie!"

Win was simply teasing her, harboring no disillusion regarding his baby sister's culinary skills. She cooked when and only when she felt like it and that time was not the present. In the present, she had retreated into her favorite thinking spot, a small pallet tucked between the eaves and windows of their ancestral home, where she had gone to smoke reefer in high school and lie back to look up at the stars. She and Atticus, another of their brothers, had both been very guilty of that. Then again, who in their small South Carolina town wasn't guilty of a little rebel rousing every now and then?

This time, though, James Winter—who hated the formality of that name—knew Cara Spencer wasn't just shooting the shit. This time her struggles were weighing heavily on her shoulders, although what her struggles were, she was never apt to voice. Sister preferred to carry her burdens in secret, seemingly afraid that her predilections would be ill received by the family. As if they didn't know. They just couldn't *say* that they knew. That made things too weird.

"Sister, I know you can hear me!" Win carefully picked his way over the artisan shingles his mother had insisted upon, taking deep, gusty inhales of Marlboro with each step. "I'm serious about that pie—"

"Oh, shut up," came Cara Spencer's light reply. "And get down off this roof before you hurt yourself. You're nearly forty years old."

Scaling one of the window formers, Win let one leg fall on either side of it and looked down to find his sister exactly where he knew she would be, dog notwithstanding. It was exactly where she had been—in an identical, criss-cross-applesauce post, on an old corduroy cushion, hair blowing in the breeze—when he had been dispatched by unpopular vote to tell her that their parents had been killed ten years before. Only this time, she was in an old Columbia jacket, with the elbows worn through, and a pair of mud-stained jeans, with red toenail polish glinting on her bare feet.

"I am a spry, thirty-four, thank you very much. And I'd wager I'm a lot quicker on my feet than you are. I am said to be an excellent dancer," he lied.

The Right Kind of Woman

"You are an awful dancer," Cara Spencer snorted, taking a sip of the Terrapin in her hand. "You were the laughingstock of Greentown High School's 1999 Senior Prom."

"On the contrary," he winked, because he knew she was looking at him, via peripheral vision. "I was prom king, if you'll recall." He and Allisan Crabshaw had been crowned King and Queen together. What a sweet piece of ass she was. Too bad she moved away to Wilmington and married a mechanic.

"You only won because they all felt sorry for you. I wish I had been there, but I'm afraid I was only a baby—" his sister regaled, placing a hand sarcastically over his heart, playing up their seven year age difference.

Win stubbed his cigarette out on the side of the dormer and flicked the butt off into the bushes below, watching the white filter as it bounced down the brick exterior, piece by piece. It was something he never would have been brave enough to do in the presence of his parents, but with them having departed for the hereafter ages ago, he felt somehow safe to smoke and litter on their boarded up property and in their yard.

"Be that as it may, I never felt sorry for myself, which is the exact opposite of what you're doing right now."

"Oh, fuck off!" his sister snapped, although she knew just as well as he did that she couldn't argue his point, no matter how much she didn't want to hear it. She was indeed feeling sorry for herself, drinking alone and on the roof over the bedroom she had not occupied in easily a hundred years.

"I was raised to call a spade, a spade, sister. Now save us both the trouble and tell me what the hell's got you up on this roof or get the hell off of this roof. Either choice is fine by me, I've got a free afternoon." Twenty-seven years into their relationship, he knew Cara Spencer

29

Madeline Holloway well enough to be at peace with the fact that she would never tell him what was bothering her unless she was ready, and she clearly wasn't ready. She was still too busy skirting around and assuming her brothers were either too self-absorbed (which was partially true) or too stupid to figure out what she was, for all intents and purposes, gay. And, not only was she gay, but she had been secretly involved with a woman from a nearby town for approximately six months, if Link's estimations were correct. Atticus and Win deferred to him only because he made no bones about the fact that he spied on her and claimed her driveway had been traversed by the same Chevy Equinox every weekend. That is, until about two weeks before, when all travel and illicit encounters involving the Equinox suspiciously ceased.

Cara Spencer had been in a foul mood ever since. A trained monkey could have put it together. Three dim-witted brothers at least made quick work of it.

"Nothing's goin' on, Win," she lied. "I'm just... I don't know. In a weird place."

"Seems like you've been in a weird place for a while," he hinted.

Like maybe the tenth grade, he wanted to say, but didn't because their relationships had all become incredibly complicated in the wake of a single-engine plane accident on an otherwise unremarkable April day. That was when he had figured it out, though, the tenth grade. His parents had taken much longer to clue in, but eventually they realized just the same, and it never affected their relationship, though they were never able to *tell* her that, which was what created the rift. They had been denied the opportunity to accept her and she had forever been denied the acceptance, through the hand of untimely death. Cara Spencer had always been her own person; free, wild, and unchained. But now, in the decade that had passed, she had become inherently more introverted.

"Listen, Sister," he continued, "I don't know what you're struggling with, 'cause you won't tell me, whatever the reason, but it'll get better."

It had to get better. Or she would retreat even further into herself, and spend all of her time on the tiny farm she had created, growing vegetables, tending chickens and goats, and drinking in isolation on her dead parents' roof.

"I know," she chimed in, which honestly surprised him. "Granny says change comes with the seasons... I guess I'm just waitin' for spring."

That sounded a lot like Granny, weirdly prophetic and nonsensical at the same time. Although, nearing in on ninety, Win figured that if anyone had earned the right to be absurdly visionary, it was his mother's mother, Granny McLeod, who parlayed her nickname into a string of profitable apple stands in fourteen different counties. She grew no apples. She bought apples and then resold them under the moniker "Granny's Apples." And she was practically rolling in dough, no pun intended.

"Come on down and have dinner with me," Win offered. "I've got three Lean Cuisines in the freezer at the house."

That got Cara Spencer laughing. It was laughable that her brother, the well-to-do restaurant owner (at least by Greentown's stringent standards of wealth and accomplishment), had no real food to speak of in his tidy, brick box home. "You spare no expense, do you?" she joked.

He stood, shaking the tension from his legs, which did feel more like forty than thirty, and held out a hand. Begrudgingly, she took it and leaned forward just a stretch. In silence, they began to make their way down the ladder, and Win wondered if he would really have to feed her. The Lean Cuisines had been a lie. Usually, she just—

"I've got a ham thawed out," she told him, saving the day. "Why don't you come on over to my place and I'll bake it off."

This was a good start.

"I'd be delighted," he smiled.

On the ground, Grey Baby howled like the little dingo she wanted to be.

"Although," Win mentioned, casually, "If that fucking dog doesn't stop barking at me every time I come near you, I'll just eat *him*."

"Grey Baby is a girl, Win," Cara Spencer explained patiently, as if she had been forced to do it a hundred times before. "And she's a guard dog. Her reason for being is to protect her home."

Yeah, Win mused internally, *that's my reason for being too, most of the time.*

On the Road

"Jesus Christ, if I get cut off one more fucking time," Dre cursed at the minivan in front of her, bedecked with soccer alliance stickers and a stick family with too many kids, and felt incredibly tempted to give the dad-perm driving the finger.

It wouldn't have been the first time in the past seven hours. It wouldn't have been the first time in the past seven minutes. South of the Mason Dixon Line, it seemed, interstate driving took on a whole new meaning. In Virginia, she'd almost been sideswiped. Twice. Now, in… Where was she? South Carolina, it had escalated even more due to rush hour traffic and she was tempted to pull over and stop for the night simply because she was sick of being in the car. She'd stopped the day before, somewhere in the lower part of Pennsylvania, in order to plug in and finish the bid for a new web contract. Shane Bryant, her "boss" at Corso, had called her on it just outside New Jersey. So she really shouldn't stop again. One hotel stay was enough. She could feasibly make it to Florida without stopping.

But she really didn't want to.

Really. Really. Didn't want to.

She wanted french fries and something really southern to eat. Like a deep-fried Twinkie.

"Buddy?" she called, lowering the rear view mirror to see the backseat, where the behemoth of a dog was dripping drool down the seat cover like wet paint, arms and legs everywhere. He lifted a head and flopped an ear sideways.

"Buddy, should we stop?"

He was nonplussed and in no way motivated to respond to her query. "No opinion either way?"

She had no idea which way she was going, no GPS to estimate her arrival time. She only knew that I-95 South would take her right into Florida, and from there, she would use signs.

There had been relatively few identifying features visible from the highway, but the regulatory green rectangles told her she was in the bottom of the twin Carolinas, and it was hard to gauge an area's level of hospitality from farm land, one factory, and a sundry of barren fields.

Dialing her cell phone with her right hand, she pressed send and felt guilty that she was engaging in an activity that was probably illegal. Tris picked up after three rings.

"You there?" her friend laughed. "Enjoying the sand?"

"Not yet," Dre heaved, as she passed the minivan that had cut her off only moments before. "I'm in South Carolina."

Tristan coughed. "You've been driving for two days and you're only in South Carolina? Call me crazy, but shouldn't you be further?"

"I had to stop in PA. I had to do a bid."

"Oh. Well, how far are you driving?"

Two college guys in a Jeep with the top down sped past and Andrea could not help but smile. At least the weather in Bum-Fuck-Nowhere was pretty. "I don't know. That's why I called."

"I don't have a map handy, friend," Tris quipped, trying to sound like a cowboy and failing miserably.

Dre snorted. "I know you don't have a map, asshole. Am I safe to stop in South Carolina? Will they burn me or run me out of town?"

Gay prejudice was a fact of life and she wasn't so much worried about herself, but more for Buddy. Buddy was so old he wouldn't survive long without his food source and pee cleaner.

"Are you asking me if they like gay people there? Because, you know, you're more than a label," Tris laughed.

"I don't need the pep talk now, Dad. I just need to know if this is a good idea or not." God only knew what the world was like outside of South Waterton.

"Not, definitely not. That's Fox News country."

That was not what she wanted to hear, not after her multiple near death driving experiences and the cramps in her legs and the hunger in her belly and her need for a really good IPA. "Like how bad of a decision?"

"Worst decision ever."

Greentown NEXT TWO EXITS the green sign to her right read.

Greentown. Greentown sounded nice. Polite. Friendly. Green. And all Southerners knew how to drink. There would be beer somewhere. She could pretend she wasn't gay for, like, thirty minutes. Long enough to get a drink, walk Buddy, and check her email. No one would know.

She readjusted the mirror and took in her reflection. Boy's haircut, white t-shirt, suspenders, skinny jeans, tits strapped down. Everyone would know she was gay. It was as good as written on her face. She had on fucking suspenders, for crying out loud.

"You stopping?" Tris was breathing heavily on the phone, like she was on a treadmill.

Dre flipped on her blinker. "Yeah, I think I am." What could it hurt? No one would kill her, right?

"Well," Tris said, just before hanging up, "if you hear banjos, run. Let me know you're not dead in the morning."

Apples for Sale

"You need to make a damn family of your own or you'll be takin'
care of those rat brothers of yours for the rest of your life," Granny
Holloway foretold as her svelte, tawny granddaughter bent over a giant vat
of shiny, green apples wearing nothing more than cut-off shorts and a tight,
white tee shirt that read "Get Your Eyes Off My Apples." "You can't be
carryin' on like you're their mama forever."

She was leaning against the makeshift counter that was really more of
a sheet of plywood stretched over two rain barrels turned upside down,
counting a wad of loose cash from her fanny pack with gnarled, spindly,
translucent blue fingers. The bills were all jumbled together, wrinkled and
sweaty and stinking of salty boiled peanuts and Coca Cola. It had been a
long day of apple hawking at the Greentown County Farmer's Market; a
long day of old man ogling, old man haggling, and listening to the
muscadine wine salesman liquor up middle-aged moms in order to sell
overpriced bottles of sugar-laden moonshine in the booth next door.

Righting herself, Cara Spencer Holloway, only female progeny of the
entire Holloway clan, juggled three apples in her hand and stood, with one
hip sticking clean out to the side. "What was that, Granny? Something
about me pretendin' to my mother for the rest of my damn life?"

An elderly gentleman across the stall chortled and handed her a fiver.
She winked and quipped, "These firm enough for you, Mister Muldrow, or
did you wanna squeeze 'em a few times?" Flirtation was a game they all
played at and, frankly, male seduction sold a hell of a lot of overpriced
apples.

Coming up behind her, her brother, Atticus, cursed. "Easy, Sister, you'll give Muldrow, here, a heart attack."

In his own Granny's Apple tee over a tan as deep as the Sahara and a pair of ripped khaki shorts, he was the male equivalent of Cara Spencer, all wild and dewy sun-kissed with an air of irrationality. "And don't feign innocence, Granny," he said, learning over to kiss his grizzled matriarch's forehead. "You know exactly what you're doing parading my sister around in a shirt three sizes too small." He propped casually back against the pole that denoted the center of their apple stall and munched on his own Red Delicious, which would not doubt be subtracted from his meager paycheck. "Men like Muldrow are paying for the privilege of staring at her."

Granny *tsk*ed him. "Don't be crass," she denied. "And don't begrudge an old man a little fun, Atticus Caleb. Men like Muldrow have grandchildren in the state Senate. All I'm doing is looking out for the little princess's future."

Running a damp rag over her workspace, Cara Spencer winced. "I'm right here, y'all."

Conversations about her future always made her squirrely, and not just because it was awkward to be set up by your grandmother. Her future was…complicated. Multi-layered.

"I think she can handle herself," was all Atticus could muster.

The mere mention of his sister's future had become increasingly more stressful. He and his brothers were stuck in a time-space continuum of wait and wait and worry (and occasionally spy). When would she 'come out?' Would she 'come out?' Everyone in the whole damn town knew she needed to 'come out.' He had his own suspicions that Granny knew—why the hell else would she say grand*children* in the State Senate and not grand*sons*—but Cara Spencer was content to shove her head in the sand

and leave it all in limbo, spending year after year on her hole-in-the-wall farm with her goats and her chickens and her dogs and her solitude.

How would she meet anyone that way? Who would she meet? A census taker? The tax assessor from the county? A lone lesbian farmer from FarmersOnly.com? Never in a million years had he wished she was straight, but he had sure wished she were brave more times than he could possibly count.

"I can handle myself," she smiled at him and he'd been so stuck in his own thoughts he had forgotten to what she was replying. "I do just fine, Granny. I'll find somebody when I'm ready."

Read: NEVER.

"You'll never find anybody living on that goddamn farm alone," Granny turned her back to the family and addressed a customer, sliding her false teeth back into place. "How dee do, Mister Carraway! It's been a month of Sundays since I've seen you last! What can we get for you today?" Only old women with partial bridgework could get away with phrases like *month of Sundays*.

Atticus rolled his eyes and slid nearer to his sister, who snuck a sip of Coca Cola in the shade behind their counter. Of the premiere tier of stalls, Granny's Apples was one of the largest, having been earned over the past decade of weekend produce sales that were anything but casual, and it encompassed a garden shed they all used as an office, along with a small portable toilet and a generator. In the shadow cast by these makeshift buildings, one could feasibly send text messages out of sight of one's militant grandmother, or drink Coca Cola and spin bullshit. Or sneak cigarettes, even though the spinster must have known they were all practically Marlboro ads.

"Don't you light that thing," Cara Spencer chastised when he pulled a bent cigarette out of his pocket. "That's disgusting."

Well, they were all practically Marlboro ads except Cara Spencer, otherwise known as the Cigarette Police.

Her closest brother shook his head, but lit it anyway. "You sound like Mom."

"Somebody needs to. The three of you will smoke yourselves into an early grave."

Somehow the intrigue of inhaling cancer had stopped with her, as she had never expressed any interest in nicotine aside from the occasional stress puff. Alcohol, sure. Marijuana, only sporadically, but no real interest in cigarettes. She said they made her teeth feel like sandpaper.

"I'm twenty-nine years old, Sister. I am old enough to make my own decisions." There was playful ice in his voice.

"Try saying that with a stoma in your neck," Cara Spencer answered. "Plus, you'll stink up my hair. Go stand somewhere else."

"I'll stand wherever I damn well want to."

The irony was in the knowledge that their childhood bickering had never really ebbed, not since the days of fighting over the good seat in the way back of their parents' station wagon, or arguing over whose turn it was to use the old rotary dial telephone in the kitchen. And their proximity only made things worse. While a makeshift will (no one plans to die in a plane crash, leaving four unruly children only on the cusp of adulthood scrambling behind), had divided the Holloway lands equally among them, Win, Link, Atticus and Cara Spencer all lived one on top of the other, always having the option of moving away, but never doing it; always having the option of spreading further, but never expanding.

The Right Kind of Woman

Win was the oldest, with an actual home that was new, brick and mortar, and a small, hard-side pool they all wanted to use but never got around to using. He owned a restaurant, but it was, for all intents and purposes, a dive. Link was next in line, but he lived closer to their parents' old house, in a tiny cottage that once housed a property manager of some kind back when the whole of the homestead was an actual operating tobacco farm, with a gravel drive that split off halfway to lead visitors toward his sister. It was a tidy one bedroom, one bathroom, but Link was a perpetual bachelor with about two millimeters of responsibility in the bulk of his body so there was no real chance that his status would change anytime soon. He worked as a bartender for his brother, but called himself "bar manager", which sounded pretentious to anyone who actually knew that all he did was chat up girls and open Bud Light bottles with a keychain suspended from the ceiling.

Atticus was an artist, by trade, but a jack-of-all-trades by necessity. Until he made a real name for himself, he could not live solely off of the profits of his paintings, despite limited success in regional markets like Charleston and Savannah, so he took shifts as a server, cleaner and apple hawker. Accordingly, his house was more transient, and he made no bones about living in a repossessed mobile home with a disconnected back staircase and rust all down the sides. All he needed in life to be happy, he said, was a roof over his head, food in his belly, beer in his fridge, oil paint and a blank canvas. His driveway snaked around the small pond at the turnoff near the main road, but his house was, by order of proximity, the closest to his sister's ramshackle old farm house that had once been Granny's before she wised up and moved into the Methodist Senior Village in order to make macaroni noodle crafts and dine at four in the afternoon. There were three bedrooms there on the property, although one hadn't really been used since God was a boy, and both of the bathrooms were more dust than retro. Whitewashed and formerly elegant, Cara Spencer's home was surrounded by chicken pens, goat pens, and an overgrown barn that kept all of one cow sheltered inside, and while she certainly wasn't the only Holloway who owned and cared for animals, her passion for them had earned her a reputation as a softie who would take in and nurture anything, except a man.

The rest of the hundred or so acres remained rustically native, with sandy, hill-like mountains that wound around the river that split Greentown veritably in half and served as the perfect distraction on a warm spring day, and lush primitive woods where the local chapters of Girl Scouts were allowed to camp in the spring.

Back in their former lives, they had all run from their upbringing. Win had been an accountant, Link had gotten a teaching certificate in Atlanta, Atticus had spent two years in New York, Cara Spencer had been to Burning Man. But they were all home now, all on top of one another, meddling in the affairs of their siblings, casting aspersions and conducting recon missions in the dead of night to see whose car was parking alongside their sister's rusted yellow Apache truck—the one she had begged their father for, promised to fix up and restore, but never did, choosing to ride around with no seatbelts and no radio and only two gears and a starter that sometimes just didn't want to start at all.

"Remember that time I pantsed you in front of Mary Ann McCutcheon?" Cara Spencer taunted him, as Atticus puffed away on his cigarette. "It'd be a real shame if I did that in the middle of the Greentown Farmer's Market."

He cocked and eyebrow. "Remember that time I—"

"Who's smoking? Is that smoke? That better not be smoke?" Granny hollered in an owl-like screech, her craggy voice filling the silence in the air. "You know I hate smoking, Atticus Caleb!"

Brother and sister burst into giggles as Atticus hurried to out his cigarette on something that wouldn't catch on fire.

"Oh my God," called a heavy, familiar voice, as they both stood there, blankly staring. "Put it out on the bottom of your fucking shoe."

Win winked as he strolled up, with Link following close behind. They were both wearing restaurant uniforms, or what passed for restaurant uniforms in their neck of the woods: ratty khaki shorts, gym shoes, and t-shirts emblazoned with the tried and true A.B. Lincoln's logo. Link wore a ball cap, facing forwards, Win's head was bare, but his hair was overly coiffed, in the manner of a fraternity pledge.

"What are you, like, twelve?" Cara Spencer quipped, as Atticus straightened his shirt. "What's with your hair?"

"Asks the girl hiding from her grandma while her brother smokes a cigarette," her brother fired back.

"He better not be smoking a damn cigarette." Granny prepared to swat with a rolled up newspaper she had acquired, more than likely from the depths of her ever fashionable fanny pack. "He knows how I feel about smoking."

"We all know how you feel about smoking," Link interrupted, hugging her while she swatted at Atticus through his arms.

Two or three vegetable vendors called to Win, who waved in response. He was notorious for using fresh, local ingredients and his appearance at the farmer's market set the vendors on edge. He had no favorites and played no games. He went for the cheapest prices and quality products. It was a conundrum in the small business world of Greentown, guided predominantly by nepotism.

"What brings you here? Not the apples, I'm sure," Granny cut to the chase. She propped her saggy elbows up on the plywood counter behind her and adjusted her Granny's Apples visor.

"Actually," Win boomed, "I could do with a pound or so. Link's gonna try sangria for ladies night. He thinks the soccer moms will drink it up."

Lincoln beamed at the brilliance of his own plan, all "Mom, I made straight As" about it.

"And," Brother Boss continued, "I could do with my sister."

"No," Cara Spencer bit out before he was finished.

"Yes," Win didn't take no for an answer. "I'm shorthanded and I don't have to pay you as much."

"Well, when you put it like that…"

"I'm serious. I'm not trying to harangue you into leaving the house because I'm worried you spend too much time alone, I really am shorthanded this time. Debbie called in sick. Denita's pregnant and slow as hell. Brenden can't serve the entire restaurant."

Denita *was* slow as hell and Brenden put his order book down every time a decent pair of tits walked in.

"Make Link do it."

"Link's not good at anything other than talking to strangers. When people drink, they want to talk, so he's in the perfect position. He can't possibly wait on anyone. He's an idiot. No offense," he looked at his younger brother, younger by three whole years and a lifetime of responsibility.

"None taken," Link supplied. "I accept my shortcomings."

Setting the Coca Cola bottle down, Cara Spencer considered the proposal. Working at A.B.'s was torture, of sorts: while not awful, it was mind-numbingly boring, and she was well aware that the whole 'shorthanded' thing was probably an elaborate ruse to get her out of the house so her brothers wouldn't have to worry that she would end up dying alone for one entire evening. They desperately wanted her to find a man and make some babies, learn to cook, and be taken care of. That seemed to be their guiding mission in life more and more, as she got older, although the only thing she worried over, the older she got, was when and how she would ever tell them that the last thing she wanted or needed was a man. Or if she would tell them. After Caitlin, she was resigned to spending the rest of her life alone anyway, and they had not even been 'serious.' They had only been 'friends,' according to Caitlin, who had decided to work things out with Mike. Friends who spent the night, naked. They were only friends and the whole thing had been a phase. It had never been real.

It sure as hell felt real to me, Cara Spencer thought bitterly. But, then again, where would it have gone? What would she have done? Would she have shown Caitlin off to her family? Introduced her as a partner? Or girlfriend? Which term was correct?

Obviously, the situation was far better this way, better that Caitlin and Mike would be happy in Bridgewood and continue trying to have a baby. There could have been no future in it, for either of them. Not in Greentown, not in South Carolina, not where people still went to church three times every Sunday and kids still said their prayers at night and having babies before marriage was still frowned upon. There would be no time where being openly gay (even thinking the phrase made her cringe inside) would be accepted, understood…allowed. Her brothers would never understand, Granny was too old to adapt to something like that.

There were no "out and proud" gay people in Greentown. *Real* gay people lived in Massachusetts and New York and California. They did not raise families and work at apple stands in the armpit of the Red Republican South.

"Come on, Sister," Win persuaded, "It's Saturday night. You'll make decent tips."

"I don't need money," she lied.

There were approximately twelve dollars in her bank account, sitting there waiting to be overdrawn when the water bill rolled around on the fifteenth. The free range egg market had been down in the past month and Granny had gotten stingy with the apple profits.

"You always need money," Link made his point succinctly. "All you do is sell eggs and apples."

"And goat's milk," she amended.

"Oh? Has the market for that increased to two customers?"

"That's enough," Win chewed his bottom lip. "What if I let you play? Would you do it, then?"

The one thing Cara Spencer loved more than her animals was her guitar, and she had one hell of a voice, and her brother was well aware of her sweet spot. As her eyes lit up, he cocked an eyebrow. "You can play *only* when Mad Dog is between sets or in the bathroom. Three songs, max." She had a tendency to go a little overboard. "*Only* between sets, Sister. Last time, you sang him off the stage and he threatened to quit."

"He should quit," Granny giggled. "He sucks."

"He's cheap and he's entertaining," Link justified. "And, for the most part, he shows up when he says he will."

"When he's not busy sitting around the house being drunk," Granny nodded.

Win pegged his little sister with his stare. "So, will you do it?"

Really, what would it hurt? She was only trading one three-sizes-too-small tee for another, and it would be nice to get out for a while, not that she would ever admit it to Larry, Curly and Moe.

"I need to go home and change," she relented, as every Holloway brother breathed a sigh of relief. Their secret plan to reintroduce her to the world and somehow give her the confidence to be who they knew she was had worked. Well, step one had worked: GET CARA SPENCER OUT OF HER DAMN HOUSE.

"And I need to get my guitar," she winked.

"*Only in between sets!*" Win called in her wake.

Dinner for One

Four hotel stops into her trek through Hell, Dre was beginning to wish she was dead. Or, at the very least, sans dog as it turned out most hotels in the Greentown, South Carolina area either were not dog friendly (the bastards), or had very stringent policies regarding the size of a dog you could have in your room—twenty pounds or less.

Who in the hell had a twenty-pound dog? Twenty-pound dogs were for rodent collectors and sorority girls and neither of the two would be found in any of the motor lodges she had stumbled across.

"If I had a twenty-pound dog, I just wouldn't fucking say anything," Dre said to herself, pulling up outside what she had deemed her last option, the run down and independently owned Carolina Inn, with a large red blinking vacancy sign and a large red blinking Pet Friendly sign. And a large red blinking BAR sign, which didn't hurt either.

To avoid having any misconception about the size of her dog, she simply opened the back passenger door and Buddy slid right on out onto the pavement, tail wagging, tiny rivulets of drool leaving puddles in his absence. Hooking him to the leash in her hand, Dre hauled him through the double doors and into a marble-tiled lobby that looked like a redneck version of the Taj Mahal and smelled like an ashtray. A rusty brass bell clanged over her when she entered. Still life paintings of fruit and wildlife prints of ducks mid-flight peered down at her from the walls.

Classy, classy...

Buddy looked up at her, as if to say he didn't particularly care for classy anyway.

"Hello?" she called, foolishly assuming the clinking bell herald to her arrival would alert some worker person to come running out and ascertain that she wasn't a robber. "Anybody home?"

That was a gay thing to say, she laughed. "Hello?"

Off to the right, a toilet flushed, and then a frazzled, overly blonde woman in her late forties popped out of a doorway, rubbing her hands with a duck-printed hand towel. Her leathery face betrayed a dependence on nicotine and her lips were far too pink, with pink running into the crevices surrounding her mouth. Her crimped hair appeared to be trying to leap from her head in a desperate plea for freedom and her eyelashes were sparse, but coated in mascara that gave her the illusion of being a doe-eyed, retired pirate.

On her black, uniform vest, the name PAM was emblazoned in maroon embroidery.

"Oh, sweet Jesus, you scared me!" she all but shouted. "That was the first time I've peed all day and a customer comes in!"

Laughing at herself, she finished with the towel and tossed it down beside her on the looming, lacquered counter that spanned the length of the small nook.

"Welcome to the Carolina Inn, I'm Pam. How are you doing? Been on the road long?"

Given that the clerk at the Comfort Inn and Suites had barely glanced up in her direction, and the manager at the Holiday Inn was less than pleasant, Pammy's attitude was like a breath of fresh air. Dre couldn't help but smile.

"Not long. All day—"

"Is that a chocolate lab?!" In two seconds flat, Pam was around the partition and on the floor, rubbing Buddy behind the ears. "I love me a chocolate lab! My ex-husband had one for all the years we were together and it liked to kill me to let that dog go. Mango was her name. Prettiest eyes in the world. You got 'em too, don't you?" Buddy was instantly smitten by the mysterious stranger and her lascivious attentions. "Where y'all drivin' from?"

Dre cleared her throat. "Massachusetts. Stopped in Pennsylvania last night, though. I had a job."

"Phew girl, you must be exhausted! What kinda room y'all want? One bed or two?" She had yet to look up from her canine nuzzle fest and Buddy was now openly licking her mouth.

"One is good. Downstairs, if you have it. That way I can take Buddy out when he needs to go." A ground floor room wasn't really necessary but it was the only way Dre could incorporate the fact that Buddy would be staying with her into the conversation. She had no concept of how bright Pam truly was, and couldn't make assumptions. Short of saying CAN THIS DOG STAY IN THIS PLACE she had no idea how to proceed.

Brushing off her vest, Pam stood and made her way back around the desk. "Absolutely. We're just shy of empty at the moment, so you can have pretty much whatever you want. One bed, two beds, big TV, small TV, smoking, non-smoking."

There were smoking rooms in South Carolina. Interesting tidbit of information, that. Perhaps some of the rooms came with deep fryers and a big, right wing Bible.

"One bed is fine, no TV preference. Nonsmoking."

"Gosh, you're easy," Pam giggled. There was lipstick on her teeth, but her mannerisms were nothing short of welcoming. "You hungry? We got a pile of restaurants right here off this exit."

"I saw," Dre tried to decline.

McDonald's, Hardee's, Chili's, Ruby Tuesday, Longhorn, Olive Garden... This exit was a quintessential interstate exit. Every chain in America was located here, except maybe In-And-Out-Burger.

"Most people like the familiar," Pam kept on, as she filled in a white cardstock form with a bright, pink gel pen. "Especially Northerners. No offense. They think we'll poison 'em or somethin', if they eat local food. And it's a shame, too. We got a great lil' place right about nine miles that way." Her arm flew up and went behind her. "It's a hole in the wall, alright, but they make a mean hamburger and they got about every beer on the whole East Coast, and they have live bands and stuff on the weekends."

Andrea could barely recall the last time she had eaten a real hamburger, one grilled with the fat and the grease and the cheese and the meat. South Waterton didn't really *do* hamburgers. South Waterton did soy burgers, turkey burgers, veggie burgers, but no hamburgers. Hamburgers were far too basic.

Basically delicious...

"How far is that place, did you say?"

Pam looked up, finally. Her face beamed and Dre wondered if she received a cut for referrals.

"Well," she put her hands on her hips. "As the crow flies, it's only 'bout nine miles, but on the roads it's more like eleven or twelve. Not a bad little drive through the farmland, give you a chance to see what Greentown really is."

The expression 'but on the roads' stumped her and Dre felt like most of the people who lived in the mysterious world of Greentown more than likely drove ATVs or horses. And while it would be fascinating to study them in their native environment, it was probably much faster to pick up a to-go salad from the Ruby Tuesday and a six-pack of beer at the Pilot

Travel Center. There was absolutely no reason to get attached to a dumpy place like Greentown, not when she was on the way to Florida to change her life for the better.

Once inside her ground floor, one bed, small TV, nonsmoking room, she sent Tris a text.

STOPPED IN GREENTOWN, SC. NOT DEAD. YET.

She tried to take a picture of Buddy, but he busied himself making a home on the floor, next to the sliding glass door, and then promptly fell asleep with his head curled up on the sagging edges of the duck-printed drapes.

Tris texted back half an hour later.

PRETEND TO BE A SOUTHERNER WHILE YOU'RE THERE.

Looking back on it, it was that specific sentiment that inspired Andrea Marie Martin to do just that.

* * *

*Do I own anything that makes me look **not so gay**?*

Turns out, Dre did not, and after agonizing over putting together the least lesbian outfit using accouterments from her plain, navy duffel bag, she ended up cloaking her sexual orientation in a slight variation of the exact same thing she had been wearing all of her life—a white button up, suspenders (because why not?), jeans, and loafers.

Loafers are super gay. What shoes did straight women even wear? Heels? That would never happen on her toned, hardened body.

As pleased as she could be, she sought out Pam, who scrawled a set of ridiculous directions on a paper towel during a commercial break in the B-Grade SyFy movie she had, apparently, been looking forward to for weeks;

so much so that the front doors were locked and the lights in the lobby were dimmed as she sat, hunkered down in front of a small TV behind the counter, using an office chair as a recliner. To any passersby, it would appear the hotel was closed for business.

"I just hope Old Paul don't drive by and see what I did or my ass is grass and he's the lawnmower," she cackled, while making notations on the Brawny like, "When you see a lot of cows, make a right." Presumably, Old Paul owned the hotel.

"Is this how straight people normally present themselves?" she should have asked, but did not. That would have been too gay—not that there was anything wrong with being gay on any level of the rainbow spectrum. She just didn't want to stick out, which was ridiculous given that having all of her teeth in a place like this Greentown would naturally make her stand out. Plus, being gay was who she was. Fuck the haters.

Following Pammy's easy-to-decipher instructions (surprise), she took the first right past the Carolina Inn and drove 'for a while' before making that right beside the 'lots of cows.' The road was serene, bare, and the farmland on either side was plentiful. There were dozens of cows, pigs and horses and almost no people. For the duration of the drive, she passed one truck. *One*.

Twenty minutes in, she thought for sure she was lost. This could not possibly be eleven miles 'on the road.' But, low and behold, she saw the 'big red barn' alluded to on the towel, at the 'kinda big intersection' and, at long last, there was the beacon of the 'matching street lights' that signaled the turn off for the restaurant: A.B. Lincoln's. Pam just called it "A.B.s" and pronounced it "Ay Bees."

Pulling her ostentatious SUV into the gravel parking lot that was more dirt than gravel, Dre paused to wonder what the fuck she had just come to.

The Right Kind of Woman

Ramshackle, beat down, and isolated, this A.B.'s was not just "off the beaten path," it was in the middle of nowhere. Correction, it was in the middle of a tobacco field, or a field of something that looked like the pictures of tobacco Dre had seen. Literally, it was flanked on three sides by tobacco plants. By the road, tottered a large, chalkboard sign that bore the name, the hours of operation (10a.m. UNTIL for Saturday), and a daily special that looked like it hadn't been updated in about a year. To the right was a pole shed with a rusty boat underneath, and a passel of burn barrels in varying degrees of rot. A tin roof hung over the front, covering a smattering of industrial spindle tables surrounded by stools. There were three other cars in what was masquerading as a parking lot, and of those three cars, about two cars worth of people were milling about, leaning against the poles and one truck smoking cigarettes by the dozen.

In a moment of indecision, Dre wondered whether or not she would actually go inside. This was not the southern fantasy she had concocted in her head, shortly before changing to go seek directions from her new BFF, Pammy Pam Pants. This was not a cleverly concealed culinary experience, sequestered between outbuildings on a working plantation where women fanned themselves with antique lace and said quaint phrases like "I swaney." This was the third rung of hell in Dante's Inferno, otherwise known as a country and western bar.

These people could kill her and chop her up and dispose of her body in one of those barrels out under the shed and it would take weeks for anyone in South Waterton or Saint Augustine to find her, if they ever did. These were the people who voted down marriage equality acts and were not in favor of legalized marijuana or ObamaCare. These people were lying in wait for the South to rise again, with their rifles and fallout shelters hidden in rabbit holes on the farm.

Her stomach gurgled.

Was she seriously about to do this? Walk in all alone and all gayed out, parading her sexuality in front of people who would literally hate her before they knew her, requesting a well-done burger and pitcher of beer?

Yes, yes she was. Because she was hungry, starving actually. Because she wanted a drink. Because she was a good person with nothing to hide. And because she was a woman who was expecting a great change that could not possibly come if she continued to do the same old shit in the same old places, safety notwithstanding.

With a large intake of breath, she pushed open the door of the Explorer and strutted into the tumbledown shed that was A.B.'s, haters be damned.

Immediately, she bummed slam into the hostess, who looked about sixteen and utterly befuddled by Dre's gender-neutral aura, or perhaps her loafers.

"Um…" she stumbled, dropping all of her laminated menu sheets. "Welcome to A.B. Lincoln's, I'm—"

"Party of one," Dre said, assertively, with a level gaze and a no-nonsense attitude. This was her life and she would own it.

"Ooookay," the hostess, muttered, slipping the menu sheets into the holder on the side of her cleverly decorated hostess platform. "You want a table or…like, the bar?"

For the first time, Dre surveyed the interior of A.B.'s and was pleasantly surprised, relieved even. The walls were clean, corrugated tin. The ceilings were high. There were a smattering of large canvas paintings suspended from the rafters—one was a field of cattle that looked unbelievably like the fields she drove through to reach this destination, one was a sunburst of red and orange and lilac and peach, one was an expertly

54

drawn profile. Just before her, a series of small, round tables were surrounded with small, round chairs. Against the walls there were booths that were shiny and empty.

Pretty much every table was empty. Even the bar, which was a bit further back, to the left of the stage, and hung with small, golden orbs that cast more of a retro air around the area, bathing the heavy, metal stools in the warmth of what must feel like southern summer sun.

"I'll try the bar," Andrea said, decisively.

The hostess smiled, her lips ruby red and her pubescent acne covered by a heavy paste of makeup. "Take one of these menus with you. Mister Win says Link never puts 'em behind the bar like he's s'posed to."

Link? Link was a weird name. Short for Lincoln, maybe, like the namesake of the place. It sounded more like sausage or chain than President.

Was it weird that the local watering hole was all but dead on a Saturday at suppertime?

Was it weird that she wanted to be at the bar? What if a cowboy sat down next to her—real one, not like the women dressed in plaids and flannels in South Waterton?

Toting her menu in her clammy hand, Dre sauntered to the bar and took the stool furthest in the corner, allowing only one possible seat for the previously theorized cowpoke in case the bar filled with outdoorsy miscreants in the next ten minutes.

There were pictures covering the grain of the cherry wood, 1940s still shots of couples, post cards from Florida and Alabama and Louisiana. Everything was covered in epoxy and the edges were shorn. In the center, behind the bar, hung a French mount deer skull adorned with Christmas lights. There were double doors beneath him—why she assumed it was a him, she was uncertain—that allowed a view of the kitchen, in which people milled about, doing things associated with food service. Someone was bellowing orders, there were several female voices.

"I don't give a shit what *you* want, Sister, *I* want you to get out there and help Natalie," clamored a large, thirtyish man in a pair of ratty shorts and a stained white, A.B.'s t-shirt, as he pushed through the double doors, his back to Dre. "She's only been here three days and it's Saturday and she can't handle the front alone. She ain't but fifteen."

Well, that made Dre feel like a huge bitch. Poor hostess kid hadn't even been employed a week. She was more confused about her job requirements than the dyke before her.

"Fuck off," proclaimed a distinctly feminine, husky voice that did not provide a face, but was intrinsically listenable all the same. "I do what I want. I don't answer to any of y'all."

"You do and you will—" Arms laden with freshly washed bar glasses, the man in question stopped short when he turned fully and saw Dre pretending to study her menu sheet. His big, brown eyes were devilishly sincere. "Shit. I'm sorry. How long you been sittin' out here?"

"Not long," she said, truthfully.

The unlikely bartender shelved his burden. "Natalie's new. My idiot brother hired her as a favor to her daddy. She's still in diapers." He looked around and saw no trace of the object of his opinion. "Poor girl's as sweet as she can be but she don't know her ass from a hole in the ground. I apologize for the wait."

His blatant honesty was refreshing, as was his open-faced nature, which was apparent in his mannerisms. He had taken in every aspect of her, she had seen it in his eyes, and yet he was the same as she suspected he would have been toward any other customer.

"Now, what can I get you? And don't ask for a Cosmo. Please."

There was a laminated sign hanging from the post against the wall that clearly stated 'This Bar Is For Real Drinks Only. No Cosmos. Except On Ladies Night.'

"It's not Ladies Night?" she joked.

He narrowed his eyes and grinned from ear to ear. "I love a woman with a sense of humor."

"You love all women, Link Holloway!" a voice hollered from the back.

"This is also true."

"You're barking up the wrong tree," Dre stated, without thinking, not that it would have mattered. She couldn't even attempt to pass for straight, with a boy's haircut and an undercut, in men's pants and a pair of suspenders. "I doubt you have what I'm interested in."

Link winked and put his hands on his hips, ignoring her comment in its entirety. Unless the wink was his response?

"What IPAs do you have?"

He slammed his hand down on the counter. "Dammit, didn't I just tell you I loved a woman with a sense of humor? Only thing I love more is a woman with good taste in beer. You name it, we got it."

"Now you're speaking my language," laughed Dre. "Give me something hoppy, but not too hoppy. Local, if you have it."

"Do we have it?!" Link turned around, reached for a cooler hidden under the bar and pulled out a rainbow lineup of cans ranging from green and dark blue to purple and yellow. "Westbrook, Dale's, Goose Island, Hopsecutioner—that one's from Georgia, but we keep it around—HopArt, BoltCutter, Total Eclipse. You pick, you saucy nymph. I'll even buy it, solely to prove to you that we brew the best of all IPAs right here in the South, which I'm guessing by your accent, you know very little about."

His condescension was oddly endearing.

Dre shoved the blue and red can backward. "Dale's isn't an IPA."

Link covered his heart with his hands and feigned a deadly wound. "Woman, you wound me with your knowledge of beers! Your taste is astounding."

"I'll take...green can."

"Westbrook, it is. Now don't leave. I want to learn everything I can about this intoxicating woman with the common sense and quick wit."

There was nothing sexual or demanding in his request, but he was unapologetically flirty anyway, with an undertone of lighthearted and silly appreciation. Link Holloway seemed like a man who enjoyed his life, enjoyed his job, and enjoyed his beer, which was something that Dre could definitely connect to. From high school forward, all she had ever wanted to do, really, was web design. It both riveted and infuriated her, and completed her in a way that nothing else ever did. She could work for hours, alone in her apartment, listening to music, occasionally pacing the hardwoods, or cuddling with Buddy. She never came home exhausted and angry, like Tris sometimes did, complaining about everything her students did not know or did not have. She never came home sore, like Sam, although wearing a baby twenty-four hours a day was beyond any realm of her comprehension. What the hell would she do when there were two? Wear one in the front and one in the back? Obviously the lesbian-owned coffee shop wouldn't give a damn how many babies she wore to work, they had made that clear from the beginning, so elated were they that lesbians were furthering the lesbian agenda by producing children. But still...

"This is good," she told Link when he returned. "Much better than I expected."

"From our cotton-pickin' reputation and our general lack of class and breeding," he supplied.

"Obviously, all of that."

A couple came through the front door and he waved in forced jolly. "Hey Marlene! Didn't think you'd make it back after last night!" To Dre, he whispered, "I can't figure how she's standin'. She passed out and slid right off the bar stool last night. Atticus had to call an ambulance." He backed up to the swinging doors and tapped them. "Atticus," he hissed, "Come here, you gotta see this!"

Three seconds later, a younger version of him, scruffy and wearing an apron and a hairnet, came forward. "What?"

"It's Marlene Denato. Back. After last night."

"You're fucking kidding me," he stiffened when he saw Dre. "Sorry."

Link slapped him. "You should be sorry, fucking cursing in front of a lady. This is my brother, Atticus Caleb."

"Nice to meet you," Dre deferred.

"Atticus," Link said by way of introduction, "this is my new friend, Hannah."

Dre shook her head. "Not even close."

"Sadie?"

"Nope."

"Magdalena?"

"Andrea. But I go by Dre."

"Nice to meet you, Dre," Atticus chuckled. "Keep an eye on my brother. We rarely let him out of the bar. He has no social skills."

A third person emerged from the back, wearing a fleece vest over his A.B.'s t-shirt, and carrying a clipboard. He was the same harsh man from before, who'd been yelling at someone before stalking off. "No social skills at all. One step above a monkey. Where's Natalie?"

Looking toward the door, Dre could see the illustrious Marlene and her man friend still standing by the front entrance, making eyes at the empty hostess stand.

"Jesus Christ…" The third man disappeared toward the door, and proceeded to seat the couple himself.

"That's my oldest brother, Win," Link explained. "He owns this place."

"He thinks he owns us all," Atticus griped, before slinking back into the kitchen.

Three brothers, all sun-drenched and earthy, all charismatic, all charming, all bearing romance novel names and biceps—what was in the water down here? Even a lesbian could spot the good fortune in the Holloway family.

"So, Andrea who goes by Dre, where are you from?"

"Massachusetts. South Waterton, Massachusetts. I'm on my way to Florida." She drank more of her beer. "My father's there."

"Mine's dead. Mom too."

Didn't that take the wind right out of a woman's sails? "I'm sorry," she mumbled, because having someone blurt out MY PARENTS ARE DEAD left her stammering for the appropriate response, as it would most normal people.

Link shrugged. "It is what it is. And it was a long time ago. Plane crash. Luckily, they left us all in charge of one another and we haven't managed to fuck that up too badly. *Yet*." He laughed, and his laugh was heavy and sated, like a man who was used to getting what he wanted out of life, no matter how badly the hand. He wasn't pretentious, in the least. His hands were calloused from work and there were scars down his arms from a rough and tumble childhood—the kind you develop after sliding down hills and sword fighting with sticks. His nails were dirty and his hair was frayed and in need of a trim.

"So, you're Dre from Massachusetts on her way to Florida to see her dad. That sounds like a country song."

"It would if someone died in the middle," she blurted and then really felt like shit because he had only moments before told her that both of his parents were deceased. *What kind of an asshole—*

"Or a dog was hit by a car."

"Ouch." More beer drinking intermingled with awkward silence. "Animal hater."

More customers entered while Win stood stiffly at the hostess stand and Natalie was nowhere to be found. They all chose tables or booths rather than the bar, where Dre noticed there were high spaces for patrons near the stage and along the side where the bathrooms were.

"Now you sound like my sister. She's obsessed with her dogs. With all dogs, really. She bought a cow on Facebook."

A sister, you say?

"I just like *my* dog," Dre elucidated. "I've had him for years. Saved him from the animal shelter."

"What kind?"

"A lab mix."

"We had a lab growing up. He stayed with Win for a while, after he moved out, but I think he died. At least, I haven't seen him in a while. I should put that on my list of things to ask him at the next family meeting."

Link had systematically cleaned every surface around him, and now fished a beer from the cooler, popped the top and took a swig.

"Tell me you're not serious." No family in America had Family Meetings. Those existed in the graveyard of classic 1980s TV sitcoms only.

"Oh, unfortunately I am. They were Win's idea. He thinks it keeps us all in the loop about one another's lives. Like living on the same fucking farm doesn't do that."

Dre snorted and nearly choked on her beer. When she set it down empty, Link produced a second while nursing his own. The byproduct of her childhood, she was reasonably certain all farms were run by Old McDonald and women who wore bonnets and overalls, not by men who looked like they spent most of the day day-drinking out of a pickup in the woods while shooting a rifle at nothing in particular.

"Yes, we live on a farm," he answered the unasked question. "Holloway Farm. It was my great-great-grandfather's land. Now it's ours."

"Must be nice…"

"Oh, it ain't free," Atticus spat in contrition, emerging with a load of rolled silverware in a basket. "It comes with conditions." His hearing and timing were beyond compare. "And chickens and family meetings and a sister."

Again with the sister…

"How many of you are there?" she solicited, incredulously. Most of her friends were single children. Her parents had both been single children. No older sibs, no younger sibs, just the one-and-done. And, selfishly, she pondered whether or not this Holloway girl child would have inherited the same ruddy, well-lived coloring and demeanor her brothers seemed to have perfected.

Atticus held out his fingers, as if he were counting. "Win, Link, me, and Cara Spencer. Maw needed helpin' 'round the house, I reckon," he jested.

"And you all live on the farm? Together?"

"In separate houses." This time it was Win, who was back with his clipboard and his very managerial expression that did not quite line up with the rest of his presence. "I couldn't live with the rest of them. They're pigs. Where's Sister?"

His younger brothers exchanged a glance and then both shrugged. In a glimmer, they were no longer adults, but babies, covering for one of their own.

"Lincoln," he reprimanded, in a paternal tone.

"James Winter," Link retorted. "I seriously have no idea. Last I saw her, she was bitchin' at me *and* you in the kitchen."

"Atticus?"

Atticus looked at the ground. He rubbed one hand through the back of his hair. The fact that he knew more than he was letting on became the general consensus of the party. He was the quintessential sheep, surrounded by wolves.

"I swear to god, if she left *again*—" Win was in the process of saying. And then the back door slammed open, rattling the neon bar signs that somehow still looked tasteful in the din of the movement, and in walked what Dre would describe as a she-devil, wily and tempestuous, in faded, low-slung jeans and a v-neck bar tee that left very (very) little to the imagination. Her fingers and wrists dripped with turquoise and her skin was golden tan, freckled and…tight. *Was tight the right word?* Tight was the first word that came to Dre's mind, as it raced with incalculable possibilities that would never come to fruition. Bathroom stalls and fields of flowers, sweaty sheets—

"Oh, hell," Link laughed, backing away to dispose of the beer he'd started no less than ten minutes before. "Here comes a hurricane."

* * *

So consumed was she with the woman before her, Andrea could only guess at to what he was referring. A hurricane of temptation, naturally, a hurricane of hair and smell and irritation.

She had seen *women* before. She had seen hundreds of women before, thousands, even, but nary a one held a candle to *this* woman. Her hair was a lion's mane of colors, all auburns and browns and blonde highlights, tendrils that wound in all directions, falling down past her shoulders in a cascade of unruliness. Her features were soft, her dye-eyes brown and thick-rimmed. She wore no makeup, at least none that was perceptible, which could also have indicated makeup prowess, really. That wasn't anything Dre had much experience with. She preferred fresh-faced girls, girls she could kiss close up, whose cheeks she could hold or stroke or nuzzle against.

Full, round breasts dipped in the vee of the A.B. Lincoln's billboard squiggled across her chest, her hips tucked into a round, shapely waist like an hourglass.

"What the fuck are y'all starin' at? Jesus, I had to go home and change clothes," the banshee barked, in an accent that was heavy with unsolicited vowel sounds and extra syllables. "I came in. I told you I would."

She pegged Win with her stare and he flushed red. Then he shuffled his feet. If Dre didn't know better, she would have sworn he was intimidated by her.

"Yeah, well, I told you to be here an hour ago," he stammered.

The Hurricane didn't back down. "I *was* here an hour ago. I was in the damn kitchen, washing your damn dishes and rolling your damn silverware. I didn't much think you'd want me sweatin' all over your customers after that."

All three brothers were frozen.

"You just gon' stare at me all night?" She pulled an order pad out of her back pocket and put a hand on her hip, raising an eyebrow. "Or you gon' tell me where you want me to go?"

When Win got heavy into his instruction and ushered her past, reminding her that she needed to help the hapless Natalie, Dre thought for certain she would say something. Anything. Hello. Fuck me. Something. Only she opened her mouth and no sound came out. Which was probably for the best.

Women who looked like that had nothing to do with lesbians who looked like Andrea Marie Martin. Women who looked like that ate men for breakfast, lunch and dinner. That woman was built for adult film and a senator's downfall, with lean cut legs for days and lush, pliable skin that would—

"Don't go getting' any ideas, now," Link was again in her corner, wiping and shuffling and rearranging, masquerading as someone who had not just likened homosexuality to a disease of the mind in one inane statement of offense, as Atticus poured himself a Coca-Cola. "I know my sister."

The unexpected nature of his comment was shocking, but his message was loud and clear, a blatant reminder of her surroundings and the red conservative carpet she had ridden in on, pretending that she would blend in and relax. It made her angry and it made her scared and it made her embarrassed.

"I'm sorry?" Playing dumb seemed like the best option. "I didn't catch that."

"I said don't get any ideas about my sister," Link repeated, again like it was harmless and mundane when what he really meant was *KEEP YOUR DYKE HANDS OFF MY KIN FOLK.*

"I'm not contagious," she mumbled, before she could stop herself, cheeks mottling at the affront. "I'm a lesbian, not a leper."

Gone were the cornball jokes. Now she just felt humiliated and...silly. Silly for thinking she could walk into a place like this and be anything other than an oddball who looked like a girl but dressed more like a boy. Silly for looking at a girl who was a hard ten when she was little more than a confused queer. Silly for being awestruck and turned-on all at once for the first time in...ever?

Jesus, why had she come here? She could be in Florida already-

"Cool your jets, that's not what I said at all," Lincoln was back-pedaling. "If I had an issue with you, which I don't, it would be because you're a Yankee, not a lesbian. I love women just as much as the next red-blooded American and I have nothin' but love and respect for anyone else who does the same."

"Then why would you tell me not to get any ideas about your sister? Why say anything at all?"

Atticus cut her off with a succinct and acute rejoinder. "'Cause we like you so far, and Cara Spencer's a hurricane, Dre. Hurricanes are hell on anyone in their path. She'd just as soon ruin your life as look at you."

Hurricane Cara

'Cause we like you so far…

It was an odd thing, this sudden familiarity that Dre felt in such a foreign place with these veritable strangers. Not quite like she belonged, but then she had no frame of reference for what that would have felt like, anyway. That, according to the psychologist her father had insisted she see as a child recently made motherless, was the lingering result of losing the nurturing influence in her life; like a baby bird falling helplessly from the nest, she would be forever plummeting and forever alone. Sure, there would be Tris. There would always be Tris, no matter how many children Sam wanted to have, no matter how many hair-brained schemes Sam would come up with to set her up with professor after professor, Tris would always answer the phone and always text back. And there would always be Michael and Ami and the twins, despite their proximity and despite their differences. They were good to her and they were…present, in a way. But belonging? No, she didn't belong at A.B. Lincoln's, but she wasn't unwelcome, either, despite her misgivings about Link's hurricane comment. She wasn't a pariah, not really. She liked beer and funny people and listening to a family make jokes about universally understood sibling behavior that she would never experience. She liked the background noise, the people shuffling and milling about, she just hoped Buddy would be fine in the hotel room for a little while longer.

Shoving the wooden bathroom door open, she checked her watch. It was the one truly nice thing she owned, aside from the MacBook, which was more necessity than status symbol; a platinum Rolex with a large face and diamonds. Stupid thing made her feel like a rapper and a small hidden part of her loved it.

"Shit." She'd been gone three hours easily, though the night was still early, yet. Tables had only begun to fill up, the bar remained empty. Cara Spencer dawdled in her section, giggling and patting backs and rubbing arms as the men around her became blobs of puddle infatuation and the women seethed in the way only southern women could seethe.

Link claimed it was her downfall, the way everyone stood up to take notice of her when she walked into a room.

"It's like a disability, honestly. Every boy she's ever dated's fallen plum in love with her," he expounded, three beers into his shift. "And she never gave a shit about any of 'em. She couldn't stand a one."

In and out with grunt chores and clean dishes, Atticus paused to guffaw at a sudden memory. "How many proposals, now? Six? Seven? Nineteen?"

Win slapped his clipboard down on the bar and took a seat near Dre. "Four. Steven, Ben, that tool from Charlotte—the one with the beard and the gecko? And Mark Hillcraft."

Without having asked, Link delivered a screwdriver to his older brother and then continued on in his rehashing of the Holloway kids' tumultuous love lives. There'd been a few pregnancy scares, all on Atticus's end, one secret girlfriend who worked at a strip club in Myrtle Beach on the weekends, one girl who set a truck on fire, all of Cara Spencer's hapless beaus, and one wheelchair-bound para Olympic contender.

"And yet none of you tied the knot?"

No was the ready declaration. *Or was it a HELL NO?*

The Right Kind of Woman

Wouldn't your parents have cared? For some reason, the northern presumption was that all southerners either wanted to get married at eighteen, or were forced to get married at eighteen to legitimize babies. College was just a formality, or a hunting ground to lance that special someone, but it was widely accepted that in South Carolina and North Carolina, you usually married your high school sweetheart, or your cousin, on that magical day upon which you could vote in primary elections.

"That was the best part of Clyde and Donna." Win explained he had long ago dispelled of calling them "Mom" and "Dad" because he had reached the point in his life when he realized he had been without them longer than he had ever been with them. "Clyde and Donna never would have given a shit about anything we did or who we dated."

"They voted Democrat," Atticus whispered, winking. "But don't tell nobody or they'll run us all out of town."

Dre wasn't sure that part was a joke—

"Should I buy the wedding gift now? Or wait 'til one of 'em makes it official?" a throaty, confident voice sniggered behind her in the bathroom, shaking her inner dialogue loose and reminding her she was very much in the present, in a bathroom staring at a blank yellow wall.

In the mirror over the pedestal sink, she saw Cara Spencer, hands on her hourglass hips, skimming the half-inch of exposed flesh just below her navel. The scent of lavender and yellow jasmine hung in the air around her and her stare was intense; however, intense did little to describe the feeling of being nailed with her almond, obsidian-black eyes. Severe? Critical? Daring?

Her deep and even breaths stole the air from the room and Dre put her hands to her own throat, heart racing.

What was it with this woman? It was like she'd never really been attracted to anyone before, never fully had any appreciation or desire for a woman's body until the moment she laid eyes on the dominant female standing in the lone stall doorway with a paper towel in her hands.

"Hello?" Cara Spencer tittered. "You can't possibly be that blind."

"Blind?" Was something on her face? Shit, was she blushing? *Shit, shit, shit...*

"They're all smitten with you, honey. All of the Holloway boys. Like you're the last steak on the savanna."

Gross. Dre didn't want to be anyone's steak, least of all the steak any man wanted to sink his teeth into. The one male experience she'd had, back at Northwestern, had been far less than satisfying, not that it was any of *his* fault. Greg was his name, Greg Fillman. The only guy dumb enough to think the girl who shaved her head and dressed in men's pants would ever want to be his girlfriend. Nope. It had been the one time in her life that Andrea had convinced herself to try a penis and see if the sensation was one she could live with. Hadn't gone well. Had gone laughably unwell. Had necessitated ringing up Tris in the middle of the night, *after* she'd driven Greg home.

"Your brothers aren't really my...type," she slurred.

Cara Spencer winked. "Ya don't say..." Her hips swayed past and she put her hand on the door. "And what *is* your type?"

"You are." *FUCK* why had she said that? Why had Dre said something so stupid?

Fuck this was embarrassing.

Dre had never so much as approached a woman like this for a quarter at a pay phone (were pay phones even a thing anymore?) and here she was, doused with liquid courage (how many beers had she had now?), and flinging about pick-up lines in a public fucking bathroom. *What the fuck?!*

Thankfully, and by the grace of God, Cara Spencer laughed, and not in a mocking way. Not *at* her, but with her. Like it was a good attempt, not a corny attempt. Like it was a real pick-up line. Like she was really, in fact, picking her up and it wasn't wholly *un*successful.

Thoughts poured in at warp speed. Was Cara Spencer a lesbian? Obviously not. No. But she could be adventurous. Maybe she'd never seen a real dyke before? Maybe there weren't dykes in Greentown. Was Dre willing to be that test? That phase experience? Was Dre a dyke?

When Cara Spencer turned to her, hand off of the door, hair in her face, eyes somehow warmer than they had been, lips parted...

Fuck yes, I will be your dyke experience! her brain yelled, winging from the neurons of her subconscious and conscious and fantasy. *Fuck yes, I will show you what it feels like!* What a sellout she was! Sam would wither in disappointment at her wilting resolve for the cause. But Sam wasn't in this bathroom. Sam was at home, pregnant and married and not confronted with this. Whatever this was. Sam had kissed her frogs and picked her mate.

And now it was Dre's turn to make-the-fuck-out with this frog who could never be her mate. It was Dre's turn to live *this* life.

With no hesitation (or beating back the hesitation she felt), she closed the distance between their two bodies with brazen assertion and, placing her hand on the back of Cara Spencer's neck, coming to her full height, crushed against her mouth in excited passion. The second their lips touched, she knew she had succumbed to some higher fate.

The other woman, too stunned to react, stood motionless. For three point two seconds. And then let loose with a moan so low in her throat it set every inch of Dre's skin on fire, igniting secret wants within her that was thus far untapped. She wanted this woman, but somehow, she *needed* this woman, right in this moment. Arching her back, she slipped her pelvis into Cara, feeling her woman's heartbeat and her shallow breaths, breasts straining against fabric, hands seeking skin. Her untamed mane fell over them both, her fingers lacing into the waistband of Dre's jeans.

Cara tasted of sin and fervor, she thought, lapping gently, coaxing with her tongue what she yearned to taste; sin and fervor and hot sweaty promise. Adventure, ecstasy and—

Her body stilled as two tiny, tentative hands found the pale flesh of her stomach, shirt untucked and left to hang in wrinkled abandon, suspenders unfastened.

Was it possible that Cara Spencer wanted this as much as she did?

"Yes...." the goddess whispered against her mouth, as her gentle fingers found the coarse hair at the juncture of Dre's thighs. "God... Yes... Please..."

Like liquid lava, she undulated in rhythms, free with abandon and want. She ran her legs up Dre's calves, sucked her bottom lip. Her touch was electric. Taking temperate hold of her jaw, Dre guided her to the wall, for her support, holding her gruffly still as she moved to the embroidered teal belt and the button-fly jeans. Pulse racing, she felt she would suffocate if she didn't taste this woman right now. Right here. Right in the thrill of this moment. It was the most recklessly exhilarating moment of her life. Droll, sensible, dependable, responsible Dre—Andrea Marie from the Italian neighborhood—who went on at least three dates before spending the night and took Buddy for a check-up every six months and worked from home only because she was so structured it was damn near painful to make it through the day. Who planned her meals a week in advance and saved ten percent of every paycheck and loved sparingly and took a shower after watching porn and...

Andrea, who was wrapped up in a stranger against a bathroom stall. Andrea, who was kneeling on a grungy tile floor, pulling at white lace panties with her teeth, growling as they slid down Cara Spencer's svelte, tan legs and landed in an unladylike puddle, leaving her bare under a wolf's gaze of possession that was unfounded. Heat surrounded them, enveloped them. Swaddled them.

The very first time she'd tasted a woman, Dre had grasped with crystal clarity that she was done for in life. Ruined. Like a bargain drinker in Italy, swirling the thick, heady mixture of Merlot. There would never be a contrast, never a comparison. For her, the taste of a woman would be the only taste she would ever crave, the only taste that would keep her up at night, keep her moving, keep her working, ever improving.

She'd been alone for so long and Cara Spencer was so achingly beautiful, so smooth, so perfect. The folds of her sweetest place bare and tan and weeping, her lips apart, swollen and pink, her hair in all directions, deep eyes glazed and impetuous.

She had only come to Greentown for a night. She had only come to A.B.'s for a drink. She had only come to this bathroom to—

It didn't matter anymore. Nothing mattered anymore.

Temptingly, with agonizing slowness, she brushed one finger over Cara's cleft. One finger, one stroke.

Holding her balance, she took hold of Cara Spencer's hip with her left hand.

"Will you..." The question was little more than a whisper, hoarse and panting, belabored and weighty with anticipation. "...will you..."

"Do you want me to?" On a base level, she needed to hear the answer. She needed Cara to want to be licked by a woman. Not any woman. She needed Cara Spencer to want to be licked by Andrea who went by Dre.

Sheepishly, Cara nodded, and then looked down. The longing in her eyes was a tangible thing. It was all Dre needed to—

"Cara Spencer! What the fuck are you doing in the bathroom!?" Link's voice thundered with terrifying proximity. His plodding footsteps stopped right outside the swinging saloon-style door, barely three feet away. "We got three new tables out here!"

"Don't come in here!" his sister squawked, scrambling to step into both her pants and underwear. "I'll be out in a minute!"

There was no disguising the embarrassment in her voice, nor the trepidation it contained.

"Jesus, what are you? Taking a shit or something? Fucking relax," he cursed, footsteps retreating. "She's in the fucking bathroom, Win, I can't go in there, she's taking a shit or doing something girly!"

Something really damn girly...

"Shit," she was saying, more to herself than to Dre. "Shit, that was close. What the fuck..." Her belt loop caught and she sputtered in irritation. "Stupid fucking belt. Stupid fucking shoes..."

Her struggle was oddly endearing.

"Fuck."

Standing, Dre took hold of her waist and she stilled. Her cheeks were flushed, her eyes wide with passion, pulse quickened. She looked like a woman who needed to be loved and loved well.

"Let me," Dre's voice was quiet. With nimble fingers, she threaded the loops of the belt and fastened the metal hardware in a moment's time.

"Uh, thanks," Cara Spencer mumbled. "I, uh…I gotta get back to work…"

In the emptiness that descended in her absence, Andrea wondered what in the fuck she had gotten herself into. What roller coaster ride had she boarded? What point was she trying to prove?

You'll never change if you keep doing the same old shit, she told herself. *That's what this is… This is me trying to step out of my comfort zone.*

Only it didn't feel quite that superficial. It felt…visceral.

Washing her hands, she splashed water on her face and straightened her shirt, refastening the suspenders that were ridiculously flapping in the wind. She was, frankly, an idiot, but she didn't want it to show.

* * *

"Hey Link," Atticus Caleb whispered, watching Andrea who went by Dre slink out of the bathroom clearly only thirty seconds after Cara Spencer. "I don't think she listened."

"About what?" Link was far too busy hitting on twenty-something students from the local cosmetology school who had only recently passed their state board exams. One was in a tank top, despite the not quite summertime weather, and the other had on cowboy boots with a skintight pair of daisy duke shorts because, you know, you never could tell when the opportunity to rope a calf would present itself. In a bar.

"About Cara…"

That got his attention. He even dropped his bar towel. But all he said was, "Hmm…"

Atti nodded. "I hope she's got experience with hurricanes."

The Right Kind of Woman

Moving between tables, Cara Spencer could barely remember her own name, let alone any of the detailed orders she had only attempted to copy down.

What in the fuck was she doing? What had gotten into her? Making out with a girl in the bathroom? Anyone could have busted in on them, any number of the female patrons who would all run back and tell their husbands and friends or her brothers. Anyone could have seen what they were doing.

What they had been doing sent shivers down her spine again, and she was already soaked, thankful she was wearing denim, which was thick enough to absorb her stupid attraction. Who was this Dre woman anyway, that her idiot kin were fawning all over at the bar because she knew enough about beer to order something other than Bud Light? What made her so special?

Her ass, for certain.

Stop! She told herself. *None of that, you're at work.* Work was a place for sweat and tasks and false niceties and female flirtation that her heart would never be a part of so Win would make money and she would make money and A.B.'s would stay open another day and their lives wouldn't all be pointless. Work was something she did to make them happy; it was not really a place she ever intended to be happy. Or wet. Or have her tongue in another woman's throat in the bathroom she had to clean at the end of the night.

Stupid Dre. Stupid, oddly sexy, oddly inauspicious Dre with hair that felt good to run her fingers through and a body that was hard in every place it needed to be hard while maintaining a woman's gentle curves. Stupid breasts—

"Sister!" Win screamed, clapping his hands beside her head to get her attention. He was less than three inches from her face and annoyed. "I've been calling you for ten minutes. Where's your head?"

Between another woman's legs.

"Oh, shit!" She snapped at herself and then realized he hadn't heard her internal peanut gallery. "I heard you the first time. What do you want now? Slop the hogs? Dance onstage?"

"Get your guitar," he enunciated, as if she were a dunce. "I asked you to get your guitar."

"My guitar?"

"Mad Dog is late. You've got ten minutes. I'll take your tables."

My guitar? He wanted her to sing? Right now? After what had just happened in the bathroom that he was completely unaware of? He wanted her to crawl up on the stage and stand under a light with soggy panties and croon to the crowd of six?

A crowd that included Dre.

"Cara Spence! Guitar!" Win shook her shoulders.

"It's in the truck," she whispered.

"Then go and get it out of the truck and get your ass on that stage. What is *with* you?"

* * *

Sliding back up to the bar, still dizzy from exertion, Dre requested her tab and Link handed her a bill for only about half of what she'd consumed.

"What the hell?" she demanded. "This is nothing!"

"'S on the house, my love," Lincoln laughed. "And I took the liberty of packing you a sixer for the road. Figured you could enjoy the cornucopia of alcohol we offer here, in the great old South, for as long as you're in town…"

"That'd be one night. Buddy and I are clearing out in the morning." Florida was calling. There would be far more women in Florida.

"Oh, you can't leave *now*," Atticus waved his arms around as he carried three plates into the kitchen and held the door open with his foot. "The music's just about to start."

Perplexed, Link checked his watch. "Mad Dog's late, though. He called and said it'd be, like, half an hour—"

Atti cut him off with a grin. "Not Mad Dog. The house musician."

"We do not have a house musician— "As his words jumbled out, the fluorescents switched on above the stage and a round, woman's body whisked up from the side with an acoustic Washburn strapped to her chest. In her right hand, she carried a stool and in her left, she cradled the guitar, an intricate beaded leather thong keeping it close to her.

Dre took in the sight of Cara Spencer and flushed. Link put his hands up, like a five year old. "I forgot my sister was the house musician. Win rarely lets her sing."

"Why?" Jesus, she was stunning, the strands of light playing up her hair and her cheekbones and her eyes and basically everything else about her.

When she looked right at Dre, the whole thing felt shockingly intimate.

"Is she…bad?" She attempted to maintain the conversation.

"God, no," Atticus was in and out with plates of food again. "She's just a little too…deep for a place like A.B.'s. A.B.'s needs an old redneck drunk who sings David Allan Coe covers and Wagonwheel eighty times a night. Songs everybody here knows."

"Cara S is more into soul, if that makes sense," Link completed. "Soul is *not* what people come here for because we don't cater to the intellectual community, no offense. Most of the people who end up here are the same people who end up here every night. They like to drink cheap beer and hear the same songs and see the same people and escape."

That was ironic, given that Dre had driven hundreds of miles to do just the opposite and ended up in the same space. The frightening thing for her was understanding that she could, in another life, be very happy in a place like this, that seemed the polar opposite of what she was accustomed to: slower, perhaps more methodical. Looser. She could be happy with food like she had eaten, although her cholesterol would be appalled— Atticus was a culinary genius with burgers. She could be happy with the ambient sounds and the lilting accents. She could be happy with these mellow men and their intoxicating sister.

Another beer slid across the counter and when she turned to question Link, he looked up toward the stage, where Cara Spencer settled on the stool and began to croon in a hauntingly smooth Jeff Buckley melody that sucked all of the nervous tension from the room and left her heart splayed and open on the floor.

"Hey, can Buddy swim?" Atticus asked, back behind the bar, mixing a rum and Coke for a girl not a day over twenty-one. "All Labs can swim, right? I read that somewhere."

She bobbed in the affirmative, but her ears were too consumed with the sultry power of Cara's husky voice. "Buddy loves to swim." When she went him to boarding in the summer, he swam in the concrete pools. The vet said it was a great exercise for his aging joints, like water aerobics for elderly ladies.

She sounds like an angel. Her fingers were masterful on the strings of her guitar.

"I'll bet Buddy would love Holloway River," Atticus continued, trading the plastic concoction of brown liquor and soda for a smile and a Wells Fargo debit card.

"I hadn't thought of that," Link concurred. "Cara Spencer's dogs love Holloway River."

Cara Spencer could sing and Cara Spencer had dogs. That made her even more perfect.

"What's Holloway River?" Dre didn't want to seem too interested. Having only met briefly outside the first stall of the ladies room, it would have been incredibly foolish to get any of her hopes up about this strange fairy goddess. Besides, in all likelihood, Cara Spencer was incredibly straight and engaged to the next Mr. President of the Southern Colonies, a man with three-piece suits and a Range Rover and three ice cubes in his mint julep.

"The river that bisects our property. It starts about forty miles away, but runs for eleven miles on our land." Elucidated Lincoln. "A lot of people use it for kayaking and water sports." concluded Atticus. Then, they looked at one another for a solid three seconds without saying a word and it was the second time in one evening that Andrea had the distinct impression that they both knew more than they were letting on.

"That's cool," she narrated, because she couldn't think of why they would be telling her all about their river or why they insisted on talking when Cara Spencer was starting a second song, just as haunting as the first.

"Say, we're going kayaking tomorrow, Brother," Link furnished, all too eagerly. "I think we're leaving at ten in the morning. Should be a beautiful day for it. Highs in the upper seventies, coolers full of beer."

Dre had never even seen a kayak in real life, outside an outdoor store or a television commercial, and she was a shit swimmer. But this river, and its family of inhabitants, was quite intriguing, as was the possibility of growing closer to *all* of them.

"But you don't happen to have an extra kayak, do you?" Atti's smile was like a Cheshire cat. "I can't figure out how we'd even include Dre, and here we are telling her all about how awesome it is."

"I don't kayak," she interposed. "I don't even swim."

"Life preservers," the brothers said at the same time. Then, Link added, "You know, we do have that big red kayak. Perfect size for a girl about five feet, ten and a big, brown Lab?"

"Perfect size, perfect size."

"I don't kayak and I don't swim and I'm leaving in the morning." Funny. Her statement sounded a lot more hollow than it had earlier in the day.

What was her hurry? Her father would still be there in a day or two. Her job would go on, regardless of location. Sam would water her dead plants for however long she wanted, her rent was paid up. Surely, Pam at the Carolina Inn would be accommodating if she desired to stay an additional night. There was no way in hell the place would completely fill up in twenty-four hours.

In the back of the restaurant, Win led the audience's applause at the completion of Cara Spencer's second song, and then unabashedly ordered her from the stage as a largish, burly man in Hawaiian shorts and a board shit bounded up with a one-man-band of sorts strapped to his person in an uncomfortable fashion.

"Well," Lincoln told her, as serious and calm as he'd been when she'd first sat down hours before, "if you change your mind—and I'm not saying you should, I'm only saying that you'd love it—my number's in the bag."

He produced a folded brown paper bag the size of a six-pack and shoved it toward her.

"We leave at ten."

"At ten, I'll be on the way to Florida," Dre was still telling herself, belted into the driver's seat of the Explorer, following a better map drawn by Win that would take her safely back to the hotel in half the time.

At ten, she would be on the way to sunny Florida, where her life was sure to change. Unless Greentown counted as a change. Did Greentown count as a change? Unsure, she dialed Tris and turned beside a closed-up AME church with a fire pit in the side yard.

"Heellllo?" her friend answered, groggy and obviously formerly asleep.

"Were you asleep?" *Stupid question.* "It's only midnight."

"We have a baby, Dre." There was scratching on the other end of the telephone, and then Tris walked into another room, her feet thumping quietly on the creaking laminate floors of their apartment. "What's up? Did they kill you?"

"Yes. I'm dead. I had a good time."

"Then why are you calling? Calling people with a baby after nine indicates emergency."

"Should I stay here another night?"

"That's an emergency? Are you out of money?"

"No, I...I met a woman." That felt extremely unfamiliar on her tongue (how she wished something else was on her tongue). "I met a woman and we almost had sex in a bathroom."

"Shut. The. Fuck. Up." Wave the yellow flag, time out, slam dunk.

"No, it's true. I'm a whore."

"What stopped you? Your conscience?"

"Her job."

"And you want to stay another night to finish the job?" Tris could always see through the bullshit.

"No." *Yes. Very much yes.* "I want to stay another night to go kayaking with her brothers."

Pause. Creaking floor. "You don't kayak."

"I could."

"You don't swim."

"I could learn."

"In a day?" Touché.

Approaching an unfamiliar stoplight, Dre wondered if she'd gotten turned around, but in the hazy distance she spotted the dilapidated Carolina Inn road sign. "I want to stay and finish the job," she relented. "She's amazing."

Tristan laughed and covered it up with a cough. "You just met her."

"So? What's that joke about lesbians? What do we take on a first date?"

"A moving truck."

She decided it was prudent to leave out the bit about not really knowing if Cara Spencer was a lesbian. That was more than Tris needed in this exact moment. Honest. And Sam would have none of it. She had no

84

patience for those who posed as lesbian, but were long-term heterosexuals. Those, she harbored an intense hatred for.

"Well," her friend sighed, considering all sides in the manner she always did, "if you're looking for a change, I can't imagine one bigger than South Fucking Carolina."

That was the last thing on her mind when Dre fell asleep that night, cuddling against Buddy and wishing he was someone else, twisted up in the itchy down blankets of the Carolina Inn, printed with mallards and ferns, just like the walls and the curtains.

If she wanted a change, South Carolina was a start. She'd never so much as driven through the place prior to that afternoon. What were boiled peanuts? Where did pimentos come from?

What was Cara Spencer doing? It was an attraction she really could not illuminate, a pull that was magnetic on a primal level. In all of her past, there had never been a woman like Cara Spencer. Not those trial runs in college, the practice girls who would help her discover the type of lesbian she would become. God, not Mare. Mare had been more man than woman, right down to the underpants she refused to take off in bed, even *en flagrante delecto*. As the captain of their collegiate softball team, she'd had her pick of straight girls to plow through and plow through them she did, always feeding Dre lies about her involvements. To cap it all off, after five years of on-again-off-again BS, she cut the cord and told all of their mutual friends that Andrea wasn't 'femme' enough for her. After Mare had come Stephanie and Stephanie was just…vanilla. Nothing even close to Cara. Cara was fresh summer air on a frigid morning, water on a dry plain.

"You're an idiot," she told herself, when the alarm went off at eight a.m. "You're an idiot and you're in love with a woman you know nothing about." Was she in love? No. She wasn't. She was intrigued. Enthralled. And it was completely unrealistic.

"One day," she said, brushing her teeth. "You get one day and then it'll be out of your system. She'll pick her nose or be incredibly stupid."

Buddy seconded.

"One day and then you'll cut your losses, say goodbye your new friends, and haul ass to warmer weather and Jimmy Buffet fans and grilled ahi tuna."

Be Careful, Or You'll Tip

"You gonna tell her?" With a kayak slung over his shoulder and a life jacket hanging from his arm, Atticus looked every ounce the outdoorsman his brothers so wanted him to be, minus the paint smeared in his rangy hair.

The weather was stunning, the temperature was rising and he was planting seeds that would grow into a great day. He had beer, two sandwiches, a battery-powered radio, and Lincoln had yet to mention to Cara Spencer that he'd invited her girl crush along for their weekly Sunday sojourn down the Holloway River. All of the boxes were ticked for what they affectionately referred to as 'hurricane season.'

"Tell her what?" Win asked, further down by the water's edge.

He had on swim trunks and a long-sleeved advertisement from the Nantahala Outdoor Center, which he'd never actually been to but pretended that'd he gone a million times when it came up in conversation with patrons. His Ray Bans hung carelessly around his neck.

When Link failed to respond, he turned to Atticus, who mentioned, in a falsely nonchalant tone, all bravado and careless intonation, "He invited that girl from last night to go with us."

"Shit, Link, not the one with the cowboy hat. She couldn't'a been more'n nineteen."

"No, no, not that one," Atticus clarified. "That one had a boyfriend. He invited Dre."

Win shrugged. "I like her."

"That's exactly what I said," Link was defensive. "She knew beer, she was funny…"

Atticus dropped his half of the sea green kayak. "She's obviously into Cara Spencer."

"She's *what*?" Win balked. Of the three remaining Holloway males, he had always been the most protective and, by far, the most inclined to being nosy although he vehemently blamed Link for carrying out the plan to spy on her driveway or google license plate numbers.

Shaking his head, Lincoln drank from the water bottle he kept in hand at all times. "Relax, *Dad*. We don't know that it's anything serious. We just know that they were in the bathroom together."

"They were *what*?"

Atticus scoffed. "They're both girls, Win. It's not a crime. And we don't know that anything happened in there. We just know that they came out looking…a bit like they'd been interrupted."

"That's disgusting," grumbled James Winter, who hated his formal name. "That's our sister. I don't want to think about her being alone in a bathroom with anyone."

Looking every bit the troublemaker, Lincoln Andrew scrunched his nose. "She could do a lot worse than Dre. I like Dre."

"Is that what this is? Are you trying to set her up?"

Atticus shook his head and stalked back to the truck, having always preferred to allow his sister the limited illusion of privacy she maintained. While the other two grannies were as tactless as the gossiping old biddies who frequented their grandmother's retirement community, he had simply assumed Cara Spencer would wander out in her own sweet time—not that it hadn't been interesting to speculate for the past twenty-odd years.

"Would it be so bad if I did set her up?" he heard Link hiss. "She spends all of her time ALONE."

"Well, what happened to that last girl? The one with the Equinox?" Win countered.

"Went back to her husband. I checked."

"How'd you check?" They were untangling ropes and strapping in seats, and picking out the remnants of sparrow nests, which was a monotonous but necessary task. "D'you run the plates or something?"

"Maybe."

Maybe... Lincoln was a *bona fide* idiot with a capital I. "You ran an innocent woman's plates?" Atticus felt himself accuse, as he lugged a cooler down the sandy, ant-ridden little beach their father had constructed in the late 1990's when building codes and ordinances were far less strict and sand was fifty dollars for a truckload.

They were nearly in his front yard, but he still felt the need to drive down in his steel gray Ford Ranger that was a hundred years old and still kicking.

"You mean the innocent woman who went back to her *husband*? Doesn't sound very innocent to me."

Win and Atti cracked up and called their brother a bitch, who then admitted that he was a bitch if a bitch was someone who 'cared for his sister.' In the space following, he lit a cigarette and leaned against a tree. "I just hate that she's still alone. I always figured she'd find somebody 'fore now."

"But she's gonna stay alone, until she decides to say it out loud. Until then she'll keep hiding, skirtin' around." Win lit his own cigarette and mumbled something about peer pressure. "Maybe Dre will pull it out of her. At least she ain't like the rest of 'em," with *the rest of 'em* being a litany of girls who wanted to play at whatever Cara Spencer wanted in the moment, but not provide emotional support in the long run. Those were the only women she would attract, having hidden herself so deep in the proverbial closet that she could barely see the light of day. They were mainly straight girls, unhappy spouses, or women who had seen too much porn to know being gay was a birthright, not a trendy choice in a bathroom stall.

Off in the distance, Atticus heard a door slam and a cow moo and dogs bark while tromping through the low vegetation that filled the entire parcel. He closed his eyes and said a silent prayer that God would find a place in his heart to forgive the Holloway boys and the mess they were about to make of their sister's love life.

"Here comes Hurricane Cara now," he said, through clenched teeth.

* * *

Stupid alarm clock. Stupid kayak trip, Cara Spencer muttered to herself as she bounded out of the back door of her tattered, hundred-year-old farmhouse and down the back slope with two dogs at her heels. The smaller canine, a herding dog by nature, was a ball of unhinged movement from sunup to sundown, with squat, stubby legs and a central girth of thirty five pounds all in tones of black and white and speckled heather, lending validity to her given name of Grey Baby. She loved running, eating, ripping, chewing, nibbling, swimming and Cara Spencer. Her larger counterpart, a shaggy white colossus dubbed Greg Allman, despite her ovaries, was more of a chowhound and rarely got out of bed unless the Threat Level on the property rose above Red, a purely speculative assumption as she had never actually done it. She loved naps, collard greens, and lying on the banks of the river watching her family engage in watery pursuits, and her only active period of the day was first thing in the morning, when the aforementioned *stupid* alarm clock clicked on to a shriek and a whine.

Stupid fucking alarm clock, Cara whined again, running a hand through her jumbled mound of curls, piled up high atop her head in a loose bun that had been hastily secured with a newspaper rubber band while mid-pee.

Bleary-eyed and cranky, she was wiped, exhausted, devoid of rest, and there was no real reason for it. She had not worked too terribly late. She had not been out drinking. It was not as if she were meeting Link and Win and Atti for a sunrise service, it was a quarter after nine. That was actually late in her life, yet her eyes were filled with sleep and her blood ran antsy.

This is probably what you get when you almost let a stranger stick her face in your pussy in a bathroom.

"Nope," she held up her coffee cup as she sidestepped a mole hole. "Not doing it. Not going there." Whatever had happened the night before had been. Whatever. It was over. Dre was gone. It was fun and it was over. Super over.

Her brothers were already gathered at the water's edge. Kayaks had already been dumped. The two boards—hers and Win's—were laid out in the sun. Grey Baby was in the throes of a snarl at Win, who may have become her least favorite person in the world; Greg Allman was pawing at a chunk of wood in the sand, looking for a bug snack or a speck of leftover food.

"Y'all ready?" she called, because she knew she needed to be polite and not inflict the monstrosity of her mood on them like she always did. *Look at me, turning over a new leaf and caring and shit...*

Batting his eyes, Link held up a mug of java that read A.B. Lincoln's: Your Home Away From Home. "Need to finish my coffee first."

"Finish it on the boat," she told him.

Every Sunday they pretended to drink coffee and then switched to beer, chucking the mugs into the woods to be retrieved at a later time. That custom would have driven their dead father crazy, the largest citation on his ghostly list of complaints as to the nature of their care of the property: there were coffee mugs and cigarette packs and beer cans littering the woods that his grandfather had purchased from the Cherokee.

"I like this mug," he lied.

"Whatever, asshole," her mood peeked through. Or was it her lack of sleep? For what had felt like hours, she had simply swaddled in the afghans that Granny deemed too ugly to take with her into retirement and stared at the glow-in-the-dark stars painted over the cheesy popcorn ceiling. What was wrong with her? Why was the Dre thing such a big deal?

Because it's not every night you get accosted in the bathroom. By a woman, she should have finished, but even in her own head she was afraid someone would hear and string her up for slaughter. There were two gay people in all of Greentown, and no one spoke to them and they didn't speak about it.

"Tell her," Atti coughed, when she came closer, kicking off her Rainbow flip-flops in the bushes, tugging at the hem of her long-sleeved tee. She hadn't even bothered with pants. The weather would warm, like it always did in spring, and then she'd be forced to keep up with them and everyone knew they'd just end up in the woods. Instead, she was in a red bikini that tied around the neck and a cotton shirt from the Apple Stand, with ripe Braeburns stamped on her tits.

"Tell me what?"

No one spoke. She reached down for Greg Allman's thick, cotton ball coat, straight off of the Pyrenees. "Spare me from the bullshit. It's early. I haven't had any coffee—"

"Link invited Dre to come paddling with us," the youngest of her older brothers furnished, looking pleased with himself in spite of the dollops of green and yellow paint that were stuck in his hair. "She's on her way."

"What the…" *Hell were you thinking?* She wanted to scream. *Why would you do this? Why would you make this more complicated for me? I didn't sleep at all last night after what happened!* Only, they didn't know what had happened, and they certainly didn't know that it had kept her up for ten consecutive hours, and they sure as hell did not know the *why* of why it was a predicament. None of them were in the least bit aware of that unexplained bathroom sojourn. None of them were the least bit aware that she was a muffeater, behind closed (and locked) doors. None of them had any indication that she had developed a crater-sized crush on the bar's one-night-stand with the patroness from Massachusetts.

Was it a crush? It was feelings.

Whatever. Her brothers were unaware and that was totally her fault. They were her family. They had been there for her as far back as her conscious memory had existed. They had taught her to ride a bike and climb a tree and pick off a doe at seventy-yards with a twenty-aught-six. And, when their parents had been killed, they had rallied around her to give her the best of everything in this world. She needed them. She couldn't push them away, and away was exactly where they would run off to if they ever found out about her proclivities. So, she swallowed her feelings and gathered her thoughts and took great gulps of her Folgers Columbian Dark Roast and finally said, tersely, "Fine."

Lincoln looked at Win, who looked at Atticus and then looked back at him. "Fine?"

She nodded. "Fine."

No, not fine. Not even a little fine. Furthest fucking thing from fine, actually. I barely shaved my bikini line. "What time is she meeting us?" *So I know when to expect my heart to beat completely out of my chest?*

Her male doppelgangers kicked at the dirt and she wondered which of them had set the wheels of this debacle in motion. "Ah, ten... So I figured we would come down and get the boats ready." Which had taken them about ten minutes, so...

"That's a good plan," Cara Spencer lied because she was weaseling out from between a rock and a hard place. "That was smart." And, for the next one thousand, eight hundred and sixteen seconds, they simply stared at one another, awaiting the derailment of the train car.

* * *

"This is really stupid," Dre lectured Buddy, as she squirmed in the driver's seat of the Explorer. "I can't even swim, really."

More to the point, she had never *tried* to swim, really, not since swimming lessons at the YMCA pool off Huntington Ave back in Boston. But those had been successful, hadn't they? She had not drowned. *How hard can it be? Jump in, move your arms and legs and you float...*

"I probably won't even have to swim, though."

The big chunk of Lab was unimpressed, content to stare out of the windows while he sat like a grown man in the passenger's seat, occasionally growling at cows and horses contained by barbed wire near the road.

"I'll just stay in the boat. Are they called boats? Kayaks?"

Skydiving would have been a much more dangerous pursuit, in the scheme of her life, but this adventure was equally as dumb. She had no suitable kayaking clothes. She had never worn knit shorts, she had not packed any shorts (laughable given that her destination was the Sunshine State of balmy low-seventies year-round), and she had planned on purchasing a bathing suit in Florida only if it was absolutely imperative for her survival, primarily because she would not even know where to go in South Waterton to buy a suit, but also because she had no idea what type of suit she would need. A bikini? Not happening. A tankini? When had she become a middle-aged mom of two?

After less than ten minutes of skepticism and introspection, she had settled on jeans, because all she owned were jeans, and a *Drive by Truckers* tee shirt, with Toms, which were ugly but she knew she wouldn't be heartbroken if she fell in the river and lost them. And sunglasses. She owned one decent pair of Aviators that she treasured almost as much as T.I.'s rap star watch. No suspenders. No socks.

A secondary reason she had convinced herself this was truly a shit idea was that she had the insane tendency to over analyze each and every situation that unfolded before in the miracle of her life, and she was bedeviled with the view of looking quite like a jackass in front of a woman she was so stupidly attracted to. She had nearly broken the cardinal rules of hygiene in a public bathroom. This had the potential to be beyond miserable, unconscionably miserable, made more so if Cara Spencer played no part in the trip.

Buddy yelped and she looked over to see a rustic, half-rotten, white-washed sign that said "Holloway Farms" in a childlike, all-caps scrawl.

95

The misbegotten road that ran off to the right like a lone child streaking through the woodland was littered with stumps and unkempt vines.

I am crazy. She had no idea if Cara Spencer would be a part of this and, she was forced to admit to herself, the only thing worse than over-analyzing her every single movement where that woman was concerned, was *not* having the option to over-analyze every single movement where that woman was concerned. Spending time with Link and Win and Atticus for the day would be a wicked way to pass the lazy Sunday morning, she knew. There would be beer. She had garnered that much from the texts they had all exchanged earlier. There would be laughter. But there would be no fire, no passion, and after a lifetime spent in the shadows, she wanted the intoxication even if it led to the slow burn of letdown.

* * *

"Aren't you a fucking Nora Roberts," she quelled her own verbosity. *The slow burn of letdown.*

Down the pothole-laden dirt path, she wound around a small front pond—that must have been Win's house, neat and trim with bushes and a mailbox and a picnic table—and then moved further into the brush. Pine trees loomed overhead, animals jiggled the low-lying greenery, birds darted from one side to the other, and the whole of the place felt very much like an entirely new world. Rolling her window down, the air smelled of clean, honest freedom and sweat and work and the blossom of spring flowers. It was the furthest thing from city life she had ever experienced.

How was this real?

Little more than a mile onward, she saw what could only have been Link's modest hut, all windows and empty beer cans and a grill, with a

Dave Matthews poster strung up in place of curtains. His yard, if the term could be applied in a loose variation, was all windswept weeds and dandelion blooms, interwoven lending an air of quaint charm to a glorified hovel of bachelorhood. Following his explicit instructions, she took the sloping curve of his driveway and saw that it split from an uneven farmhouse with a pole shed, which she knew instantly as Cara Spencer's. Even from a distance, Dre could tell that the back porch was organized, if a bit dusty, and her steps were flanked with tender sunflower stems. There was a birdfeeder hanging from the eave of the home and a yellow flag bearing a snake and a set of words had been tacked up in the screen.

"Keep going around the bend after the two houses and the trailer. You'll see us," she echoed her directions. "We'll be down by the water's edge." *Trailer, trailer...* "Yep, that's a trailer." Rusted and orangey, Atticus's humble abode was lying in a heap in a cleared field, surrounded on three sides by tobacco stalks that were nearly as high as the roofline. Pallets and long sheets of plywood were scattered about, and open paint cans formed a bit of a design in the dying clumps of grass, some waving in tufts of purple or grey. She had never seen a trailer before, and it made quite an impression.

Looking up, she turned a sharp corner and nearly careened into open water before skidding to a stop. There, she found them, frozen in conversational silence; Win, with his arms over his chest, dangling a coffee mug in one hand and a Marlboro in the other, Link, looking out over the slow moving brown wrinkles in the wide, clear cut river, Atticus, wiping boats and boards with a washcloth, and Cara Spencer, hands on her hips, defiance in her stance, taking them all three in as the risen sun poured down on the wave of eddies in her serpent-like bun.

At least this dispels Worry Number Three. Here was her woman, and here was her chance.

* * *

"Mornin'!" Link cried, all rise-up-and-greet-the-day-like-it-could-be-his-last. He was such an asshole first thing in the morning.

His legs nearly fell over themselves in a venerated dart to Dre's lifted Explorer. Yanking her hair down from its' nest, his sister rolled her eyes. He was just too Opie Taylor for words, always the chivalrous man boy, always rushing to the aid of a damsel in distress. Even when the damsel was more of a man than he was.

Coming up behind her, Atti smoothed the sand from her paddleboard with an understated grace, "Why'd you take your hair down?"

"No reason," she lied like a dog. "It gives me a headache sometimes is all."

Blah blah blah. She took it down because more people paid attention to it when it was down. It was unbearably hot, sticky, wet and sweaty in the Southern blanket of humidity that would roll in in a few short hours, but it would beckon notice. Even from Dre. Especially from Dre.

"You remember my brothers, Cara Spencer you met briefly."

Briefly? Too briefly. *Way too briefly.*

"Good morning," her Yankee accent was more pronounced that it had been the day before. "Thanks for inviting me."

"Oh, no problem," Win stepped forward to show her down, as if she needed a damn escort to move three feet down a bank that wasn't even really that steep. Behind her, a dog lumbered out and took his place at her knees. "Who's this handsome little fella?"

"That's Buddy," and submissively, the mud-toned Labrador placed his body between hers and the alerted frames of the other two dogs present, then without ado, he lay right down on the sand and wagged his fluffy, chestnut-lightened tail.

"He gets along fine with other dogs," she stated, although it wasn't necessary. Grey Baby and Greg Allman were direct in their estimations of others, human and canine alike, and their complacency belied an acceptance rooted in platitude. Concisely, Buddy and Andrea were good people, posed no threat to their property, and could be trusted beyond measure.

"Well," Win pointed at the deceptively docile grey beast, "these are my sister's kids, Grey Baby, who's a real pain in the ass, don't you dare let her fool you, and Greg Allman, who's about sixty pounds too heavy to do anything other than sit in the sand and pant."

When she lowered her hands, both animals approached Dre, tongues wagging. "Are they both girls?"

Cara Spencer shook her head in the affirmative and wished she could make them do a circus routine just so something she had would seem cool for thirty seconds.

"A girl named Greg Allman?" Andrea commended, laughing a little. "I can't say I've ever met one before." Link clapped her on the back and steered her toward a giant, red, canoe-like kayak that was the size of a small cruise ship. "Dre," he said, in all fairness and ease, "it goes a lot easier if you stop questioning why she does what she does and just accept it. She drives a truck that won't run and she named a perfectly sweet girl dog Greg Allman. Let's get you outfitted in the boat, shall we?"

Coffee, a life preserver, and approximately one hour later, they were up and moving, having lost a good bit of time trying to instruct Dre on the finer points of turning, remaining upright, dispensing beer (because her gargantuan craft was the only one large enough to hold the cooler) while remaining upright, pushing off the bank to stay clear of rocks and branches and snakes (with the last bit only glossed over), and lounging in general to allow the mild current to carry the entire party from one spot to the next. She was a quick study, stiff as a board, but a quick study, and once they were a mile in, all of the Holloways backed off, having deemed her sufficient enough behind the paddle to right herself when need be and to make an emergency exit when nature called, or fell off of a low-hanging willow branch.

The sun was out in full bloom, the trees were brilliant green, and Cara Spencer lost the apple shirt at the first opportunity, trying not to look like she wanted Dre to see her body, and trying desperately to conceal the fact that it was a bit too chilly for a fully exposed bikini and her nipples were rotten little buds at full attention. She laid flat on the Oxbow paddleboard—the more rectangular cousin to a traditional surfboard— wiggling her toes, and traced lazy ripples in the dirty brown flux that carried her ragtag party forward, using peripheral vision to spy on her unlikely (and uncomfortably comfortable) companion. Dressed in pants— PANTS, for god's sake, who went out on the water in pants?—with a band swag tee shirt from a group she'd never heard of, Andrea was so far out of her element she may as well have been in a different realm. But she was smiling. Legs splayed out, hanging off of the tips of the boat, cuffs rolled up, toes touching the water but only slightly, she was looking up at the ominous Holloway tree line, grinning into the sun while Buddy slept in the shallow opening behind her, having proved himself a born water dog. Poor dog was way too big for that red boat, despite its massive size. She couldn't figure on why Link had loaned it to her when she had a much bigger one—an 18 footer—in the barn, with the cow. The size of the Royal Caribbean fleet, she took it out only when Greg Allman wanted to ride, inhibited as she was by the immense girth of Great Pyr. Grey Baby barely needed a foot and much preferred swimming to riding. Greg? Not so much. The Queen of Sheba demanded a full catamaran, with pedestal and buffet.

"Absolutely beautiful," Dre breathed, quietly enough to have been a private sentiment but loud enough for Cara to hear.

"Oh, you like what you see?" she poked, fully intending the double entendre to stand on its own. She was in her lucky bikini, oddly because it was the only thing clean in the house, and she hoped like hell it was doing its job.

"God yeah, this place is fantastic," Dre assured her, not looking at the assets that were intended to be viewed.

Well, Andrea's attitude was borderline infuriating. Where was the passion from the bathroom? The 'take no prisoners,' no holds barred, pants on the floor, ankles wrapped around her head demand? Had she just been drunk? And wasn't that the way it always played out? Every girl wanted to be a lesbian at the bar. Sporadic girl-on-girl action was half the reason Win had any male clientele. But this girl *had* to be a lesbian, for real. Had to be. Cropped hair, A-cup, athletic build, boxer shorts that hung low on her waist, skinny jeans, suspenders, thumb ring.

What a stereotype you are, her subconscious screamed. Here she was trying so hard to blend in and she was using their ideas—the hetero majority's—against her own kind.

Wait.

Did she have a kind?

"No," she told herself, not realizing she'd said it aloud. She wasn't one of *those* gays. She was... Cara Spencer. She wasn't really anything, except herself, and currently, herself was confounded.

"No what?" Dre's voice was full of lazy curiosity.

"No...I...don't want a beer."

"I didn't offer you a beer."

Dammit. That had been a really stupid thing to say. "Well, maybe you should have." Moody Belle was definitely the way to go when deflecting attention.

"What the..." Dre reclined backward in the black, detachable seat. "You make absolutely no sense." Buddy huffed in agreement. Someone laughed, whole-hearted and open, behind them and Cara Spencer turned to see her brother, Win, speeding up to cut them in the center. He had his own board, lighter and less stable than hers—an Almundson 13" to her 30"—but he'd been riding for years and could balance on a wire in a pinch. Beer in hand, he saluted as he passed. "Andrea-Dre, my friend, we've been saying that bit for years but, fickle, thy name is Cara Spencer."

Branches hung down in his path and he jiggled one loose, tossing it aside, using his paddle to keep erect. A tiny black snake splashed to the water near Dre and she recoiled.

"Relax, he's leaving," Cara said without looking. There was no point in telling her they were pretty much everywhere. She'd only fall in and the water was a bit cold yet, no matter what lies the sun told.

"*Leaving?* Where is he—"

"About that beer?"

"Would you like a beer?" Dre offered, baffled

Getting her mind off of the snake was probably the best bet for all of them. She made sure their legless swimming companion was gone and shrugged. "If you insist. But something light."

"If you want light, drink water!" Link hollered, reinforcing the notion that they weren't even slightly alone. And reinforcing the fact that he had no faith in her alcohol selection abilities, which was par for the course. Her blood didn't run IPA brown like her brothers, so she stuck with Corona Light and was mocked for it.

"I agree with him," Dre said, all 'by-the-by' about it as she wrenched a slender silver can from the dry bag filled with ice wedged between her body and her dog's, sitting in the vee of her thighs.

I wonder what else is between her thighs, Cara slyly thought and then blushed. All by herself, on her OxBow, she blushed like a damn virgin. She'd been with tons of women (maybe not tons but a solid five). Maybe she hadn't been with them the "right" way, maybe she wasn't doing it right. It certainly wasn't as if there existed a copious amount of legitimate, mainstream, lesbian porn. Okay, mostly she just made out with girls— *women*—but whatever, she knew her way around a crotch. When her hand touched Dre's, who leaned precariously over to hand her the Corona Light, heat seared her and set her spinal cord on edge.

Shit. "Don't um...don't roll too much. Or you'll fall out," she cautioned, like a lame.

Don't roll too much?! What the hell...

Chances were, Andrea had a girlfriend anyway. If she were really gay, which was at least a ninety percent certainty given that she hadn't made a move on a brother. She was a catch. All dark hair and olive skin lightly dusted with freckles that were visible only on her neck and gave the impression that they hugged a region much more interesting. The muscles beneath her sleeves rippled when she moved, strength evident in every nuance, and she walked like a panther, all grace and underlying authority, caught in a special space that existed somewhere between man and woman. She was confident, calm—

Cara snuck a glance and found Dre staring at her, a smile on her lips.

From a more practical standpoint, she had a car, a job, an apartment, a dog. Buddy was reasonably well taken care of, even though she let him eat whatever he wanted. Poor Grey Baby was an enforced vegetarian, and an angry one at that.

Speaking of, Cara Spencer nudged the feisty grey matter at her feet. The cattle dog gurgled a response that could have been either positive or negative depending on the weather and the sun's trajectory, and wagged her heavy, fat tail.

"Grey Baby, swim," she instructed. The thirty-pound lob rolled obligingly into the water, popping up at the surface immediately. When Dre stared in disbelief, Cara hefted her shoulders. "She loves to swim. It's good exercise."

"But how long can she do that?"

Oh baby, I can do all night...maybe. If what she was doing was doing it correctly. And by 'what she was doing,' she meant being a little on the gay side.

"What? Swim? Couple of miles, I think. She'll get out when she's tired."

Ducking beneath the board, Grey Baby rolled and kicked and barked, more like a toddler in swim class than a canine. Her strokes were even and well-rehearsed and she fancifully bit at droplets of water created by her own doggy paddle.

"That dog's got energy for days," Atticus methodically dictated, as the heeler swam past his Hurricane and bit his paddle loose. "Damn thing won't let me get within twenty feet of your farmhouse."

"That's her job, Brother. She's a guard dog, emphasis on the *guard*."

"But what the hell's she guarding? Her mama packs one hell of a punch," Link preached with pride. "Little sister's given more than her fair share of ass whoopin's in this county."

Something about her illustrious past didn't suit her current situation and Cara Spencer tried to look unfazed. Or maybe she should look fazed? It was difficult to tell what type would be more suited to Dre—damsel or badass. Why was this so hard? At last, someone else who could understand, as if that were possible. Why was she being anything other than herself? *Maybe you don't trust that she understands,* Inner Drama Queen relayed. And that was, partially, the truth. Cara felt that gay people (if gay was what she was and she had never referred to herself as that) in other places, larger places, more populated places, progressive places, had it much easier than gay people (or confused people) in holes like Greentown, where marriage and kids and kindergarten carpool were the status quo. There were gay bars in larger cities. *What the hell even went on in a gay bar?* Gay pool? Gay day-drinking? There were gay clubs, gay churches, gay parent groups.

"Are we still on your land?" Dre wanted to know, ignoring the reference to her misdemeanored past.

Cara looked haphazardly around and nodded, praying her skin didn't burn under the glare of the sun. She'd only just gone to sleep when the alarm clock had jarred her awake again and she hadn't remembered to grab sunscreen.

"Yeah. For a long while more. Our boundary ends just beyond the overpass for Hwy 151. You'll see it. We'll move down a tributary there and circle back around on a creek that dumps out near the far pasture." Every other year, the far pasture nurtured soy beans but this was an off season, so Win used it to shoot at broken restaurant machinery when he had a bad day behind the griddle, or the cash box.

"So you own the river?"

That was a more complicated question. Thankfully, James Winter had a less than complicated answer. "Yes and no," he cut circles on his board because he was so good on the damn thing he got bored floating, "The river is just...a river. 'S been a river for hundred years before our time and our names on an easement don't mean much where it's concerned."

"Our great-grandfather used it to move tobacco," Atticus recited like a Mina bird. Someone grumbled "dork" and he threw up the finger. "What? He did."

Discreetly this time, Cara Spencer watched as Dre made the connections, traced their lineage back to some comportment of time in which tobacco was grown for wild profit in the continental United States and tiny, sunken rivers were used for large scale transport and pissing away time on a Sunday. Her bloodline was so severe, so settled, so chiseled in the Rosetta Stone, she mused that it would have been utterly foreign to her to be new. Or singular. Part One of One. Generationless, ambivalent.

"Do you have brothers? Or sisters?" she blurted, facing her guest, eyes drifting over the other woman's unsteady but cautious movements.

"Ah, two, actually. Brothers. They're six."

"Six?!" Win, Link, Atti and Cara said at the same time.

"Yeah. My dad got started late, after me. His new wife's only, like, forty."

"Your dad is my hero," some Holloway man-child snorted.

They neared a bend in the river and three of the five of them disappeared around it, leaving Cara stalling her own progress so she could stay near Dre.

"He never really dated much when I was a kid. He saw women, but not, like, seriously. And then he took up yoga and met Ami."

"Yoga?" Cara Spencer giggled. She couldn't see a sixtyish man in yoga sweats and a t-shirt. Her father had whittled away his life in fly-fishing shirts from Columbia and pressed shorts with cargo pockets. "I thought only hot girls took yoga."

"Do you take yoga?" Dre questioned, ever-so-quietly. And didn't that strip the paint off of her closet walls. "You can't tell me you didn't enjoy last night."

They were coasting a safe distance from her brothers, who were otherwise engaged in a race to the big stump half-submerged in river water and notoriously home to beavers they could fuck with. Also, she had no clue how to be "lesbian sexy." Granted, she had rehearsed this in her head a million times as she'd stared at those stupid glow-in-the-dark stars, but now that she was face to—well, side by side with it? *Don't blow it.* "I enjoyed it, alright."

"I thought so," Dre's voice was hoarse. "I could smell you in my sleep."

Between her legs, Cara felt the same rush of slick heat she'd felt the night before, only this time the illicit nature of their surroundings intensified the emotion to an almost unbearable level.

"Did you like it?" She wanted so much to be as seductive as Andrea was. "Did you like the way I smelled?"

"Oh, I can't wait to taste you. Feel you run down the back of my throat."

* * *

Dre couldn't have been more shocked to hear the words come out of her own mouth. Who was this vixen that mouthed everything she was thinking, so ballsy all of the sudden? So forthright?

"You sound like you know what you want," Cara Spencer's voice wavered.

She was such a conundrum, so very perceptibly straight and yet so very responsive. So very willing. Dre could smell the attraction.

"I want you," she groaned, softly. "All over my face, in my hair. I want you liquid and screaming."

Her own body was beginning to react as the pictured Cara spread out before her on the fluffy white bed in her own shuttered apartment, pushing her legs further apart, giving herself completely over. She could see Cara's lips, open, as she bit and pleaded. She could feel her hands light as they ran through the short stalks of her black shock. She wanted to push this woman to the edge and seek the glory thereafter, which gave her boldness not necessarily at the surface.

"I've wanted you since I first saw you, watched you move. Your hips sway when you walk. When you sing, you set my blood on fire—"

"I wanted you," Cara cut her off, uncertainly. "I wanted you to see me."

"You wanted me to want you." It was more statement than question, with the carnal honesty between them sheltered by the draping cypress that tickled the tops of the river. "You wanted me to think about the slow dip of

108

your belly and the curve of your hip." She had an immaculate hip, one that beckoned to be kissed and touched and felt, with nails sinking into the taut flesh of her stomach, pulling her forward.

Looking over, Dre watched as she fingered a strand of her hair; hair that was as stunning as the resplendent light after the sadness of an inky black night, a crescent moon on the horizon. Her thin fingers, so elusive and intrinsically female, kept the curl between them, twisting, as she stared into the sun, hiding behind the drugstore sunglasses she'd had to make one trip back to the house for before their departure.

Hiding was a good description for her.

Ahead, Link and Win and Atticus were so far gone they were but shadows on the water, with Grey Baby perched on the back tip of Win's lithe Aldmundson, evidently *not* being hated. Their laughter was unrecognizable mixed alongside the chirping of the woodland birds and the lapping of the tiny waves upon the untamed shores. Leaves rustled, cars drove off in the distance.

"Show me how much you want me," Dre coached. "Let me see you."

"What—No." Cara Spencer sat upright quickly, rocking her board. "My brothers—"

"Are a mile away. Easily," Andrea finished. "Show me."

She could only hope the rasp in her words acted as a clever disguise for the urgency she felt, the overwhelming and insatiable need she had to be inside this woman, to unlock doors within this woman that were bolted to their hinges.

"Show you what?"

"Don't play dumb. Dumb is for teenagers and party girls."

Steeling herself against rejection, she turned her head and looked out over what appeared to be barren and free-ranging wilderness, for all practical purposes. Trees that were decades old, unruly vegetation—it was all…magical on a level that Dre had never realized she could appreciate. South Waterton was faux-industrial, refurbished industrial, industrial with a familial edge. But this…this was space and air and independence. This was feral and wild and strangely welcoming.

Taking a deep breath in, filled with humid heat and mosquitoes, she turned and nearly toppled right into the water she was ninety percent certain contained every strain of bacteria necessary for initiating an infection of flesh-eating bacteria.

Back arched, swells of her breasts reaching, Cara Spencer's left hand fell to her side, in disharmony as her right slipped easily beneath the low waist of her bikini. Tiny white teeth bit at her bottom lip, her eyes closed. And then her hand began to move.

"Yes…" was all Dre could say, as the air left her lungs in a rush of unexpected and visceral reaction. "Show me. Oh, show me, Cara…"

Bearing an achingly precise anticipation, Cara Spencer slipped her bottoms down, balance inhuman as they moved right along. The top of her mound, bare and bronze, was out for all to see.

No, not all. This was a sight intended and demonstrated for Andrea alone, skin that seemed to exist for her pleasure, a small and wholehearted gift.

"Pull over," she flubbed, sticking her paddle down to her left and shoving in the five feet of muck. By all the gods of all the places, she would get this woman into her mouth and out of her head if it would be the last thing she accomplished. Jarred, Buddy stood at attention and his weight threatened to dump them.

"Stop! You'll tip!"

Luckily, Cara took over, ducking under a protruding limb that stretched nearly six feet out, and reaching over for Dre's hand. The charge that existed between them, or perhaps was set off between them, sent chills in both directions as they worked together to pull the boat and board up on the neatly secluded lagoon-like beach.

Jostled, Buddy leapt to his feet and trotted off into the surrounding woods, happily hunting smells that must have seemed inordinately fantastical to him, so secluded he was in his kennel club lifestyle. In his absence, Andrea wasted no time. She stepped right out into the sand and pulled Cara to her, once again crushing her mouth in a kiss fueled by passion and hunger. Hands entwined, she stole possession of Cara's neck and lips and fisted her hands in that riotous mane. Her tongue fed on sweat and sweetness and eager exploration. Stars exploded in her brain. This, *this* was a kiss. This was union. This was everything that every kiss before had been lacking.

"More..." Cara Spencer said against her. "Give me more... Touch me..." The *please* was understood.

Trailing the pads of her fingers against nubile skin, Dre made her beg, tracing the outline of her shoulder and forearm, the tuck of her waist, up from her knees. Gentle and starving, she ran her open palm over the belly she had seen in her dreams—dreams so dirty she blushed, eyes closed and tongue extended. The navel, soft, inviting navel, hips made for riding.

When she dipped lower, seeking the source of her heat and the calm in her storm, she nearly came right there, so amazing was the sound her touch elicited from the wild-eyed subject of her physical adoration. Spreading her legs further, Cara wiggled and rode, rubbing herself in futile demand against Dre, who pressed on, inch by slow and painful inch, crawling toward the crevice she had been barred from enjoying the night before. The buildup was an epic torture for both of them, the smooth folds of the shorn skin soaked and dripping.

"Touch me…" Cara whimpered. "Touch me, Dre."

It was the advent of her name, the guttural croak of her, that drove her in, first with one finger and then with two. It was the ragged and sensual satisfaction of hearing her name on the lips of a woman who tasted like fire that pushed her inside.

"Fuck," she breathed, dropping Cara's neck to steady herself against an obliging tree. "You feel like heaven."

They were half-standing, half-leaning, and with no preamble, she lifted her companion and set her smoothly on the base of the gnarled limb that shielded them from view, reveling in the feel of rounded ass against her wrists and the solid cushion of Cara's weight in her arms. With legs open wider in a seated position, she moved deeper into sex, deeper into desperation and deeper into Cara Spencer Holloway, who slid the bikini bottoms down off of her ankle and twisted a leg up to wrap around Dre's waist. Locked on one side, she lifted up with her bottom, wrapped her right hand around Dre's shoulder and began a relentless ride of her own, bucking wildly against the cypress. Bucking wildly against the other woman.

* * *

It was the most wanton experience of her life, hair flapping, breasts shaking, muscles screaming, leg locked. Cara threw her head back and moaned, feeling the ecstasy of Dre's fingers inside her. Fingers? How many?

"Give me more," she wheezed, locking eyes with the inception of her need.

Andrea's gaze was hooded, her cheeks flushed. Fully clothed and barefoot, she bore the bulk of their weight and had lifted her as if she weighed no more than a child of ten. The cords of her forearms tightened and rose, sweat breaking across brow. Her shoulders strained.

"You want more of me?" she murmured. "Tell me you want more of me."

"I want more of you," Cara's voice poured out with no hesitation. She was completely and utterly unabashed, for what was perhaps the first time in her life, sexually speaking. She didn't want more fingers, she didn't want more sex, she wanted more of Andrea inside her. More of this heady woman who spoke to the passion that rose inside her body.

"Deeper." As the third finger slid into place, she cried out and felt her release barrel up from the depths of her soul.

Catching the sound in her mouth, Dre supported her once more and tongued her as the orgasm spun madly around her, earth-shattering in its intensity and depth, fingers so far inside she could no longer tell what was her and what was not. It was the most intimate moment of her life.

After a year of pleasure, she pulled away and rested her forehead on Andrea's chin. Her heart was racing, her legs like rubber. She didn't think—

Dre set her down carefully and she unlocked her leg, daintily feeling the sand between her stubby toes.

"Turn around."

"Wha—Huh?"

"Turn around for me, Cara." The shortened variation of her traditional double name sent the hairs on the back of her to parade rest. Never in her life had she favored it. Never used it in school, never used it with a girlfriend—she hadn't really had a girlfriend. Ever. But when Dre used it, clinching the intimacy that shrouded them. She was putty.

Willingly, she spun and put her hands on the branch, it landing right at a convenient waist height.

"What are you—"

Pants unzipped, boxers dropped to the ground. Shirt flew off.

Afraid to turn around, she knew her expectation would drip down her leg, an anticipation of what this woman would do to her next, what part of this woman she would feel.

Dre's arms encompassed hers, hands coiling together, those tight, high breasts running against the naked coils of her own shoulders. She could feel the taut firmness of each nipple, the clammy skin, cool to the touch. She could feel Dre's breath hot and serrated in her ear. Hips met her rear, hardened edges against the softness of her curves, legs pressing against hers. She looked down to see their feet side-by-side, all of her exposed and waiting.

Softly, Dre ran her lips down Cara's neck and spine, tongue following beads of sweat, greedily drinking from her skin. Below, she used the yielding support of Cara's cheeks to rub a thoroughly different set of lips. When the secret skin made contact, both women cried out. When Dre reached forward with her left hand, finding Cara's cleft of pleasure, already sensitive from their first experience, it was Cara's voice that yelped alone, Cara's words that were eaten by the wild around them, and hungrily, they moved against one another.

"That's right, Cara," Dre scratched in her ear, still holding firm with her right hand while her left hand called forth another in a stream of orgasms that seemed to last for days. "Come for me. Let me hear you scream again."

Gone were any worries about being heard or seen or suspected. Gone were any worries about not being discreet enough, ladylike enough. Straight enough. Cara gave herself over to the torrent of emotion and sensation that was Dre's onslaught on her body. The impression of Andrea's clit at her ass, the subtle and demanding tickle of Andrea's hands in her treasured spaces, the feral cries in her ear, the push of woman at her back, the feel of skin on skin, the slip and slide and flow of *everything around her*.

She shattered into a thousand pieces for a second and third time, riding the waves of bliss as they broke over her one after the other until there was no her and there was no Dre, there were only colors and sounds and—

Jesus, I can't come agai—

"Don't stop," Dre told her, her own pulse thundering as she neared the finish line. "God, don't stop." Her vision dimmed and she sagged as her sex throbbed with life, contracting deep in her womb, as words poured of her, unintelligible words that meant nothing and everything all at once. "It's right there." Dre's left arm snaked around her, holding her close, closer than two people could be, and she felt as the tension and ride released in her, the garbled sounds of her ecstasy like a warm blanket of acceptance.

* * *

"Cara…" Dre felt the woman in her arms still as she came, racked with an orgasm that was larger and more powerful than anything she had

115

ever even dreamed up before. "Oh, Cara." They were silly words, stupid words, a girl's words, but they were out of her mouth and down her lips before she could stop them.

And then there was quiet, both of their bodies humming with spent energy, knees weak and buckling, the intake of air coming in craggy gasps.

She gingerly turned Cara Spencer around and hefted her back onto her limb. Touched her face, pulled her close.

Kissed her.

They were riddled with sweat and sex and sand.

"You're amazing," she almost didn't say.

Her companion laughed and stretched those thick and curvy legs. "As good as you wanted it to be?"

"Better. Way better." She should have felt foolish or foolhardy, standing naked on the beach of a river she did not understand, but she was entirely unselfconscious.

Can we do it again?

"Have dinner with me," she said instead, feeling like a recharge would be only necessary if there were to be more sex later, and, come heaven or hell, there would be more sex later. Lots more sex, if it would all be like that. Hell, even half of that would have been better than any of the pre-existing sexual history. With Mare, sex had been a chore—a scary chore, but a chore—and one Mare did with her pants still on; very little chemistry in the beginning and all of that fizzled after a week. With Stephanie, sex had been about as interesting as shopping around for gas. *This?* This was out of this world, romance novel sex, and she wanted it every night for the rest of her life, even if she had to do it against a tree, on a mealy beach, covered in army general ants and weeds with snakes hiding in the branches overhead.

But that wouldn't happen.

Because tomorrow she'd be on her way to Florida.

Cara Spencer bent and retrieved her bikini bottom, shaking out the sand. "You askin' me out on a date?"

Dre tugged on the shirt she'd ripped from the brambles near the surf. "What if I am?" There was still the chance that this woman was a poser, enamored of an experience rather than the gender of a person, disinterested in the actual life and livelihood of a gay woman.

"That's a little backwards, ain't it?" she wisecracked, grammatical shortcomings be damned.

Boxers went back up her rangy legs, and then jeans, which were halfway soaked with water, not that it mattered. Her pussy would leak for hours afterward, primarily every time she looked over at Cara. "Is that a problem in this neck of the woods? Having sex before the date, I mean?"

Her newfound candor was growing on her. Maybe that was the change she had needed all along, the door she needed to open.

"Tell you what," Cara Spencer stepped into her then, putting the curves of her body against Dre's stiffness. "I'll make dinner for you."

BINGO! "One of those real southern deals? With the fried chicken?"

Cara nodded. "One of those real southern deals with the fried chicken."

Mockingly, Andrea put her fingers to her lips and thought it over. "Fine, well...if you insist, but there's not much of a kitchen at the Carolina Inn."

There wasn't even a microwave at the Carolina Inn.

Helping to right the boat and bracing if for entry, Cara Smiled. "Oh, believe me, I do. Wouldn't be right to send you home without a real taste of the area. Come on over to my house."

Yes, Dre's saucy thoughts molten lava as blood raced through her veins and her breath caught in her throat, *I'll come over to your house and get a real taste of the area.*

One of Them Real Southern Deals

Once they caught up with the Holloway brothers, who were an hour deep into an argument about the plot direction in a Marvel film about a superhero named Deadpool that sounded about as badass as he did lame, Dre did her best to pretend that she hadn't just fucked their sister in the woods on a cypress tree, which was easier than she had anticipated, though her pants were still soaked in two separate and distinct areas. Cara Spencer put her shirt back on, which helped some, and Link kept her supplied with beer, which helped some more. Buddy rejoined them after a while, with Grey Baby in tow. In a moment of weakness, the heeler had bitten Atticus in the ass when he stopped to pee and had been subsequently deposited on a deserted bank.

Win intimated that he and his brothers had a standing date at a fried oyster dive joint that served all of its meals outdoors, but Dre declined his invitation, simply stating that she was pretty tired. She had no idea whether mentioning her dinner plans with their sister was warranted, but played the whole thing close to the rainbow vest just in case.

"I imagine you'll need to get some rest," Link said, vaguely, but specifically.

"Yeah," Win cut him off. "You got a long drive in the morning. Saint Augustine, right?"

"Yeah," Dre nodded. "My dad's got a bakery there. It's like a neighborhood market."

They turned the boats down the tributary and followed it around before they pulled out in the shallows by a tire swing, a picnic table, and a rusted metal dock, in a field littered with metal parts. Atticus relieved her of her kayak, and pulled out another beer. Up from the mini-landing, a Dodge Durango was parked beside a banana yellow Chevy Apache.

"I can take you back in the Durango," Link explained. "We just gotta get the boats out and hosed off—"

"I can take her back, Lincoln," Cara cut her eyes. "It's on my way. You put in in my backyard and I left my truck here last night."

"We put in in *my* backyard," Atti, who was aptly named, as it turned out, in honor of a character he appropriately represented, corrected.

"Should we get out the property map and decide?"

With more puffing and teasing, the Holloways decided amongst themselves that Cara Spencer's idea was probably the most direct way of returning Dre to her Explorer so she could trek back to the Carolina Inn and call it a night, but none were too happy about it—the bit about her leaving, in general.

"It's been a real damn pleasure," Win told her, side-hugging her gruffly, between puffs of his cigarette. "I hope we see you again real soon."

"Keep in touch," Atticus chimed, giving a fistbump.

"Almost felt like you part of the family, there," Link winked, before giving her a bear hug. "Take care of my sister on your way back."

Little did he realize, Dre fully intended to take care of his sister about a dozen more times before she cleared out in the morning—once before they even made it in the back door.

* * *

"So your family's been here forever, you love animals and you have a box of recipes that your mom left you," Dre surmised, after eating her fill

120

of fried chicken and cornbread and a casserole she did not understand but could not put down.

They were facing one another at a small, metal-topped table with a dent right in the center, seated in mismatched chairs squarely in the middle of Cara Spencer's yellow painted kitchen. Grey Baby and Greg Allman and Buddy were scattered lazily around, two candles were burning on the windowsill, and music played from one of the back bedrooms. The sliding glass door was open and a humid, homey breeze blew in through the patched screen, carrying with it the distinct smell of what could only be called Deep Southern Spring.

"My family *has* been here forever, I *do* love animals, and yes, I have my mama's recipe box, which I think you appreciated quite a bit." She ate one final spoonful of cryptic casserole.

"Tell me something else."

Squinting, Cara stood and collected the plates from dinner. "Like what."

"Something that nobody knows. A secret."

"I fart in my sleep."

"Not *that* secret, a good secret."

Setting the plates down in the apron sink, Cara gasped. "I know! I have a pretty big secret. I had sex with a woman in the woods today while I was supposed to be kayaking with my asshole brothers."

Dre stood and dropped her beer can in the tin trashcan by the seafoam green refrigerator. "Helluva secret. How long you plan on keeping it?"

"There are more beers in the door," Cara pointed. "And probably forever, lest I develop a fan club of old men who want to camp out on the riverbend with binoculars."

The Right Kind of Woman

Is that the only reason you'd keep that a secret? Dre wanted to ask, but chose her words more carefully. On the ride back to the farmhouse, Cara Spencer had been oddly quiet, almost like the reality of what they'd done had been too much for her. Then, once inside, she had busied herself with meal preparations (of which there were many) in solitude, having all but retreated into herself, which was odd for someone who had been so willing to disrobe on a tree trunk and ride three fingers in veritable reckless abandon only hours before.

"Care to give me a tour?"

"Ah, sure." The modest catch in her voice was too much.

"Listen, Cara…if this got weird, for whatever reason, my car's parked down the way. I'd be more than happy to go—"

"I don't want you to leave." She stopped covering the casserole dish, aluminum foil hanging in her hand. "It's not that. I just…"

"Need some space? Need to fart?" Her attempt at an ice-breaker went unchallenged. "Do you need to find the tools to murder me and chop me into little pieces and throw me into the backyard?"

"I don't need tools. I have a gun safe." That was far too matter-of-fact for comfort.

"Ooookay."

"And I'm not going to kill you." Cara Spencer covered the casserole dish and placed it in the refrigerator, retrieving a slim can of Corona Light. "I just don't know quite what came over me down there."

"On the river?" *When you rode me and felt me come up behind you?*

She nodded and Dre felt like shit. Here she was planning their evening like a tiger stalking a dying gazelle and what she should have been doing was backpedaling, actually getting to know the woman before her who was a hell of a lot more than a nice pair of tits and a round ass.

"Me either," she said, honestly. "I've never done anything like that in my life. I'm…practical." *Internal, thoughtful, analytical…*

"I've never been called practical in my life, but what happened down there was about the furthest thing from what I saw happening today when I walked down there this morning." The Corona Light can cracked open. "I thought I'd be babysitting again, watching my brothers do some dumb shit and bandaging wounds."

"Sounds like you enjoy being a sister."

Cara reached into the fridge and got another beer for Dre (which was a good sign), leading her out onto the side porch through the waving, stretched screen. It was small, rustic, and felt like home, with wood beams making a frame that at one time held a more solid netting, all painted gunmetal grey and all hung with wide-bulb Christmas lights. There were two chairs and a card table littered with cigarette butts that Cara said belonged to Atticus.

"I like it well enough sometimes," she expanded. "My parents have been dead for so long, they're all I have. But sometimes, they smother me."

Taking a seat opposite her, Dre took a swig of Rebel IPA and nodded sympathetically. "I can't really fathom what that would be like, to have *real* brothers. I've always been on my own."

"And I can't fathom that. I've had Win and Link and Atti forever. Even when they're pains in my ass, they're *here*."

"And you've always been close?"

The other woman shrugged. "As close as you can be to a pack of pricks who party too much."

"I hear you." That was how Dre felt about the bitches in her building, with their lesbian trendy outfits and hipster hats. She should have gotten close to them, dyke-to-dyke, but... It was hard to have a rationale conversation with someone who was more interested in jello shots and tequila than the current political climate and the push for Marriage Equality. A safe assumption would have been that Win and Lincoln and Atticus were the straight, boy equivalent of belly chain-fedoras.

"You wanna see the bedroom?" Cara piped up.

"What?"

"Do you want to see my bedroom?"

Is this a trick question? "Thirty seconds ago you said you weren't the type of girl who got naked on a beach."

"I know." There was no apology in her voice, almost as if it all made perfect sense in her head, the head of a woman who named her female dog Greg Allman and said she didn't want to have sex when she really did. "I'm not the type of girl who does that."

"Your mixed signals are killing me."

"They're not mixed. I'm not the type of girl who has sex on a beach in broad daylight. But, I am the type of girl who has sex in a bed in the dark."

What the—

Dre stood up. "Show me your bedroom, then."

* * *

"This is the single dumbest fucking plan you've ever had in your entire goddamn life," Win slurped through fried shrimp from a big red basket covered in brown, charred French fries and tartar sauce. "It's ridiculous. It's more than ridiculous. It's so underhanded I don't know if I can safely call you my brother from now on."

The Right Kind of Woman

Across the cloth-covered picnic table, in the back of the outdoor lot where they came to pass the time on Sunday evenings when every other decent restaurant was closed, Link sipped on the beer he'd brought in his own cooler and blinked in a series of *I don't give a shit* successions.

"Call it what you will, but it's working, so I don't give a damn," he released, propping his feet up on the end of his empty bench seat. "Dre is over there right now, sweeping poor Cara Spencer right out of her self-imposed closet."

"You orchestrated this whole fucking thing to push Cara out into the world?" Atticus was dumbfounded, not that he should have been. Lincoln Andrew Holloway had been a master manipulator for the thirty-one years he'd been wandering earth. Why would his sister's homosexual love life be any different? This man could sweet talk a male police officer out of writing a traffic ticket for a frat boy. Obviously, he could sweet talk a lesbian into making it with his adult sister.

"I can't take that much credit." Link was at his beer again. "I couldn't have controlled where she would stop or how she would find out about A.B.'s, although when I find out, I'll be sure to thank whoever pointed her in that direction. I merely set the people in my disposal in motion."

"Inviting her to kayak." Win nodded. "Leaving them alone for a bit."

"You even warned her," Atticus deduced. "Back before we left. You warned her. When she thought Greg Allman was a dumb name—"

"For a female dog," Lincoln finished. "I gave her the only piece of advice I have, concerning Cara Spencer Madeline. She doesn't make any sense at all."

Spearing more shrimp with his red plastic fork, James Winter, Jr. ate them whole and then reached for his own beer. "And you hope this does what? Makes Cara *officially* gay? She's been *officially* gay her entire life."

125

It had been slow going at first, picking up the signs of what had been ingrained in her DNA, but it had always been there, as sure as the sun rose in the east and set in the west. Her first crush had been a playmate, Laura Tipton. Big brown eyes, long brown hair. The boys had seen it all over her face when they snuck off to the barn to play for hours in the twilight. And they should have addressed it then, forced her to label it, accept it. Maybe then she wouldn't be so hell-bent on burying it or running from it, or hiding it away in the old farmhouse that needed about a half million in repairs, but would do in the now.

"I know that, Win, but this," Lincoln could be long-winded when he was on a roll. And buzzed. "*This* one, Andrea Dre, will show her that it's okay to be gay."

"That's cliché." Ever-the-gentleman, Atticus lifted his shoulders in the universal symbol of *YOU'RE AN IDIOT FOR NOT SEEING THAT!*

"Cliché, whatever, it's the truth. If she just sees someone being all gay and walking around in the world, maybe she'll get it."

The artist didn't seem to be buying it. His interest was vested enough, his time and heart all balled up together, but he had a bad feeling that this fucked up sub-scheme to set his sister up with the cryptic Yankee queer, would blow up neatly in their faces.

"Wouldn't it be easier if we just sat her down and told her we knew?"

The other two stared at him, blankly.

"Atti, if it were that easy, wouldn't we have done that years ago?" Win *well duh-d*. "She don't listen to us. She ain't picking up on any of the hints. Even Granny's tried bringing it up, but all she does is slink away."

Lincoln snagged his beer can and held it up in salutation. "A toast." He proposed, elbowing the others until the joined suit. "A toast to Cara Spencer Madeline Holloway." Only when Atticus finally lifted his own can, in supplication, did he continue. "May she find some form of happiness in this life, preferably sooner rather than later."

* * *

With her face firmly between Cara's thighs, knees planted on the maroon-toned carpet, hands full of that delicious backside, Dre found herself unable to fathom what any alternate version of heaven would look like. In her nose was the smell of an enchanting woman. In her mouth was the sweetness of soft, private skin. In her throat was the saccharine nectar she was after and in her ears. In her ears was the prevailing sound of her own name sprinkled among an inventory of curses, praises and incoherent sounds.

"Make me... Oh god, please, Dre..."

Cara Spencer's hands reached blindly for the headboard of her lumpy queen-sized bed, for the metal bars sprayed with lacquer or the wood-stained mahogany. Her breasts, free at long last from the layers of clothing she had constricted them in, relished the breeze from the open window and the thrum of air circulated by the ceiling fan.

"I'm so close...." A solid five minutes she'd been whining, struggling to push her flushing body further down when Andrea moved backward consciously dragging out the culmination of her efforts. It had been...hours? Since dinner. Since mixed signals and a tour of the bedroom. Hours since the muted sounds of a classic rock station led them to embrace, lips brushing lips. Hours since hunger overtook the parameters of polite conversation. And Dre had yet to have her fill of this woman.

"Dre… Oh baby, please…" Somewhere in the time, she had become *baby*, noticeably more empowered than Andrea or Dre. "Baby, I'm gonna come."

Snapping to attention, Dre lifted her head, eyes glazed over, drunk with lust. "No."

Cara sat bolt upright. "No?"

"No," Dre reiterated, forcefully. Then she prowled up the bed, shaking off the dead weight in her knees, displacing those breasts she had been watching from a distance, the wide deep brown areolas calling her forward.

Tentatively, she licked one, inciting bedlam of a new variety.

"Baby, please…" Cara thrashed.

She shook her head. "Still no."

Hands fisted in the short stalks of her hair. "You won't make me come?"

"Not like this," she said, blowing cool air over the marks her teeth would leave.

"Not like what?" There was an underlying plea in Cara's voice, so insistent Dre looked up.

"Not like this." She splayed a hand over the belly below her chin, clenched and sweaty, sweltering. "When you come, I want you on my face."

With the flick of her wrist, she found that secret nub again and sent her paramour spinning helplessly toward the release she wanted but wouldn't get.

"I don't…I never…"

Dre flipped over beside her and dragged the body of her pleasure house closer, hip against hip, one leg thrown carelessly over the muscles of her flat stomach. Touching Cara's clit, she then pointed to her mouth.

"Put this here." She grinned, like a stranger with candy in a big dark van. "And ride my face."

Erotic interest anew lit in Cara's eyes, adding another check in the column labeled *I Do Not Think This Woman Is a Lesbian*. She sank her lips to Dre's and, for a moment, neither moved as strains of the Allman Brothers drifted in and around them from the age-old radio that plugged into the hallway socket, under the generic print of the Eiffel tower and the sconces that were cow-printed.

"Ride you face, you say?" Cara's voice was so low it could have been a manifestation of Dre's desires.

Until she pushed upward and took the headboard in both of her hands, rising to her knees like a fleshy phoenix in a pit of sexual ashes.

* * *

Feet fidgeting, throwing the knot of her hair over one shoulder, she split her haunches and looked down at the woman below her, faltering. The smoldering purpose in Dre's eyes was alarming, but in a good way. In an instant, the gap between her sex and Andrea's mouth was closed and her head lolled back, eyes unfocused. The world as she had known it, simply ceased to exist. No more peeling window frame, no more sound, no more sandpaper sheets under her knees, no more unwashed dishes in the sink, no more family, no more obligations, no more pressure.

Turning her eyes back to her unlikely beau, chills sliced up her vertebrae. That face held reverence and worship, those hands gripping the backs of her legs not roughly but in heated adulation. And when that tongue jutted outward, sneaking the hidden fissures of her hidden trove, she all but climaxed. Only, Dre wouldn't allow it.

129

"Ride me," she ordered. "Take your pleasure from me."

Through the lion's share of her lesbian experiences (and that is the term most used in her mind to describe the relationships she'd strung along), Cara Spencer had never ridden anyone in any capacity other than that of a dry-hump on a sofa or a couch. Hell, the last woman hadn't even made it to the bedroom. That had been too *much* for her. Too real. Too lesbian, or whatever. They'd rolled around on a quilt in the den, simulating positions most associated with missionaries or cowgirls.

"Cara," Dre purred. "Ride me. Ride my face. Don't think, don't worry…ride my face."

Cara wondered if she were an open book, or Plexiglas window, her soul lying just as naked as she was. She wondered if Dre could see her uncertainty.

Reassuring hands found her rear, ran up her hips to the lax spaces above her hips. Tousled her forward. Moving in tune with the motion, Dre extended her tongue, craned her neck, provided sweet friction to the pelvis as it swung.

Not one to be outdone, Cara Spencer tried moving backward.

"Oh, baby," she hissed like a cat.

The commotion created in the aftermath of that discovery sent the head board slamming against the wall and knocked three pictures loose in the opposite hallway. Like a unbroken foal, Cara bucked faster and faster, losing all perception of space and time and breathing until at long last the elusive orgasm that had been waving from the distance mounted her and left her collapsing in a soggy, worn-out mess with her legs dangling in an unladylike angle over Andrea's chest and her head lobbing off of the mattress.

Thicker fingers traced patterns on her legs, in no hurry, rubbing back and forth.

"I should change," she lied, knowing full well she was not in any shape to move off of the bed. "I'm sweaty."

"And I love it," Dre cut her off. "But I think all of the blood is seeping into your brain."

That made Cara Spencer giggle. "You really are practical, aren't you?" She used her right arm to maneuver her body parallel to her lover's. "You're worrying about my brain and shit."

"I also alphabetize grocery lists, but that's neither here nor there. What time is it?"

Panic surged briefly before Cara tamped it down. It was quarter to eleven in the evening. Andrea Dre would be leaving soon, leaving her bed, leaving her farmhouse, and leaving Greentown. This was transient, this was a one-night stand, and that was okay. It had to be.

"Almost eleven," she answered, reminding herself that she could not live solely in her head. "There's a clock on the wall by the bathroom."

"I should go," she knew Dre was about to say before she said it. "I've got a long drive back to the hotel."

"Yeah."

Awkward silence bubbled up and neither woman moved. The sounds of sleeping, contented hens and murmuring goats rode in one the breeze. Cicadas called and crickets chirped.

"But there's probably not a lot going on there. No breakfast or anything," Cara suggested, at long last, stretching like a cat.

"No breakfast?" Dre played along.

"Nope." Cara Spencer groped for her beer, which she'd left somewhere on the nightstand, lined up among various and sundry other knick-knack items. "No breakfast, no cold beer and no lumpy queen mattress."

"It *is* a lumpy fucking mattress."

"So you're staying, then?" She swigged as she heard Grey Baby baying at the moon, the same as she did almost every other night, like a vicious werewolf stuck in the stout body of a cattle dog. "I'm beat and I can't walk you to the door."

When Andrea stretched an arm around her, making her feel a little too much belonging, she knew, on some level, she'd won her prize; at least, for the moment.

* * *

Wearing all black and carrying a bulky black Magnum flashlight, Win ninja-toed out from behind a big, honking oak tree and peered out into the night, into the space stretching from Atticus's disconnected back deck— where he'd just left—to his sister's pole shed and side yard.

"Do you see anything?" Atti rustled, half lit and carrying a bong in his pocket, like a jackass with no concept of the law. "I never saw the Explorer leave."

The beam of the Magnum scanned the lot. "I don't—"

The glint of a tire caught his attention. "Well I'll be damned."

Back inside the trailer, he could hear Lincoln's mirth as it was carried by the breeze.

"I told you so, Brother! I told you so!"

Chickens, and Goats and A Cow Named Erin

It had never been a conscious decision to wake up at eight a.m. sharp on the daily, Dre thought drifting between states of mid-slumber and mid-wake. It had never been something she set out to do, specifically. No class that required her attendance, no desk that required her presence. It was simply the best time to awaken, brush her teeth, and look over the list of tasks she needed to beast before she could lay her head down to sleep again. Sad only in the idea that the steadfast institution of her alarm clock was necessitated by the ridiculously detailed lists she made the night before, and it had gone on so long that she had no concept of what time her natural clock woke her in the decades of her past. Any inherent biological analog had been trained to fit into the captivity of a pre-specified alarm, like the lame hyena in the display at the zoo, feet up and tail limp as tourists lounged on the rails overlooking a safety shrubbery, thinking "I guess I imagined them meaner, or more frightening." The hyena was her spirit and her spirit was dull, adult, and monotonous, and it woke up at precisely the same time every single day.

Measuring the minimal amount of light escaping from the dusty, wood-slat blinds that had possibly never been cleaned, it was all-too-obvious that Cara Spencer did not suffer from that same partiality (nor any predisposition toward cleanliness). Bright-eyed and bushy-tailed, she rifled through clothes left in a pile on the floor, soaked in the scant light from the swinging bulb, at the entry to her walk-in, master-suite closet, with her bare ass up in the air in a refreshingly candid display

Truthfully, there was something refreshingly candid about *her*, in general.

"What time is it?" Andrea croaked, shielding her REM-deprived face with a pillow that smelled like strawberries and Herbal Essence shampoo.

It had to be early. Her body was still stiff and ungainly, her eyes only opening a peep.

Cara Spencer sniggled, pulling on a sweatshirt with an Ivy League school logo printed on the front. Her breasts swayed, sans bra, and her rumpled hair covered her face. "'S a little after six."

A little after six was a time as yet completely unknown to Dre, whose structure included an approximate valuation of required daily hibernation. She winced, rolled over, and then turned back. "Wake me up at eight," she said, through gritted teeth. *Eight is when normal people get up. Nothing is really even open **before** eight, not even most of the schools back home.*

The scent of strawberries and Herbal Essence shampoo grew stronger and she felt Cara's slight weight dip the mattress. "I'll be long gone by eight, sweetheart."

"Long gone? What the fuck do you do with your morning?"

The weight disappeared as Cara Spencer moved, presumably, to locate pants from the same cavernous pile of vestments that littered her space. "Hell of a one night stand you are, you wake up bitchin' at me." Her legs were nothing short of miraculous, sinewy in their buxom musculature. Almost enough of a temptation to lure Dre from the sweet embrace of the cavernous mattress and itchy afghans she'd been balled up in for hours.

"Is that all I am to you?" she cracked, closing her eyes again, "A one night stand? Oh, how little you care."

Pulling on the same pants she'd worn to A.B.'s two nights before, Cara shook out one leg and released a wool sock that had been trapped in the chute. "What term would you prefer, my lady? Tryst? Secret liaison?"

134

No, Dre felt in her bones. There was something unseemly in labeling what they'd shared as casual sex. Casual sex wasn't…whatever this was. *This* was bigger. She was infatuated, smitten, and with decidedly more than the mysteries between Cara Spencer's legs or the way her cheeks flushed when she bit down on her bottom lip. The woman she'd spent the night with, held in the confines of her embrace, was smart, passionate, and incredibly funny, with her bizarre mood swings and her dogs and her disregard for orderly housekeeping. She hung wind chimes anywhere she could, even in spaces where there would be no wind. Her kitchen floor needed a good scrubbing, most of her trappings ended up at her feet rather than hanging in the closet, no part of her décor matched (ornamental Chinese vases paired with singing bass, candle holders with no candles, paintings mounted to every discernable surface), and there was dog hair everywhere. But the extent of the place, and the extent of the woman, was homey, warm, inviting, invigorating, salubrious.

"Come back to bed." Dre questioned whether there would be a time when she'd have her fill of Cara Spencer Madeline Holloway, and she felt the rush of desire flare when the other woman knelt at the bedside, placing her sweet oval face only inches away. Pink from sleep, her cheeks were dappled in deep brown freckles, and her lips were the lightest shade of rose. Her eyes, so shadowy a brown they were black, raised in haughty glee. "I can't, baby," she cooed, pushing a chunk of hair back from her gaze. "I gotta get to work."

"Work?" There had been no mention of work in pursuit of the pleasure held in a vice grip the night before. It was only—Shit, it was Monday. Most people worked on Monday—most people who weren't on a spiritual trek to Florida and could work from anywhere.

Dre felt instantly stupid for not putting that together.

"Work," her minx enunciated. "I have to work…farm, apple stand, restaurant."

Farm, apple stand, restaurant. Dre's ordinary routine simply began with washing her face and ended sitting down to plug in for a few hours at her desk.

"What farm?"

"*This* farm, dummy. Put your pants on and come help me."

One simple request, that was more of a command, and that was how she had ended up, coffee-laden and carrying an empty cat litter pail full of corn feed, while standing in a vast, chicken-wire pen surrounded by Rhode Island Reds and something called a Minorca Pullet that was named Daisy, in a thoroughly contradictory image of anything she had ever done or thought to do in her life. Sure, she had gone along on that 'working farm' field trip in the second grade, chaperoned by her feisty Italian father, but the experience was difficult to compare to the maelstrom of avian movement she was standing in the center of.

"They don't get out?" she asked, sipping from the mug in her right hand, clutching the metal bin with her left, balancing it between her arm and her hip, swaying it with her movements every few moments, as Cara had previously instructed in a hurried rundown of dos and don'ts for the chicken coop.

"They can," her instructor concurred. She was wearing a big, canvas glove and scattering whole handfuls of meal in every direction, swatting away the hens brave enough to stumble too close, or become too curious. "Thankfully, Grey Baby is a herder, not an eater, but it's rare that anything like that would happen. Chickens are relatively dumb and they associate the enclosure with food, so they never want to wander too far from the buffet."

"That makes sense."

"On a base level, absolutely. I think all domestic animals think like that, though."

Outside the flimsy metal mesh, hypnotized by the flurry of feathers and the cluck-cluck of the herd, Buddy's tongue hung embarrassingly out of his mouth while Greg Allman peed on a pile of raked leaves and Grey Baby patrolled the perimeter.

"Even Grey and Greg Allman don't stray too far from the farmhouse. They could, in theory, run all the way into the next county, but they don't. Neither do the goats."

"Neither do the Holloway children," Dre chuckled.

She could see Atticus's trailer barely an acre away, windows closed and lights still off as the sun dotted the flat land in tasteful hues of golden honey.

Cara paused. "I guess that's true. None of us every strayed too far from the home place. Odd, really. Our parents weren't the smothering type *before* they died. They had their own hobbies and their own lives. They loved us, but they weren't helicopters."

"That's hard to believe." Only it really wasn't. Michael and Ami were ultimately happy being alone, wrapped up in one another in Saint Augustine. They had the boys, who required such a large amount of time and attention as six year olds, they just left well enough alone in terms of Andrea. She was older, self-sufficient and responsible. She didn't warrant rearing any longer, had not in quite some time. And there was the complication of a May-December-stepmother dynamic to navigate.

"They were always with us when we were younger, don't get me wrong. We did plenty of regular family stuff—playing sports and going to church and taking beach vacations. But Mom and Dad were just always two peas in a pod, I guess. Always held hands in public and, at the end of the day, we always figured they would just be happier alone together, bird-watching in Costa Rica or hiking or fishing or doing whatever older, retired people with too much money do for fun. Flying single-engine airplanes with faulty wiring."

As an awkward silence descended, Dre drank her java and contemplated how different her life would have been had she lost both parents, instead of just the one; how different she would be if she were truly alone in the world, rather than partway so. Fat, black, and elegant, Daisy pecked at the ground around her Toms.

"Do you miss them?" she asked, before she could stop herself.

Wrinkling her nose, Cara flipped her hair over her shoulder. "Yes and no. I hate thinking about everything they missed out on, grandkids and stuff, although I think it's safe to say that ain't happenin' with my brothers any time soon."

"Do you want kids?" That seemed like an important enough question to ask in the moment, not that any of their naked mambo escapades in the past twelve hours could have resulted in that. Dre thought it was just one of those questions that you always needed to ask someone before you let your heart get pulled down in a mire your brain couldn't fight off.

"I don't know. I never really thought about it."

"Me either," she softened, honestly. "My friends have kids—well, they have *a* kid and Sam's pregnant again, apparently. It seems fun, but I don't know that I'm into it. It's all I can do to keep Buddy alive. The thought of being in charge of another human is terrifying."

* * *

The Right Kind of Woman

Cara threw a handful of food down and watched as her prized, fluffy hens scrambled over to it, stepping on toes and pecking heads in a line of dominance that was as old as time itself.

"Are they…gay?" She felt like a child talking to Dre. In any other subject, she would carry the conversation (more like *dominate* the conversation, if Atticus and Win were to be believed). Chicken husbandry? Goat rearing? Art? Beer? Music? But she knew so little about being gay it was astounding.

"Yeah," Dre answered, like it was no big thing. Like two women raising a baby together was no big thing, reinforcing the staggering fact that two parts of the same country were and could be so decidedly different. Freedom to marry and live and hold hands and make children and work and love and die verses. Whatever South Carolina had become, which had its' good days and its' bad days, on a state-run level.

Where would two women even get a baby?

"Most of the people in South Waterton—that's where I live—are gay. It's, like, the lesbian capital of the world. Well, the lesbian capital of the United States, at least."

"Really?" They were nearly out of food and the goats were beginning to whinny and whine.

"Yeah. You can't make it down the street without seeing a rainbow." Something in her voice repudiated the opinion that this arrangement was anything less than spectacular. But still…

"I can't even imagine what that would be like." Gay people were like apparitions in the South; some people believed in them and some people didn't and all of the respectable ones stayed firmly out of sight, opening florist stands or hardware stores and only traveling in their own, secluded circles.

139

"Yeah, I'll go out on a limb and say you probably don't have many here."

Shaking her head, Cara led the way to the clanking metal gate, anchored by two wooden posts dropped in by her brother and an auger the year before. Atop one, her A.B.'s coffee cup teetered perilously. "Not hardly," she delineated. There was another bag of feed—this one full of oats and grain and mixed vegetables—sitting in the back of her truck, which she'd parked at an angle, butting up to the pens. Stripping her hand of the glove, she heaved it up to her shoulder and strolled alongside the pole shed to the tangled web of hog wire that roped in a compatible amount of land to accommodate her growing flock of goats.

"And if there are gay people here, we never talk about it." That was probably the one fact that had done the most damage to her in her teen years. There were so many mixed messages, so many confusing developments within her body, and no one to discuss them with. No mentor, no sounding board. She had dared not bring it up to her girlfriends, all of whom were more interested in hairstyles and spray tans and dousing already-blonde hair with Sun In and lemon juice than hearing out the sexual malfunctions of their sleepover host. She had dared not bring it up to her brothers, all of whom, she assumed, would share the opinions of those around her. She had come to the conclusion that she couldn't bear for them to look at her any differently than they already did, treasuring her, showing her the ropes of life. They were all she had and she would rather live in secret than alienate them, as bizarre as that would seem to someone as cosmopolitan as Andrea.

As her body came into view, Polly and Pepper, infant Nubians born barely three weeks before, skittered over to her and began to chomp lazily on the knees of her jeans, all chestnut brown and white and floppy, with subtle amber eyes.

"We need to fill the feeders," she explained, pointing to two troughs lined up on the far wall. "They may nip but it doesn't hurt too much."

* * *

Dre reached down and touched the head of a brilliant tan and white goat, an adult with drooping speckled ears. His—her?—coat was coarse and scratchy, but clean.

"You really love animals," she stated, because it was the truth and she could tell that the topic of homosexuality in her town made Cara Spencer nervous.

Whatever her issues were, they weren't uncommon in the gay community, but thanks to the overwhelming support of her friends and her father, they hadn't affected Andrea quite so much as the woman before her. That had never been something she had known to be grateful for before. Removing her cell phone, she snapped a quick pic of her newfound friend and sent it to Tris, who wouldn't even *be* at school yet it was so goddamn early.

"I do," Cara ripped open the feed sack and emptied half of it into the first trough. Four sets of legs trotted over and began to pick out the spinach leaves. "I used to bring home strays all the time. It drove my parents crazy. Then, when I inherited this place, I figured I'd just start my own farm. Animals are much easier to deal with than people."

When she emptied the second half into the remaining trough, every leftover goat traipsed her way and the two babies, who had been steadily eating her pants, left to the join their pack with only one wistful glance backward.

"The eggs from the chickens make pocket change at the farmer's market. The milk from the goats I sell to a woman one town over who makes gourmet cheese for local restaurants. Erin Andrews just takes up space, but I can't bear to part with her. She's too sweet-natured." She learned back against the rails of the hog wire and watched with distinct pride as her goats ate breakfast.

"Erin Andrews?" Dre hadn't been sure it could get any stranger after Greg Allman the bitch Pyrenees, but Erin Andrews? The former ESPN anchor?

"The cow," came Cara's reply. "I keep her in the pole barn. She has her own stall and her own blankets. But she doesn't milk much. Win says she's too old, but I can't stand to think of putting her down, or whatever it is you do with old cows. Some guy on Facebook sold her to me for thirty bucks."

"Is that cheap for a cow?" Andrea wanted to know, before her cell phone shrieked in warning.

"That's very cheap for a cow."

"Good to know."

The face of the phone bore a picture of Willow, wearing more turd brown clothes, and laughing at nothing special—probably her sense of femininity blowing away in the breeze. Hers was the image assigned to Tristan's cell, and Dre answered quickly, putting a bit of space between her, the herd, and the pack leader who was now scratching and whispered to each individual goat.

Stepping over a pile of shit (literally), she greeted, "Hey."

"What the hell is that?" Tris screamed. "Is that a goat? When did your dad get a goat?"

Riiighhhttt...

"Um, I'm not actually in Florida. Yet," she admitted, bashfully. "I'm still in South Carolina. That's where the goats are...in South Carolina."

"Are you serious? Why? Never mind, don't answer that. How'd it go? With the girl? I guess well if you're still there playing with a random goat at seven in the morning on a Monday."

Dre took a sip of her coffee, which tasted pretty good for a grocery store blend. "They're, ah, they're *her* goats."

"Whose goats? The girl? That you met in the bar?"

"That makes it sound seedy."

"It is seedy!" Sam cried, in the background. Then, "I'm sorry, babe, I stayed quiet as long as I could."

"You're on speaker," Tris retracted, far too late. "I'm taking Sam to the doctor this morning. We get to hear the baby's heartbeat." There was an enthusiasm in her voice that had not been there, previously, when the topic of their unborn child had come up.

"Congratulations."

"No. Tell me more. What's she like?" Bossy had nothing on Samantha.

"Standing about six feet from me at the moment, so—ah—we're not going there."

With the jerk of a head, Cara put her hands on her hips, having been made aware that she was the topic of conversation. Pepper and Polly made agitated noises while Erin Andrews heaved a bovine sighing sound.

"Ugly? Fat? Dumb?" Sam continued.

"None of those things. Spectacular, in truth. Good enough to lure me into a goat pen before eight in the morning." There. That was compliment enough without betraying how much she was into Cara Spencer. It was just enough for her friends to understand, and befuddled enough for her paramour to miss.

"Oh my God, you *like* her, like her!" Sam screeched, certainly loud enough for everyone in the surrounding county to hear.

Dre blushed.

"Well, have fun!" Tris came to her aid. "Remember what I said about the banjos."

"Tell her we said hey! Tell her to move back to Massachusetts with you and make lots of gay babies and—" Willow gurgled and clapped her chubby hands and Samantha, blessedly, had to turn her attention elsewhere.

"No, I will not," and Dre hit the END button. She had had about all of the awkwardness she could stand in that moment, busy-body friends be damned.

Looking up, she saw Cara grin, like a cheetah. "Already told your friends about me, I see," was all she needed to say, giddy like a schoolboy who caught the teacher smoking a joint between classes. "I'm so flattered."

Andrea slid the phone into the back pocket of her jeans. "Well, you shouldn't be. I tell them about all the women I meet on road trips."

"Asshole."

"Hey, I'm being real. I've had so many one night stands, I can't even—"

"Are there clothes in your Explorer?" Cara interrupted. "Like, that you could change into?"

What in the hell was with this woman? She finds out I've already told my friends about her and now she wants me to change clothes? "Probably, why?" Most of her suitcase was still in the Explorer. She had only taken in what she absolutely needed for a night.

"Take a shower and come to work with me. It'll be fun."

Dre finished off her coffee. "I fail to see how working in an apple stand will be any definition of the word *fun*."

Winking in the splendor of the southern sun as it bathed her flock and her fields and caught all of the right angles of her hair, setting it ablaze, Cara Spencer put her hand on her hip, in a gesture that was swiftly becoming synonymous with her presence. "Of course it'll be fun, dummy. *I'll* be there."

And it will postpone the inevitable, Dre weighed, completely and utterly taken with the creature who stood before her caked in mud and animal feces and contented sweat, *but that might not be such a horrible thing.*

You Don't Have to Come Alone

"Hey Dad," Dre phonated, heaving an exhausted sigh as she leaned up against the back of a tangerine toned shed at the Granny's Apple Stand in some beaten down town called Kirkwood that had taken roughly an hour to get to in the yellow Apache with no A/C and no seatbelts. "I've been meaning to call you, but…" *I've been hefting apple bins and sorting apples into new bins and listening to an old lady tell me how much I looked like someone she knew a hundred years ago FOR THE PAST FOUR HOURS.*

"Jesus, kid, where are ya?" Michael boomed. "We been waitin' two days for you to pull up into the driveway." Had it really been two days since she'd left home?

No. It had been three days since she'd left home. It had been two since she'd wheeled into Greentown and been accosted by the Holloways and their beer and their apples and their sister, and plied with a good time that never seemed quite seemed to end, albeit interspersed with bounteous periods of hard, manual labor. "I'm in South Carolina."

"Did your car break down? I can come get you."

"No, no… It's nothing like that."

"Well, what the hell? Did you join a cult?"

She laughed, because sincerity oozed from his words despite their farcical nature.

"Nothing like that, Dad." She hadn't fallen in with a cult, had she? Were the Holloways a cult? "I met someone, some people—a girl."

"In *South Carolina*? And you've been there two days?!"

The more she said it—in her head, to Tris and now to her father—the sillier it sounded. *I've been in South Carolina for two days with people I do not know, sleeping with a woman I could only dream of, who may very well be an axe murderer.* Who up and drives to South Carolina, meets a woman in a restaurant, and then hangs around for days to kayak and work for free at an Apple Stand for an eighty-three-year-old lady? In any time zone outside a smut book, this chain of events made absolutely no sense whatsoever. Why had she left South Waterton in the first place? What was this overwhelming urge to seek change? This entire production was filled with gaps of common sense.

"I can't really explain it," which was the God's honest truth. She had not been able to explain any of it, from the beginning. She had no idea why she chose A.B. Lincoln's over the more traditional Ruby Tuesday. She had no idea why she felt an immediate kinship to Link (who was currently begging her via text messages to come and bartend in his stead at seven p.m. so he could meet up with one of the twentysomethings from Saturday night—like, *seriously*, he didn't even know her) or his brothers. She had no idea what had driven her to get inside Cara Spencer on a tree on a beach off a river. Yet somehow, it all felt right, and if she truly were about to be murdered by an adz-wielding brigade of Southerners holding a grudge against the lesbian culture, she had to trust her instincts enough to assume that a warning light—a *Check Engine Soon* alarm in her psyche—would have gone off by now. The Holloways had been nothing short of freakishly kind to her. Cara Spencer fed her, held her hand (out of view of anyone and inside the truck, but still) and Granny seemed to be on her best behavior. According to Atticus, who was huffing and puffing and lugging right alongside her at the apple stand, it had been years since he had seen her carry on a conversation that did not include a string of less-than-ladylike, four-letter words.

"Well, are you okay? I mean, do you have everything you need?"

"I'm fine. Really. I'm having fun. I fed goats."

"And it's not a cult?"

"Nope. No cult."

"And you say you met a girl?"

"I met a girl," she blushed. And felt foolish. "She's smart and funny and smells like strawberries and Herbal Essence shampoo."

In twenty-eight years, she never so much as described a girlfriend to her father, and now she had flagrant diarrhea like a kid. *She's smart and funny and smells like strawberries and Herbal Essence shampoo. What a fucking tool, I am.*

"I see."

"Don't be weird."

"I'm not the one on sabbatical in South Carolina."

"Fair enough."

She traced the splintered wood of the makeshift shelter with her right forefinger and, for the first time in her life, wondered if she would ever have had conversations like these with her mother, had she not been killed in a car accident. Would she have had a relationship like this? One where she could ramble on about her new girlfriend and talk in glittering generalities and explain, calmly, that she was in South Carolina for an indefinite amount of time.

"You know, your mom was from South Carolina," Michael divulged. "Some tiny shit town outside a place called Georgetown."

"Really?" Dre didn't remember her mother having any sort of accent, but then... She didn't really remember her mother's voice, did she? She only knew the quick imitations her father had given her, repeating words and phrases, but not really syntax or cadence.

"Oh sure. Her parents moved up to Boston when her father got a job with a bigger company. Never really had any extended family so there was no real reason for her to back."

"I never knew that." There must have been a lot about Caroline Faye Martin she didn't know, most of it inconsequential, but the peace in her soul that hadn't been there up North? That bit would have been enlightening. "My mom was from South Carolina."

"That's my fault, kid," the craggy stillness in his voice told her he had not, perhaps, intended to go quite so deep into their joint past on a Monday afternoon. "There's a lot I never thought to tell you. There's a lot I buried somewhere, kept it all down. When you get here, I'll show you. Assuming you're still coming."

"I'm coming," she promised, with conviction. "I'll leave tomorrow." Or the next day. What was the rush?

"I'll believe it when I see it," his tone lightened. "And, you know, there's no reason you have to make the trip alone."

She nearly dropped the cell phone. "Huh? What? I don't..."

Michael Martin was too Type A for words. Too together, too regimented. Too...not the person to invite his daughter to bring her southern fling down to his compound in Saint Augustine.

"You don't have to come alone. Why not bring your friend- what's her name? Savannah Grace? Something *Gone with the Wind*, eh?"

"Cara Spencer." Putting the words out there in the universe made it somehow all feel very, seriously, no-take-back kind of real.

"Bring *her*, if you want. No reason you can't enjoy yourself. We got a guest house. We won't even know you're out there."

"Okay, Dad. I gotta go." Hastily, Dre hit END and sat for a moment, or rather stood for a moment against a sheet of plywood poorly sanded, painted the color of a Red Delicious and weight down with apple puns. As a momentary silence descended, that could have existed only in her own mind, she processed the developments in the ten-minute conversation she had just spun with her father. A born list-maker, she felt it only appropriate to separate each development into a specific category.

A. She had been in South Carolina for two whole days, which had been a slight to her father, but a honeymoon for her soul. Had it been fair to Michael? It had not been fair to Michael. Michael had been expecting her in Saint Augustine.

B. She had met a girl and was completely smitten and had all but shouted it from the rooftops, and was curiously unbothered by the image of her father, in a rocking chair on his front porch, drinking wine and pining for her to come to him and learn all of the secrets he had kept buried for so long.

C. Her mother was born in South Carolina, which didn't seem like it would change much in her life, twenty-six years after that faithful April day, but in reality it changed more than she could have expected. Something visceral, as if all of the things she had flippantly regarded from the unsavory interstate view now mattered in a much more serious way.

D. Her father wanted to show her things that presumably belonged to her mother or related to her mother and she had not known she would ever want that. Or need that.

E. She did need to see those things. Very badly.

F. That would necessitate her leaving tomorrow.

G. It would not be the end of the world if Cara Spencer went with her.

Line Item G was the most troubling. Her heart did not so much *want* Cara Spencer to go, as *need* Cara Spencer to go; she needed the connection to continue and the laughter to continue and the sex to continue, if she "called a spade a spade," as Link would put it. Moreover, she needed Cara Spencer to *want* to come with her—to *want* all of those things—too, and not give up on whatever it was they shared because she felt a duty to stay behind. *Leave your house, leave your animals, leave your job and your responsibilities, and agree to drive six hours with me and Buddy and stay in my father's guest house which I have never even seen, which could be a hovel. By the way, you don't really know me, but I cannot get enough of your clit. Don't say no.* What a terrifically difficult position. Except... She had essentially done the reverse by staying in Greentown.

Throwing caution to the wind (because that's what this trip was teaching her, right?), she stalked around the shed/office and found Cara Spencer easily enough, measuring the ratio of Braeburns to Pink Ladies. Wrapped in fabric so tight it appeared to be painted on, Dre took in the sight of those pink delicious breasts as they swayed behind the apple stand logo, hair spilling down her shoulders and back like a tangled waterfall.

"Cara," she began.

The booth was, for the most part, deserted. Granny had gone to the bathroom, which was always an ordeal. Atti had gone as her chaperone. The farmer's market was weekday dead.

"I have to leave."

Cara Spencer did not look up, mouthing numbers. "Did Link get a hold of you? He wants you to take over his shift at the bar. He says he's dying—"

"No," Dre stomped a little, like a diva, which was uncharacteristic. "I have to leave South Carolina."

151

That got her the attention she wanted. "Right now?" Cara's eyes brimmed with a loud shout of *NO I DON'T WANT YOU TO GO*, but she quickly masked it. "You're leaving right now?"

"In the morning."

"O...kay."

"And I want you to go with me."

Brows furrowed. Hands found hips, the apples casks between them forgotten. "You want me to go with you to Florida *tomorrow*."

It was stupid and it was brazen and it was irresponsible and imprudent, but Andrea Marie who went by Dre and had only just found her voice was not about to back down. "I want you to go with me to Florida tomorrow."

"And stay for how long?"

"No clue." No planning, no preparation, Dre was flying by the seat of her proverbial pants, hoping she would not lose them in the crash landing. "A few days, I would imagine."

"But I have a job."

You count apples. "Take some time off."

"I have the farm."

Goats and chickens and a cow do not a full farm make. "Your brothers can take over."

"I have Grey Baby and Greg Allman."

Dogs? Really? That's an excuse? "Bring them."

Cara scoffed. "Bring them? Three dogs in the backseat of a Ford Explorer?"

"Bring them. I'm not giving you any excuse not to go." *If it's fear that controls you, you'll have to the be the one to say it. I took a leap, now it's your turn.*

"Dre, this is crazy," she launched and Dre found herself wishing that she had said *baby* in place of the more lackluster Dre. "I can't just up and leave for Florida and inconvenience everyone around me. I have shifts at the apple stand and shifts at the restaurant, even if they're stupid, menial jobs. I have to gather the eggs and milk the goats—"

"I have no idea how I ended up here," was Dre's only return. "I got into the car and headed for 95-South. I drove until my ass hurt and I pulled over on the first ramp I saw. I wanted a drink, I was sent to A.B.'s. And there you were. I took a big chance. I went kayaking with people I didn't know… Now I'm asking you to do the same. It doesn't make sense and it may be a shit trip, but I'm asking you to do what I did."

"Fine." Cara Spencer came around the bins and met her eyes, stare-for-stare. "Fine. I'll go."

"Fine?" Dre squinted and pushed her hand through her hair, which was a nervous habit she had only recently given birth to, like in the last five minutes. "*Fine?*"

"Fine."

Okay. Fine.

And that was how she'd ended up chauffeuring two clunky canines (Greg Allman was just too big for the car and reluctantly agreed to have a sleepover at Uncle Win's) and one snoring Southern belle all the way from Greentown, South Carolina, to Saint Augustine, Florida. And it was all just fine.

The Sunshine State

"Wake up, baby," Cara gloated with no preamble, "Ami made more muffins and they're fucking delicious."

Smiling from ear to ear, with berries probably stuck in her teeth, she flopped back down on the pillow top mattress in the guesthouse she had been sharing with her lady love for four consecutive nights. Four nights that felt like four years, that felt like forever. Four nights that had been perfect, sheltered in a guest house—not a guest *room*, but a whole building—done up in yellows and blues and patterns of china, like the rooms in *Southern Living* magazine. The breadth of the place was a gasp of fresh, Floridian air, drenched in sunlight from a pair of French doors that opened onto a pool deck with a private, intricately carved, wrought iron cabana. Photo frames in blues and greens dappled the lemon-toned walls, drifting seamlessly into an en suite with a claw foot soaking tub and etched glass doors on a walk-in shower.

Quite simply put, it was the most luxurious place Cara Spencer had ever been in, even if it was a converted storage shed in the Martin's backyard. It was unexpectedly posh, and unexpectedly private, and the unexpected combination of those two things left her free to explore each and every inch of Andrea Dre Martin, all while inhaling every sweet, gluten-free concoction Ami whipped up in her spare time, behind those high-gloss granite counters in the main house.

"I'm serious. These are better than yesterday's." Because she was staying in a four stay resort where a sinewy, hippie fed her scones each morning after lending her the space to have copious lesbian sex.

"Go away," Dre mumbled. "I'm sleeping."

"No, you're not. You never sleep this late." Feet carelessly in the air, ankles crossed, Cara Spencer seemed more like a spoiled princess than the rough and tumble farm girl she was at home. It was a change she did not completely hate, not that she would ever admit it to anyone. A world away from the dirt and the grime and the smell of feces and swamp water, life in the swank subdivision of Mallard's Crossing (seconds from the water and seconds from a pool and seconds from a community pool and seconds from a golf course) was very near heaven.

Pulling the blanket down below her chin, Andrea glared at her without heart. "Only because you *always* wake me up."

"Because I *always* miss you."

For some reason, Florida unleashed the torrent of her bottled, practically thirty-year-old feelings. It became okay to express them, for her to play at being open and honest with herself, and with Dre, which pretty much translated into nonstop sex, nonstop affection, nonstop kisses. They held hands on the beach, for Christ sake, in *public*. Where everyone could see.

At first, she had been reticent to even give the appearance that they were a couple. That was nothing she would have been brave enough to do in front of her *own* family - sharing a bedroom with a girl on vacation. She had tagged along under the assumption that she would serve as an old friend or roommate. After all, the gay people she had encountered in and around Greentown (all, perhaps, two of them) used the term "roommate" interchangeably with "partner" or "lover," almost like a code the rest of the world imposed. But, no sooner had her Rainbow-brand flip-flops rainbows hit the travertine foyer, Michael had expressed his gratitude toward her for "putting up with the likes of Andrea," who, allegedly, hadn't had a real girlfriend, one that met his sky high standards, in "ages." Once that introduction was out of the way, they were free to be seen as… Whatever they were: randy teenagers who had only recently discovered the sensation of necking. And caressing. And sneaking hands deep in bathing suit bottoms at every hint of solitude. *Every* hint.

"You miss me?" The devilish glint was back in her lover's eye, akin to the hungry glint and the desperate glint and the glints of sweaty, screaming passion.

"I do," her voice dropped about three octaves.

"Then come back to bed." Dre opened the down duvet and exposed the lean flesh of her hip, inadvertently; hips that trailed down to her muscular backside and robust legs that felt like paradise wrapped around her.

"I don't know," Cara lied, lifting the hem of her soft, white v-neck to expose the swollen underside of her breast. "Those muffins *were* pretty damn good."

Playfully, Dre reached for her, rubbed a heavy thumb over the weight of her chest, stroking nipple through fabric. "The only muffin I want is yours."

And that would have sounded cheesy—*been* cheesy, if she hadn't, in that moment, reached down and thrust her own fingers into herself, pushing back the blankets and the faux-fur throw, bending backward. Her rear dug into the mattress and she bit at her lip. "Can't you help me?"

They'd been gamboling at it all week. Teasing one another. Pushing buttons that neither knew about. Tempting and cajoling. They'd gotten hot and bothered in the Explorer, just crossing into Florida. Cara Spencer had ridden thirty miles playing with herself just to watch the expression on Dre's face. There had been the inaugural sex in the guest house; sex up against the glass, sex on the sinks in the bathroom, sex in the shower, sex out by the pool in the middle of the night. When they'd gone to the beach, looked out at the ocean, there'd been risqué brushing, accidental bumping. If the main house was vacant, as it was when Ami went to teach her yoga classes and Michael took the boys to school, they had poked around and then *poked around*. Andrea had taken her to heights so great she was soaring with the eagles and, in turn, she had done all that she knew to do. With her fingers.

"I like to look into your eyes when you climax," she fibbed, and Dre never pushed her. Oral sex was something she just…had never done? Had *never* done, though she desperately wanted to. All of the women (okay, the phrase *all of the women* made it seem like a lot more than six or seven) that she had seen "sporadically" had been sheltered, inexperienced, in a phase, trying things out. It had been enough for them, just letting her make out, never pushing for anything else. More would mean they were serious about things. About her.

Clearly, taking another woman's secret spaces in between her lips made would make her a "real" lesbian. *Fuck.* The more she thought about it, the less likely she was to do it. And she couldn't just say it out loud because saying it out loud made it a thing, much like the homosexuality she skirted with her friends and family and the general population of the non-Floridian world. *If you don't say it, it's not real.*

"Come back to me, Cara…" Dre strained and rubbed and writhed on the mattress, her naked body laid out before her, thighs split, and those perfect breasts peaking. She was fully nude and it was a heady combination, the body and the woman and the sunlight coming through the windows.

Without thinking, she ditched her tee and sweats and mounted the looming bed, splitting her legs to kneel over Andrea, balancing but not touching.

"Oh yes, Cara. Cara, touch me," she heard, letting her hands caress her own skin as they blazed a trail she wanted Dre's mouth to follow. "Touch me, please…"

If her body was soft, Andrea's was steel, all angles and edges and bone.

"Fuck, you're beautiful," she said. *You're the most beautiful woman in the world.* "Let me taste you."

Dre's nostrils flared and her eyes snapped to attention, fingers frozen. "I didn't…I mean, I don't—"

"I want to," Cara felt herself decide. She could not have predicted that this would be the moment or the time or the place, but she knew in her spine that being inside Dre was the only thing she cared about, the only real thought in her brain, and her fingers weren't enough. Her fingers were a poor substitute for enough. She wanted to feel what she had explored with her mouth and her tongue and her lips. She wanted Dre inside her, between her teeth, and down her throat. She wanted to lick until all she smelled was Dre and all she felt was Dre and all she knew was Dre.

Pushing her lover down, hand on one of those precious high breasts, she prowled backward, losing sheet and spare socks and pillows, tossing comforters aside. The doors were open and the windows were parted and she did not care.

"Cara, it's really okay," Dre mumbled, almost as if it were a contest of temerity. "I don't need it."

"I do." On her belly now, one hand parted Andrea's lean, athlete's legs, slipped overtop—

"Put your hands…under my legs…if you can."

Right. That made more sense.

"It's…more comfortable."

It was the last coherent sentence she said for a long while.

In the exact instant that Cara Spencer's tongue touched the sensitive folds of her clit, Dre knew that she was sinking in a sea of affection that she could not bail out of. She was done for, ruined, and left for dead if she were to be parted from this woman. But as that tongue began a slow and torturous rhythm of movement, anticipating what her body would want before she even knew, she realized, in the very pit of her soured, bitter soul that she was wholly and completely, one hundred percent in love with Cara Spencer Madeline Holloway. Recklessly, irresponsibly, stupidly, foolishly, unwisely in love with Cara Spencer. Crazy in love with Cara Spencer.

What came out of her throat was a low, deep, guttural, rasping and inarticulate sound the likes of which she had never heard. Or felt. Her body soaked and shook, her legs numb. She wanted more, needed more.

Grabbing a hole of Cara's hair, that hair that brushed against her when she held them both at night, she drove herself forward. When her lover laughed, pleased, she wanted to cry and scream and beg to stay like this forever, locked down, for once and truly owned by another human being.

"God…please…" she said, or thought she said, or attempted to say. "Please…" Her emotions were raw and seething.

But Cara shook her head. "I'm not done." Her breath was a cool breeze of pleasure, her words rumbling against skin and liquid.

She should have been shouting from the rooftops. It was the first time in her life, relationships and flings and encounters included, that she had ever let anyone this close into her private spaces. It was the first time she had trusted, and been trusted, and been vulnerable and open and patient. It was the first time she had ever felt a woman's tongue between her legs, *inside* of her.

At Northeastern, she had been the receiver, reserved and taciturn, unsure of how to go about being gay in the new world, the world outside the confines of her tiny childhood brownstone and the safety of those who knew and loved her. She was cynical of the lesbian community, leery of exposing her soul. And that's what this was, this beautiful moment that she had fallen so unexpectedly out of the sky: this was a significant and noteworthy moment in her life, hands wound in sheet, head kicked back, mouth parted, Cara Spencer's name on her lips.

This was her beginning. This was her change. This was where and what she wanted to be for the rest of her life, no matter how fucking stupid that sounded to the rest of the world. People fell in love on a regular basis, out in the universe, bumping into one another through cosmic mistake. People fell in love in high schools and office buildings and hospitals and over Italian food. People fell in love all around her. Tris, Sam, her father. And she was tired of waiting, tired of playing the game to try and fit in and be the type of lesbian that everyone wanted her to be. She was tired of pretending that she didn't want an all-cards-on-the-table-it-doesn't-even-bother-me-that-you-wear-makeup moment. She was tired of pretending she was into dirty hippie music when she liked light jazz and boxed macaroni and cheese, even though it was filled with carcinogens. She was tired of pretending she wanted to change the world when all she really gave a damn about was finding someone warm and open and caring to come home to every night.

The Right Kind of Woman

She was tired of the empty apartment and the dog being her only real friend. She was…tired, had been tired for so fucking long she wasn't even sure she knew what awake felt like until this one moment in this one guest house in this one town that happened to be, thanks to her stepmother's guided tour, the oldest continuously inhabited settlement in all of North America.

She was—

* * *

"I'm about to… Oh God, there it is…."

The delicate lobes of Andrea's mystery were slick and smooth like honey, the parts of her all the more mystifying because they were kept hidden. There were her most beautiful parts, wrapped in the unadulterated beauty of a woman who was so steadfast and sure in the world. They were her vulnerable parts, her uncertainties. And Cara worshipped her there, at the naked altar of power. Over and over she lapped at the beauty, tickling with her nose and her chin and her teeth. Over and over she came, in her own right, thrown by the power and fullness and breadth of what she had done. What she could do. What she *needed* for…ever?

"Oh… Don't stop… Don't—" The orgasm nailed her from behind and shook her to a buried core so deep she thought there were earthquakes in Northern Florida and almost looked around the room to see the damage.

All sound tunneled out, all movement, all sensation until she was alone with the stars and the love of her life and a blanket and a heartbeat and two hands running fingers over the outsides of her thighs. When her vision returned, she looked down to see the love beaming out of Cara's obsidian eyes, long-rimmed lashes those of a schoolgirl who had no concept of the power she wielded.

"Fuck, I love you."

* * *

The words hung in the air, just above her head, and Cara had to blink to adjust her vision. But that wouldn't really help, would it?

Shit. She needed to say something, say it back, say it was sweet, say she wasn't ready. *Am I ready?* Was she ready?

Her body still roiling, Dre didn't skip a beat. She sat up, took Cara Spencer's hands in her own, and looked her right in the eyes that needed blinking because she couldn't hear. That was how poorly her brain worked.

"I love you and I don't fucking care that I just said. I don't care that it's been, like, a week. I don't care that you live in South Carolina and I live in Massachusetts. I don't care that we're only here for a few days. It's there and I'm too old to play head games. I love you." She took a deep breath. Cara did the same. "You don't have to say it back. You don't ever have to say it back, but if I keep living my life in the same lane, never taking chances, never letting anyone in, never looking beyond what's in front of me in the now, I'm never going to be happy. With you, as un-fucking-likely as this is, I feel happy."

As confessions went, it was the most perfect one Cara had ever heard. If a train barreling down the tracks at full speed with her in its sights was perfect, which, in some ways, she guessed would be true.

Love Her, But Leave Her Wild

"Oh my fucking Christ," Tris sputtered, and that was the closest she would ever get to yelling in all of her life. "You love her."

In the background, over a grunting baby, Dre heard Sam's sharp intake of breath. "She loves who? The girl?"

"And she told her she loved her," Tris endowed.

Funny, Dre thought, as she watched Grey Baby and Buddy, outlined by the floodlights, frolic in the grass outside the three foot tall, black pool safety fence (that Grey Baby continued to attack and circumvent at every possible allowance), it was almost like they were all together, having a late dinner at the Mongolian diner down the street from the apartment building. Almost, but not quite.

"You told her you loved after, like, three days?!" Sam challenged, taking full custody of the (shared) cell phone. "That's insane. That's absurd. That's so romantic!"

"That is not Dre," came Tris. "That's not Dre at all. Dre dates women for years and years and *never* tells them she loves them."

"Because I didn't," was the simplest of answers. "I didn't love Stephanie and I sure as hell didn't love Mare."

"Mare was awful," both of her friends jibed. "She was just…awful. And confusing, and not at all someone you would want to grow old with."

"So you took this big change thing pretty seriously, huh?" Tris's voice was singular again. "I mean, here we were, thinking you were just going to head to Florida and soak up some rays and now you're got a girlfriend and you love her and you touched a goat."

Grey Baby slipped through the black, metallic slats and bounded into the shallow end of the swimming pool. Having realized the extent of the dog's paddling abilities, Dre understood it was not an emergency situation. She sat back on her heels and waited the inevitable egress and shake.

"She's not my girlfriend."

"But you love her?"

"But I love her."

"So why can't she be your girlfriend?"

"Because…" *Because* **girlfriend** *sounds like a stupid, childish word and I feel things for Cara Spencer that are far from childish.* "Because I live in South Waterton, Massachusetts and she lives in Greentown, South Carolina." That was the more practical of the reasons: logistics. Logistics were complicated little bastards.

"So tell her to move. We're nice." Sam was as blunt as she was pushy. "It'd be nice to have a distraction from the two of you and your *Chopped* marathons."

Tristan made disapproving sounds, but Dre just shook her head. "I can't do that. I can't ask her to leave her house and her family—her *brothers* and her grandmother—or her farm. I can't ask her to leave the goats and the cow and the chickens and shit." Look at her being so verbose. And shit.

No one even mentioned the probability that she would move, which was ironic given that her chosen profession could be accurately executed from a beach in Maui or a tree in the Amazon. And a small part of her really wouldn't mind waking up on that farm every morning, playing with the goats with the stupid names, fishing brown eggs from beneath speckled chickens and watching Buddy romp in the overgrown fields.

"So… What are you going to do?"

164

The Right Kind of Woman

What am I going to do?

* * *

As her admission of undying affection draped the bedroom in a stiff cloud of AWKWARD, she had taken the first available opportunity to head out and plug into her father's Wi-Fi connection in order to sift through work-related emails and finalize the contract she had initiated in Pennsylvania. Immersing herself in work always seemed to calm her down, roll her swiftly back to center. Cara Spencer had not emerged from the guest house, and she had no idea whether that was a good sign or a bad sign, but she had to relinquish what she could not control. It wasn't every day that she dumped it all out in front of someone whose mind was a practical stranger, in deference to the kinship of bodies.

No. That wasn't true at all, was it?

Cara Spencer's mind had been an open book, her thoughts spilling out in the car, in the bed, on the beach, over dinner, even while watching Michael Junior and Christian practice soccer in the roped off fields of their neighborhood YMCA. She liked bluegrass, but hated country music. She had grown up on classic rock, because her father had driven a VW Beetle in the late nineteen sixties. She liked the colors green and blue, but hated purple and loathed pink. Lincoln *thought* he was closest to her, but Atticus took the prize. She even tossed him unneeded funds (which were rare in her life) when she could so he could buy more art supplies. Those paintings suspended in the restaurant, the giant canvases hanging from the ceiling— those were his, and she was amazed by his talent. In her estimation, he was the only even vaguely artistic person in the entire Holloway family tree.

In high school, she had played in the Academic Bowl and been bullied on account of her hair. The tendrils and waves, uneven and wily, were natural, though none of her brothers inherited the trait. She kissed one boy in the ninth grade, his name was Jose, and he had been a migrant worker on the Holloway tobacco farm. Immediately, she felt guilty about it and told him she couldn't see him anymore because she knew deep down it "didn't feel like it was supposed to." She read romance novels in her spare time because she liked stories with unrealistically happy endings. Her favorite food was broccoli and her favorite meal was hamburger steak and mashed potatoes with gravy.

Cara Spencer had been her grandmother's name. She snored a little when she slept on her right side and she snuggled when the fan was on, but she woke up gooey. She never put anything back where it belonged and she was unapologetic about waking up in the wee hours of the morning to start her day. Where most would shy away from the smells and tasks associated with a goat farm, she felt the most alive when she was with them.

"Shit." *Just shit. Lots and lots of shit.* Andrea Marie Martin was butt-crazy in love with Cara and there wasn't a damn thing she could do to run away from it. "I have no fucking clue what I'm going to do," she told Tris, who had been patiently letting the cogs and wheels of her friend's thoughts run their course. "I really have no idea."

"Well," the words of wisdom poured forth. "You should go and talk to her before she thinks you're a weirdo who ran away after dropping the L-Bomb."

"Yeah." Dre called the dogs, who both came running, Grey Baby's thick tale spraying droplets of water around her. "Easier said than done."

So it came in fabulously handy when her father cornered her in the kitchen and wanted to share a moment that became an hour.

* * *

She loves me.

She loves me.

She loves… Me?

Dre loves me?

Dre had told her the news and then wafted out under the pretense of getting work done closer to the Wi-Fi signal. *Probably because I'm a loser and I didn't say anything. Probably because I have no idea what I was supposed to say!*

It was the first time in her life that anyone, aside from the people making up the consortium of her family, had confessed affection for her any deeper than what girls feel in the ninth grade when a boy slips his hand into the waistband of her Hanes. It was the first time, in all of her days, that anyone, girl or boy, had proclaimed a real love for her.

Boys never wanted much more from her, once they realized she would not consent to anything more physical than kissing. They simply settled for bragging about having had sex with her instead, when no sex had ever taken place. Any girls? They women she had been with—not that she could consider anything they had done much more than heavy petting after everything Dre had given and shown her throughout the preceding week— had all been straight, she had suspected. They had all been heterosexual, confused, hurt or experimental, and nary a one had lasted longer than a few weeks; not once they realized their illicit "relationships" (if they could even been called such things) would never exist beyond the confines of Cara Spencer's ratty couch.

But now? Cara Spencer was loved. By a real lesbian. And that made her a lesbian. And that was off-putting to a woman who had done her very best to hide that blaringly obvious fact from childhood forward.

"I'm not a lesbian," she heard herself say to the shadows on the wall.

She had spent years saying that, behind closed doors, in the shower, underwater in the river. She had spent years bluffing, covering, concealing...pretending that the woman inside her was not what she was. Had she built a life? Sure, albeit not a romantically fulfilling one. Had she found happiness in her profession as a farmer and an apple-picker and a part-time restaurant worker? Without a doubt, if she could call the complacency and comfort she found among her brothers as professional happiness. But had she ever been honest with herself? Not one single time. And had she ever experienced an actual, *real*, adult relationship, where two people combine lives and share toothpaste and the duties of grocery shopping and look forward to Friday nights in, with the Food Network? No.

She slept alone in a bed built for two, sheathed in unease and the blankets of her ancestors, dreaming of her wedding day and the blank face of Prince(ss) Charming. She went to church at Christmas and Easter, listened to the pastor spread God's loving message—the one that excluded any spelled out specifically in Leviticus—and wondered what all of the people around her would think if they knew. What the people at the apple stand would think if they knew... What the people at A.B.'s would think if they knew...

What her brothers would think if they knew...

"What do I do?" she asked everyone in her mind, except the Jesus she believed in, one who was mortified at everything spelled out in Leviticus, especially the bits about bacon. "What do I say to her?"

I could say I LOVE YOU back. She could totally say she loved Dre. It would be so easy, to run away with Dre and leave the past, the family and the pressure back in South Carolina. It would be so easy to be with Dre, once they were in Massachusetts.

It certainly was not as if she did not return Dre's affection. She loved Dre, absolutely. She had known it the very moment their paths had crossed in that bathroom, and it had slowly wormed its way through her defenses. But that was utterly ridiculous. That made absolutely no sense. They had known each other all of one week—seven nights, seven days. To think that she could know someone well enough to entwine her future and her soul and her life and all that she ever would be on a shallow statement of love screamed out during sex? That was preposterous, absurd, and wholeheartedly nonsensical. After weeks, months, year—maybe. Her own parents had been together for four years before they even contemplated marriage. Win had dated some girl named Monica for six years before she up and left him for a rodeo clown. What if they rodeo came through South Waterton? What then?

Cara could not, and would not, uproot her entire life and relocate based on seven days. Seven *days?* She did not even remember whether Dre was right-handed or left-handed. That seemed like a pretty big deal.

You can't move in with someone if you don't know what hand they write with, for fuck's sake. And who said anything about moving in? We just met! Applebee's, Chili's, Ruby Tuesday, a couple of movies, one vacation. Not BAM WE LIVE TOGETHER. Dre slept too long in the morning, and constantly picked up after her, and took really involved showers. She would be miserable living with a scatter-brained woman like Cara. Cara sped through showers like they were the plague and preferred bathing in the creek to bathing in high-gloss with multiple shower heads.

"Fuck, this is complicated. Why is this so fucking complicated?"

* * *

"Your mother was…beautiful," Michael had downed four glasses of a deep red and robust blend that smelled like a French woman's cleavage over a period of about ten minutes. He leaned across the granite countertops in the kitchen, built to his current wife's explicit specifications, and rubbed his chest, like the very mention of his dead wife's memory was painful in a way that he refused to accept for the benefit of his grown, adult daughter. "Full of energy, quirky as hell…she was bright and funny. She woke up a room when she walked in."

The outpouring of his confession served as a welcome distraction from the awkwardness that would mushroom the guesthouse like Hiroshima the moment she returned—not that Dre would take any of it back. She loved Cara Spencer and didn't give a shit where they lived. None of that mattered at the moment. All that mattered was that she finally found someone who was worthy of the words "I love you."

But what Cara did with that knowledge was out of her control.

"When I met her, I loved her in about fifteen minutes, just melted in a goddamn puddle."

Twenty-eight years had gone by and Dre oddly knew very little of the woman who had donated her egg and womb and two years of her life, or of her parents' courtship, as strange as that sounded. She knew Cara's parents had been sweethearts at the University of South Carolina, but hers? For all she knew, they met in a strip club. And it had never much bothered her, never having known the woman to feel her loss fully. Her earliest memories were of a peculiar swirl pattern in the carpet of their above-bakery apartment, or the sound of the timers on the big bakery ovens in the shop her father owned. For the majority of her childhood, her mornings and afternoons had been spent in that space, coated in flour and sugar and frosting.

"She worked in the Registrar's Office at some college I went to, back when I had decided to do just about anything *except* be a baker like my father. You know I never wanted to be a baker—"

"I know, Dad," Dre said, pouring her own glass of cabernet.

He had never wanted to be a baker, had never wanted to carry on the family tradition, had only gone back to it to support his young family and give them the stability he felt they deserved. It was the same speech he rattled off every time she brought home grades below a B. Sacrifice, hard work, menial unhappiness all so she could have the chance to further her education and pursue her own dreams. Dreams, consequently, that would take averages far higher than a B to accomplish.

"She had the most beautiful smile. I think the moment I saw it I knew I was done for. Almost like I was ruined for anybody else."

"I know the feeling."

Michael felt around for a crumb to clean and couldn't look at his daughter. "I can see that," he meandered around the point of his spiel. "And I am so happy for you. Ami and I are both so happy for you. The way you smile when she comes close to you, the joy in your eyes—it's as plain as the nose on your face how you feel about Cara."

"Cara Spencer," Dre corrected. "Double name."

Her father crowed. "Of course she does. Good old southern double names. She reminds me so much of your mother. Andrea. Willful and secret, open and closed."

The description of a dichotomy, of a woman so headstrong and yet so plagued with self-doubt, was a more fitting description of Cara Spencer than Dre knew her father could appreciate, and it was ironic that the two most predictable, most regimented, and intrinsically motivated people on the planet would have so definitively a type. It truly lent credence to the age-old adage of "opposites attract."

"That's why I'm scared, kid."

"Scared?"

"Your mother…" He took in a great gulp of air and reached behind his corded neck to rub the muscle strained with memory. "There's no easy way to say this…loving your mother was the hardest thing I have ever done in my life. Harder than raising you alone, even…staying with her, being steady when she wasn't steady. I can't— I cannot describe to you how demanding a scenario it was."

Their hallmark moment had swiftly changed direction. "I thought you adored her? And now you're saying she was awful?"

"No, no. Not awful." Michael reached for more wine and Dre couldn't begrudge him that. She had downed an entire glass in a moment, swept up in a wave of curiosity and entertaining detachment that was or was not feigned. "I loved her with my entire soul. But she was never the same from one day to the next. She was so willful, so headstrong. She refused to marry me, refused to take my name. Refused to name you after my mother, Rosaline. She could be wildly intoxicating, like a drug, but the crash was just as bad. She walked out and left us when you were three months old, and then came back a week later. She told me she just needed to be alone for a while."

"Oh… My…"

"I know. I should have told you—"

"You really probably shouldn't have." Subconsciously, she may have needed all of the years of romanticized fancy about a woman in a pale white dress with flowers in her hair, smiling and hugging and making the team snacks for soccer. Confronting the image of a crazy, selfish woman who was vaguely bipolar wouldn't have been the best path for a second grader.

"I can't say for sure that we would've stayed married, but I sure as hell know that having her, loving her, holding her…it was the best ride of my life."

Light bulbs flickered on in the recesses of Dre's consciousness. "And you're worried Cara Spencer's the same roller coaster for me?"

Michael nodded, shaggy hair hanging in a ponytail that seemed fitting for a man married to a much younger woman who made gluten-free muffins and taught yoga and wore two-piece bathing suits and looked like a model even in her forties.

"I am terrified," he relented. "I would never presume to tell you what choices to make in the life I fought to give you. I would never tell you to leave her. But, I would rather saw off my arm than watch you live through the pain of that woman walking out of your door." His added *and she will walk out of your door* went unsaid, for good reason. "She will be the most exhilarating thing you have ever experienced, but…"

"Dad," Dre reached out and grazed his forearm with her hand, in an immaterial gesture that seemed as necessary as breathing. "You don't have to worry. Cara's not going to walk out on me."

173

"But how can you know that?"

"Because we're not together." She poured more wine. "We're not a couple. We're not dating. We live in two separate states, divided by a lifetime. I'm not moving, she's not moving. The whole thing is...not serious."

"The way you look at her tells a very different story," he said, simply.

"The way I look at her is." *Is what? The way a lion looks at a well-cooked steak on the savanna? The way a shark looks to the sea?*

"I know that look, Andrea—the way I look at Ami, the way I looked at your mother. Regardless of how you deny it, you love her. You have never loved anyone in your entire life, aside from maybe me, and yet you love this woman. And I don't know how she did it, how she's done the impossible, but she has gotten that part of you—the one you hide away from the world—to flourish."

Dre blushed. She had never considered herself hidden, especially from her father, and she had to give him credit for calling her out on it. There were parts of her life that she had never shared with him—predominantly among them the gay scenes and experiences. There were chunks she left out. But she had never considered that it would matter to him.

"We just met, Dad. We live in totally different places. We have totally different lives."

"So move."

"I can't move."

"You can do your job quite well from anywhere with an internet connection. You could do your job in the wilds of Africa. Do not act as if the thought is so foreign to you." His words were clipped and he somehow seemed far wiser in that moment than he had in all of the years prior, which was quite remarkable to a little girl who came of age thinking him to

174

be a superhero who simply happened to make bread to put a roof over her head and clothes on her back. "Look to your future, and tell me what you see."

"I see an empty wine bottle," Dre answered, because it was the easiest route.

When he produced another from beneath the counter, she was forced into submission.

"What do you see when you look at her?" he pressed. "When you wake up and see her face?"

His daughter, the spitting image of him with her mother's softer features, sighed. "I see…life. And happiness and fun and silliness. I see a house…and a farm and the sunlight stretching up from beneath the blinds in her bedroom. I see a wedding and kids, maybe. Shit, I don't know. I hate kids."

"You do not hate kids."

"I don't want kids. I just like the possibility that our future might include kids. And a dining room table we purchase together and chairs we both pick out and…I see us watching television and arguing about NPR and…"

* * *

In the hallways outside the kitchen, near the tiny vestibule beside the pantry door, Cara Spencer stood, frozen in motion, just as afraid to hear the words that poured from Dre's mouth as she was to move and risk *not* hearing those words. For the breadth of her life, she had been missing something, and had never known what that was, always watching on the periphery of happiness, always the bridesmaid and never the bride, as her mother so often told her. For the breadth of her life, she had been alone, surrounded by family, when all she ever dreamed of, all she ever yearned for, all she was unwilling to say but felt all the same, was to love and be loved by a woman like Andrea Marie Martin; a woman with bravery and tenacity and fierceness who was openly gay and funny and likable and endearing, all the same.

And yet, here she was, petrified and hiding after hearing the words she longed for, only to hold in her reply because of what? Because she was scared and she felt silly and she felt defeated and cowardly, like the world had blossomed as an open oyster in her childhood but closed with severity upon realizing she would never fit the status quo of Greentown, South Carolina.

"I can't tell you what to do, kid," Michael's baritone came through, and she shrank back even further into the hall, terrified they would be alerted to her presence. "But if you love her—if you even *think* you love her—you have to consider that it may not end the way you want it to." There was an apparent pain in his words, as if he this heart-to-heart glossed over the healing scar left in the wake of his wife's death, who very much favored his lesbian daughter. "The last thing I want is to see you hurt the way I did, in the space your mother left behind."

"She won't hurt me, Dad," Cara Spencer heard Dre say with a conviction that made her queasy. "She can deny it all she wants, but she feels the same way about me that I feel about her. I know she does."

"Love is not the question, Andrea Marie. It's more a question of bravery."

"Bravery?" Of course she wouldn't understand. How could someone residing in the Lesbian Capital of the World, where all of the road signs were rainbows and all of the couples on all of the streets were fierce and determined women, ever understand the inherent bravery involved in being openly gay in the South? Being theoretically gay was all well and good, all tied up in code words and secrets and furtive glances, but being *actually* gay? Cara Spencer had never even had a girlfriend, never referred to herself as a lesbian, never identified as gay, never been to a gay party or seen a gay bar or had a real gay friend. She had never tasted the beauty of another woman—at least, not until roughly three hours before the moment she stumbled upon her future being mapped out by Dre and her father in the kitchen, over a bottle of red vintage. She had never seen gay porn, or contemplated going to a gay pride festival. *Were there even gay pride festivals in South Carolina? Fuck. Shouldn't she know that?* But she didn't, so hell bent on hiding who she was from everything and everyone. Why would she ever have taken the initiative to seek out a pride event?

"It's not as easy for everyone, to come out and be different."

"I'm not different," Dre was adamant. "I'm gay. And so is she."

Her father coughed and, feeling like she was facing the edge of a cliff, being pressed upon by a train, Cara Spencer could sense their conversation coming to a close.

"I hope it's as simple as that," Michael sighed, heavy with fear and a tinge of hope.

In the shadows, his phony faux daughter-in-law knew that it was not, nor was it ever likely to be.

* * *

She could barely contain her panic, as she rushed back to the bedroom, her mind racing with all of the things she knew she should say to Dre but alternately realized she would never be able to adequately verbalize. She was running. She was scared. She wanted to go home, and be alone, and lie low in the familiar surroundings of her homestead with her dogs and her cow and her chickens and her goats and her stupid brothers, who were understanding in all of their well-meaning ignorance.

She wanted this to be over—the whole thing. She wanted to go back into time and steer clear of that bathroom because her life had been moving in the right direction—the right, lonely, hidden direction - without all of these complications.

Was that really what Dre was? A complication?

Tears threatened to break through, spill forth, but she—

What was she doing?

Cara Spencer sunk to the ground, in a loose ball of sweaty arms and legs and horror and covered her face with shaking hands.

What was she doing?

She loved Dre.

She fucking loved Dre.

And that was why she had to leave, wasn't it? She could never be what Dre wanted her to be? She could never be gay.

She needed to get the fuck out of Florida.

* * *

My mom wasn't perfect, Andrea mused, in the backwash of her paternal convo. *My mother wasn't perfect and my father is worried that Cara Spencer is imperfect in that same, impetuous, imperfect manner.*

Cara Spencer was, supposedly, very much like her mother. Offbeat, headstrong, wild, unpredictable; it was an intoxicating combination. But, according to her old man, it was also a potentially volatile combination, which, inevitably, cost him most of his heart and that was all before her death. What did that say about her newfound love interest?

She felt like something needed to be said to clear the air, especially in the throes of their "I love you" debacle. She needed to reassure Cara Spencer that she wasn't actually *asking* her to do anything, or be anyone she was uncomfortable being. What was happening between them was new—brand new—and she had no business imposing restrictions or expectations.

That sounded exactly like the right thing to say to the girl whose brothers nicknamed her 'Hurricane Cara.'

And she would have used those words, verbatim, to console Cara Spencer, had she not walked up to the guest house just as her lover was waddling out, laden with suitcases and a wildly struggling Australian Cattle Dog, obscured from view by the murky evening ink of night. At that sight, her heart sputtered. Even Buddy froze in confused and nervous apprehension.

Catching his scent, Grey Baby growled and then barked and nipped at Cara Spencer's vice grip on her stubby body. Looking up, the two women locked gazes and a lifetime of pain and hiding and fear and loathing and love passed between them before either gave birth to the words that needed to be said.

"I don't want to have kids with you."

The words had landed heavy on Cara Spencer's heart, whilst hiding in the hallway. The picture seared her, branded her, in a way she had not anticipated back when she had been carelessly tossing things into her suitcase, calling her brother, Atticus, calling for a taxi, googling a map.

Dre was fun.

Dre was attentive.

Dre was caring.

Dre did things to her, showed things to her, opened her. But a future? A real future, with kids and dogs and joint checking? Family vacations and Christmases with Granny and Easter at the Greentown United Methodist Church?

"I don't know if I want kids at all. Or if I'm interested in marriage, or if I want to buy a table, or if I like NPR."

"Cara, slow down—"

Fuck, Dre was calm. Still. Unmoved. Like if she stayed stone still long enough the wind and rain and earth-shattering fury that was Cara Spencer would dissipate, like the hurricane would peter out around her and she would be left in the quiet to rebuild.

Fuck.

"You're already planning a future and you want me to slow down?" Grey Baby leapt down onto the ground and made for Buddy's direction.

Dre thought about moving toward her, but then thought better of it and lingered, a safe distance away. "I didn't plan our future, Cara. I had a conversation with my father."

"You had a conversation with your father about *us*. About *me*. About what you see with *me* in the future."

Dre nodded. "Because I love you. Because I want a future with you. And I don't know what that future is, and it's early to be thinking about it, but I want it and I know that and I'm not ashamed of it."

"You want a marriage. Like a Cleaver marriage, between the two of us."

"Eventually, yes."

Eventually? A marriage? Like they were normal people who could walk around do normal things? Go to the grocery store and make mortgage payments? Be like everyone else?

Could they ever be like everyone else? Maybe here. Maybe far away from all of the people who would know her, away from her family and her family's reputation and her brothers. But at home? In Greentown? That would never happen. Gay people weren't a *thing* in Greentown. And where was a future if not at home? Where was a future if not in the place where she had been raised? Where the memories of her parents were?

The world spun around Cara Spencer and she felt as if she were losing her balance.

"You just—You just can't say that! You can't drop that on me! You can't expect that from me!" she screamed, and she was very much screaming in panic now, regardless of the neighbors or Michael and Ami and the boys. "You can't expect me to be that person!"

"What person?" Dre crossed her arms over her chest, over the design on her tee that said something about horses and cowboys. "What person can I *not* expect you to be? One who loves me?"

"Don't do this."

"Don't do what? What am I doing? I don't expect anything from you—"

"You expect me to label this, define this, analyze it."

Analyze it? Define it? It was a relationship. *Right?* Two people, making love, driving to fucking Florida. Two people, lying in the sun, holding hands, sneaking kisses. Two people who had gone the extra mile to introduce one another to extraneous family.

* * *

"Don't make me define it." Cara Spencer was wild with a hundred different things: fear, anger, uncertainly, disappointment, heartache. She was a child, in that moment, in that side yard, laden down with bags, white with playground terror.

What if *they* all knew? *They*—the boogeymen of the closeted gays. What would *they* say when they found out? And how could *they* not find out? With her strolling around town next to a woman like Dre, who was identifiably lesbian, with her short hair and flannel and skinny jeans and loafers. She was everything that Cara Spencer had worked so hard, so conscientiously, so diligently, *not* to be so the looming and ever-present *THEY* would never catch on.

Being attracted to women and combatting her attraction to women while subsequently giving in to it had been the paradigms of her existence for so long, it had grown difficult to distinguish the memories in which she hadn't felt isolated or alone. There were dresses when she really probably wanted riding boots, and dolls for motherly skill-building when she had really been a little repulsed. Granny taught her to cook, the organist from Greentown Meth taught her piano, the age-old ladies in charge of cotillion taught her dance. She had been eleven when Will Turner had kissed her under the Greentown Elementary monkey bars and at 11.0001 she had begun to realize how different she was (after slugging him in vengeful reciprocity). Twelve brought a period and breasts and a dance she hadn't wanted to attend but felt very foolish avoiding. On her thirteenth birthday, Daniel Moore had put his hand in her pants and she had run away, run to hide from her sexuality and its malfunction in the way of male attention. Next came braces, then misinformed dating. Pretense, condoms, college, family dinners she struggled not to cry through. Everything nursing, creating, forming a barrage of anxiety that threatened to force her to spend the rest of her life all alone because alone was safe and secure and predictable and didn't require a fucking label that would just make everyone who knew her uncomfortable, like the only thing she was good for, or known for, or could possibly contribute to the world at large was that where every other woman she had ever known was attracted to men, she wanted to be with women. She wanted to smell the hollow of a woman's neck and trace her lips down the edge of a woman's jaw. She wanted the heavy weight of another woman's breasts against her chest. She wanted the slick rub of another woman's most intimate of spaces against her own. She wanted to brush Dre's hair from her face before she pulled her in close for a kiss. She wanted to lift the sweet skin of her rump.

But she was not *gay*.

She couldn't be gay.

God would smite her if she were gay, she thought ruefully, remembering all of the sermons and the quotes and the signs on television and the tears from men and women who only wanted separate recognition.

Greentown would cast her out if she were gay.

Lincoln would disown her if she were gay.

Win would never look at her again if she were gay.

Atticus would never speak to her again if she were gay.

Atticus who was quickly on his way to retrieve her from this godforsaken holiday.

She tried to remind herself of those things, as she left.

She tried to let them guide her, as she called Grey Baby to her side and walked off, without another thought, shoving everything she owned in the state of Florida into the back of a taxi minivan that would drive her forty-five minutes to a rest stop where she would wait on Atticus.

The Right Kind of Woman

She tried not to hear the soul-shattering sobs that came from Dre then, the sobs of a truly good woman who had not only given her love and unconditional support—a woman she did not fucking deserve, at all—as she left, under cover of darkness, because she was a coward.

You Can't Go Home Again

Atticus had known that things with Cara Spencer would only get worse the moment he pulled up in to the shady, middle-of-the-night parking lot of the Pilot Travel Stop just outside Saint Augustine, Florida, off of Interstate 95, to find his sister sitting patiently in the murky street light, on top of her suitcase, drinking a Slushee and holding on to her stupid dog for dear life, her face a mixture of pain, terror, and tear-streaks. He had known things would only get worse during that silent five hour drive home, during which she stared, blankly, out of the drizzling rain through the muddy window he never cleaned, Grey Baby settled, possessively, in her lap, though stupefied by a sadness of her own. He had known things would only get worse, yet he stayed silent, even as he opened the back door of the farmhouse the next evening, to let Greg Allman in, and found his sister curled in a ball on her rattan couch, covered in the familial afghans, staring at the framed photographs of their parents and grandparents still hanging against the dusty wood paneling of the living room. No television blaring, no radio humming, no movement. Only the stiff quiet of her weeping secret heart, the one she felt she couldn't share with them, not even with *him*, and he had always known that he was her favorite.

It had been him to whom she turned, after all, when she needed a ride home from Florida.

"Atti, I need you," she had said to him, through the receiver of the cell phone. "I need you to come and get me."

And he should have done it then, ripped the Band-Aid off of her sea of despair. He should have shaken her, when she had crawled into the cab

185

of the truck, shouted at her, forced her from the inner closet with a resounding yelp of "Cara, we know that you're gay! We've always known! Stop being so afraid!"

But he hadn't done that.

He hadn't done that at all.

He had taken the chicken's way out, driving silently, stopping infrequently for her to pee and refuel her body, asking her if she needed anything, and waiting for the inevitable muffled negative, before simply redacting his presence like he had never been there at all.

He had known that she was very nearly lying upon the craggy rock bottom of her proverbial crevasse, and he had done nothing. He had stayed away, kept his distance, not wanting to pry but conversely hating his predicament, left out in the dark.

And three weeks later—three entire weeks of nights and days and nights and days—there was no change.

In the mornings, too early for God to show his ass, she fed the chickens and the goats and the cow. She planted a tiny garden and tended her fledgling produce. In the afternoons, she worked her shifts at the apple stand. She filled in at the restaurant when she was told to, which had slowly become a full-time job, of sorts, for all of them. But her eyes remained hollow and her smile never seemed to gurgle forth from her soul, never reached up to her eyes. She barely ate. She had given up on drinking altogether, as far as her brothers could tell. On Sundays, they could see her as they drifted aimlessly down the Holloway, with her books and her coffee and her stupid dog that still would not let them within twenty feet of the property line without growling and snarling and foaming at the bit.

Grey Baby had, in a sense, become the embodiment of how badly they had fucked up with the Dre thing; whatever had transpired in Florida before her precipitous return via brother express had not been the sunny, beautiful, beach-themed coming out that he and Lincoln and Win had schemed toward. Whatever had transpired in Florida had been brutal and traumatic, leaving their already surreptitious kin in a catatonic trance that showed no signs of relenting.

Stuck on what they had deemed "Sister Watch Duty," a relegated sort of babysitting from a safe distance that no one minded and everyone thought completely necessary, Link inched closer, with a sack of apples slung over his shoulder. He was horribly hungover and sweating bullets, but he was determined to make it through the day in order to keep Cara Spencer from jumping off of a bridge or running into traffic, or gorging herself on pound cake and ice cream while weeping into her vanilla and listening to old George Jones singles. "I tried Dre again," he said, with an emphasis on *again*, "I know she's getting the messages, I just…she won't answer." She hadn't answered in three damn weeks, not one single text message.

What happened?

Are you okay?

Tell me why my sister won't talk to us. That revised version had sounded way better than their original draft of *Tell me why my sister is a sad, unresponsive mass of ice cream-coated zombie who sits in her fucking house all day and won't kayak with us.*

I know you're getting these, I can see that the message was READ.

Don't be a bitch.

How's the weather?

It was like they were both in mourning, and the somber quietude was deafening, but for what the Holloway men folk were at a loss as to produce. While it was obvious that things had not panned out in the

187

romantic sense, and that was a chance they had all taken when they made the decision to push Dre and Cara harmlessly together, this seemed so much more severe than the period of grief that followed a two-week breakup. Girls came and went in life. According to Granny, one should bemoan and fret for one day per week of togetherness. Bearing that logic in mind, Cara Spencer should have been back to normal eons ago. Still, she wasn't, and what they were witnessing was becoming more and more like a death; the slow and painful death of the one woman they had been enamored of since the moment those curls sprang forth into the big, wide world and those wide, searching brown eyes had first opened and filled with fiery conviction. Even strangers had begun to take notice of the change, with their grandmother foremost among them. Why, only the day before, she had thrown an apron at Win, along with an apple, and demanded that he "fix" whatever was wrong with Cara S.

Only, they didn't quite know how.

"Maybe you should try calling," Atti suggested, deciding it was as good a time as any to smoke a cigarette if his brother were going to stand beside him, reeking of stale liquor.

Calling was an inordinately stupid suggestion, but he was fresh out of reasonable suggestions and he was tired of watching her suffer and doubly tired of Lincoln and James Winter pestering him about what she may or may not have said during that horrendously painful and dead silent ride home from the sunshine state.

"I have," Link offered him a light for the Marlboro. "She doesn't answer. I've called, like, a dozen times."

"Maybe you should call from my phone."

"You think she'll answer that? Like she won't put it together? She's not an idiot."

"It's worth a shot. I ain't got a local number—I've had the same one since I lived in Georgia—and nothing else has worked. And…she ain't getting any better," with the *she* in question being an understood CARA FUCKING SPENCER MADELINE HOLLOWAY.

"Win says she doesn't sleep hardly anymore. Every night when the bar closes, he drives by and her lights are still on. One night he caught her sitting on the porch, just staring off into space."

Atticus sucked on the nicotine in his hand, nerves frayed. "Shit…" He was enveloped in a tremendous shroud of guilt that he could not shake. It was his fault, this giant mess that had become of his sister. Her pain was his doing. While it was true that Lincoln and James Winter were far more ingratiated in the drubbing than he was, this was the woman who forked over money to support his art and cooked for him and listened to all of his ideas, even when she must have known that they were just crap. She bought his groceries and bandaged his ego when he came home from art school, tail between his legs. He should have known better. He should have known better than to do any of this to her. He should have known then, back when they came up with such an outlandish plan, that coming out, for those in the LGBT community, was a marked and powerful step that no one could be forced into. It was something she would have to do for herself, because it was important to her.

"Gimme your phone," he huffed.

"You can't call from my phone, she'll see the number. That's the phone I've been…"

"I need the number out of your phone, you jackass." No doubt Link's mind was just as preoccupied with the tragedy before them, not to mention drowning in a sea of half toasted Jack Daniels. They all loved her they just didn't show it in the best of ways.

The Right Kind of Woman

As Link disappeared to retrieve the 4S out of his truck, Cara Spencer moved off to wait on a customer. Her hair was down, and loose. She was wearing her Granny's Apples tee, her shirt was clean, her jeans were the same jeans she had always worn. She laughed, but not really, and suggested Red Delicious over Braeburn, which had never been her favorite apple strain. From her rusted folding chair, Granny concurred and waved a dismissive hand.

For her recent birthday—the big 8-4—someone, one of her paramours from the retirement home, no less, had given her an old laptop and a Netflix subscription. Now she watched old episodes of *Friends* and just about every episode of *Murder, She Wrote* ever produced, while her third generation progeny kept things running smoothly at all of the local branches of her apple empire. Technology was endlessly fascinating to her now, and it maintained her interest for hours on end, the little laptop stretched on her knees, bobbing with sound and action while she listened through a fancy pair of Beats by Dre.

"Alright," Link rattled off, "It's one, six-nine-eight…"

* * *

Doctor Gina P. Laudsdale, Dre thought, as she skimmed the ample litany of information displayed on a Facebook page laden with LGBTQ Equality postings and photos of one Siamese cat. An enumeration of degrees and awards danced across the screen of the sleek, silver MacBook.

Bachelor's in British Literature
Bachelor's in Women's Studies
Master's in Gender Studies
Doctorate in Women's Gender and Sexuality

The Right Kind of Woman

Every accreditation so high-brow, ever degree from an old-money, East Coast school, all very polished and professional. One stemmed from a work-study institution in North Carolina that required all students to work forty hours per week on-grounds, doing everything from chopping firewood to milking cows, in addition to the hefty sixty-thousand-dollar-per-semester-tuition requirement. One bloomed from what was commonly known as "lesbian Harvard." And they were heavy degrees, very existential and forward thinking. They were the degrees of someone who wanted to change the world. They were the degrees of someone settled, someone comfortable with herself and her sexuality—someone openly gay and proud of it.

Someone who was the exact opposite of Cara Spencer.

Shit. She had promised herself she wouldn't waste any more time thinking of that today.

Cara Spencer had been fun. Sexually fulfilling. She had been a fling, down South, and she had provided Dre with valuable insight regarding what she wanted for her future, which was (or could possibly be) a woman like Dr. Gina P. Laudsdale.

Dr. Gina P. Laudsdale was political, informed, and dressed in a tweed blazer in her profile picture. She used only gender-neutral pronouns like "they" and "professor" and she distanced herself from the Marriage Equality movement, stating that marriage equality mattered very little when trans men and women were fired without cause, leaving basic human rights out of the trendy equation. On that momentous day in June, when the Supreme Court handed down a verdict that declared all marriages equal under the Constitution of the United States, Dr. Gina had, rather than post about her happiness and the weight of the accomplishment, posted a very entertaining video of her cat, Cersei Lannister, following a laser pointer on the carpet.

That was the shit Dre needed in her life. She needed a call to action and a cause. She had seen too much of what homophobia could do to a person in Cara. No more quiet homo in the corner. She needed a sign and a rainbow button and a bumper sticker.

Tris and Sam were taken aback by this change, understandably. They had let the blind date thing fall to the wayside since she had returned from her trip, not that she needed the inadvertent space in her life. She was ready, finally, to seek out a mate. Not a date, a mate. This time, she would find a dedicated partner—a woman who was mentally and physically stimulating, and who would be in it for the long haul.

This time—

To her right, balancing on a roll of masking tape that she had been using to patch one of the newer holes Buddy had taken to gnawing in his dog bed, her cell phone chimed.

It hadn't mooed in a while. That was a good sign. Link texted so much in those first two weeks, she'd gone to the trouble of assigning him a tone in order to better avoid his contact. She had absolutely nothing to say to him, or to any of them. There were no words, honestly. At the very least, there were no words any of them would want to hear.

What happened? **Your sister isn't a lesbian. She screamed that at me before leaving my father's house in the middle of the night. She can't handle the idea of being a lesbian, and I can't handle the idea of being with a woman who isn't comfortable in her own skin. I want a marriage. I am not interested in the shame Cara Spencer carries around.**

Are you okay? **Not really. But I will be, because I know who I am and I know what I want, and I have Cara Spencer to thank for that. Had** *she not yelled "I don't want to have children with you" at the top of her lungs, who knows where I would be right now.*

Tell me why my sister won't talk to us. **Probably because she confronted what she could have had in her future and proved too chicken shit to do anything about it. She'd rather spend the rest of her life hiding in her fucking closet in the back woods than holding hands with a woman who would have loved her, without question. And my love should have been enough, but it wasn't.**

I know you're getting these, I can see that the message was READ. **Goody for you, you have an iPhone, too.**

Don't be a bitch. **Try telling your little bitch sister that.**

How's the weather? **Sunny with an overwhelming chance of GAY.**

Arbitrarily laughing at her own internal monologue, she slid the screen to Answer and fumbled for the contact information she had been working on moments before her interest in Dr. Gina Laudsdale had been tweaked by a byline. She had been expecting her newest client to get in touch with her for days, had been fiddling with the logo design for a doggy day spa down near Disney World—

"Dre Martin," she spat, mechanically.

Clients were the only real people who called her in the middle of the day. Well, clients and her father, who was now obsessed with her wellbeing, given that his prediction regarding her spring romance proved to be more than a little accurate in the pain department, which was more than a little embarrassing, especially after defending what she felt so vehemently the night before. Driving home, *alone,* she had been nearly blinded by her own tears.

"Andrea-Dre," a distinctly Southern voice elicited smoothly, the three syllables of her hyphenated nickname slowly becoming ten.

"No," she pulled the phone away from her ear.

"Dre, don't hang up. It's not Lincoln."

"No, but it's one of you." Her finger lingered over the END button floating on screen and looking at the number, she cursed. She should have known better than to blindly answer a call. Those Holloway brothers would not have given up as easily as she first assumed.

"It's Atticus. I'm awesome. Don't hang up on me. I know you read *To Kill a Mockingbird*."

In silence, she stewed, because it really was a good book.

"You don't have to say anything. I mean, I'd like to know what's going on, but, that ain't my place to inquire about. Something's wrong with Cara Spencer. Something big."

"Atticus, I really don't think it's my place to say any of this."

"You don't get it, Dre, she's— It's like somebody died. It's like *she* died. Somehow, she's come back from Florida and she's walking dead, she's not eatin' and she don't sleep."

"She won't go paddlin' with us anymore!" someone shouted from the background.

"She won't go paddlin' with us anymore," he repeated, "She won't even talk to us and we're— We're scared. And if we fucked up tryin'a get you guys together, if it didn't work out, if you're not interested, *that* I'd understand. I've been her brother long enough to know she's a crazy one...but this? This is bigger. This is like her soul is gone and she can't do nothing but go through the motions and even then it ain't workin'..."

Well, good! Fucking great, really. It was great that Cara hurt the same way she did. It was great that Cara went back to her armpit town and her chickens and her goats and her cushy damn closet. It was great that things weren't the same in her soul. It was great that Atticus and Win and Lincoln

194

all thought she was the "walking dead." Maybe then, maybe with her heart ripped out and her emotions splayed out on the table, she would understand something—some grain or centimeter—of what she had done, making Dre fall in love with her when she had known all along she had absolutely no intention of staying or of being GAY in public.

"Your sister's not gay, Atticus," she blurted, the words spilling out as conversational vomit. "Cara Spencer's not a lesbian and I doubt she ever will be."

"Jesus Christ, Dre, my sister's been a fucking lesbian her whole damn life."

"But she doesn't know that! And she doesn't know that *you* know that. She's conditioned herself to avoid being gay. She's petrified of what people will say, what you will say, what Win and Link and her grandmother will say, what all of the people who go to your parents' old church will say."

"We haven't even gone to that church in a coon's age—"

"But she still fears it. She fears being different or being made fun of or being vilified. She fears not fitting in, and…Atticus, I love her." She let those words out as well, having kept them tied down and ignored for the better part of a month. "I love her, I really, really do, but she can't live that way, and neither can I. I cannot live in the shadows. And you shouldn't want me to."

That was the honest reason she had never bothered to respond to Link's one hundred and sixty character pleas. She needed them to understand her need to be respected. She needed them to love her enough not to expect her to go back into a closet she had struggled herself to break free of, burdened by her own self-doubt and feelings of worthlessness and uncertainty, though in a tremendously less substantial way than they

195

burdened Cara Spencer. They were the trademarks of the LGBTQ youth of America—the dread that comes with being a round peg in a sea of square holes.

"I *can't* live that way," she concluded. "I'm not perfect, I'm not even close, but I know who I am and I know what I want and it's not that life." For a split second, she would have given it all up, perhaps, abandoned everything in order to follow behind Cara Spencer. But with the clarity of nineteen hours behind the wheel came the recognition that she owed herself more than a half-lived life in South Carolina, where she would walk on the eggshells of judgment every moment of every new day, and introduce herself to strangers as Cara Spencer's "roommate."

Seconds ticked by as she sat, waiting for him to say something, the room filled with Buddy's soft snores as they crept into the void left by the pain of the conversation. The poor lab was, no doubt, dreaming of his taste of life on that farm, or the chickens and the goats and Greg Allman and Grey Baby and rising before dawn to watch the sun trickle in over the river. If only she could explain it to him. He'd probably stop eating his own bed.

"Listen…" she started, hoping to ditch the brunt of the convo.

"You're right," Atticus agreed, after what felt like a year. "You're really and truly more right than I can ever say."

The Cat's Out of the Bag

Once it was over, once the cat of her hidden secret was roaring free of its padded closet-bag, whole days would rise up when Atticus would catch himself wondering if he had, in fact, done the right thing—if he had handled things with Cara Spencer the way he should have.

He would wonder if yelling it at the top of his lungs was appropriate, or warranted, or sensitive to her feelings.

He would wonder if pushing her into the rainbow-toned limelight was necessary or appreciated.

But he would never, not for one red second, regret what he had done, not if it had cost them customers, not if it had cost them reputations or standing, if they had any left to spare. What was social standing, anyway, in a place like Greentown, South Carolina? If no one wanted to patronize the Holloway family in all of their illustrious business endeavors, then the whole damn town would find themselves sans apples, cold beer and a mighty comfortable swimming hole come July. He and his brothers who have thrown up a dam or a gate, blocking anyone on a boat, kayak, float, or legs from accessing the more beautiful sections of a river that carried with it his family legacy.

Bidding farewell to Andrea-Dre, he slid the cell phone into his pocket and turned, without meeting Link's expectant stare. In retrospect, he would come to know that this was out of fear that someone more rational than he was would talk him out of his hastily constructed plan of immediate action, a plan that went entirely against the guilt he felt not half an hour prior, as he agonized over the state of his sister lesbian sister's sad, sheltered life.

He swept past Granny, who was rocking and rolling to an episode about Ross and Rachel and the infamous "break," and he snatched three apples out of Cara Spencer's arms, forcing her to turn around and look at him in feigned irritation. Her eyes rounded in question, bearing dark circles beneath them. It was the presence of the dark circles that spurred him onward. "What the hell?"

"What the fuck did you do?" he demanded, his voice brokering no argument, as the only member of their ragtag family who never raised his voice, lest they were yelps of pleasure. "In Florida, Cara Spencer, what the fuck did you do?"

She flushed and backed up, and tried to turn away. Atticus stopped her, with one reedy arm. "I swam, I sat in the fucking sun," he forced her to say by keeping her there.

"And you broke that girl's heart."

Around them, the owners of the flanking stands began busying themselves within earshot with phony disinterest. In the blink of an eye, booth tidiness became a pressing priority for every hawker of peaches, collards, pumpkin seeds, ferns and jellies galore. "You went with her to Florida to see her fucking family and you broke her heart."

"No, I didn't."

"Yes, you did." Atticus had never yelled at anyone a day in his life and it felt horrendous. He was calm, patient, placid. He was not accusatory. Accusatory was Win. He was not demanding. Demanding was Lincoln. Yet, here he was. "You really and truly did."

Cara Spencer pushed her hair back from her shoulders and, had she not been a zombie, she would have come forward swinging, which he knew and had concocted his moves dependent upon. "I don't know what you're talking about."

He shook her then, wondering if he were crossing the great divide into domestic abuse, but also realizing that he was the least aggressive man on the planet, which gave reliability to his motions. "Yes, you do know what I'm talking about and I'm tired of the lying."

"What lying?"

"You still want to play dumb?" he yelled, and, all at once, the farmer's market was so deadly silent that he could have heard a pin drop from the Sunday hat of a choir robe, not that Atticus Caleb Holloway noticed. Or would have given a shit. "I'm tired of your lies about the women!"

"Holy shit," Link murmured.

"Part of that is my fault." Atti put his hand to his chest, laying it over his heart, which was curiously marked with an apple. "It's all of our fault. We should have made you feel like it was okay to tell us, like we'd love you no matter what. But part of that is your fault; your lack of trust and faith in your own family—like we'd judge you for not living your life in a certain way. Have you seen us? We're a fucking mess!"

He was only vaguely aware of Link's proximity to him, and of Link's mouth hanging open, cigarette tumbling down to the pavement. He was only vaguely aware of words spoken to him, of his brother's rough voice in his ear, of urgent whispered cautions.

"Don't do this here."

"You're gay," he delivered, in the stillness before the atomic bomb. "Cara Spencer Madeline Holloway, you're a lesbian. And we want you to be the gayest lesbian you can be, but you've got to stop lying to yourself 'cause it ain't doin' anybody any good."

* * *

199

With his bomb smoldering in the air (or was it Lincoln's Marlboro Light?), Atticus was thoroughly and completely unabashed. He had once and with finality ripped the shroud from his sister's life, and he was self-righteous enough to brandish it like a weapon.

"I'm not gay," Cara Spencer began, intending it as a declaration of the heterosexuality no one bought into, regardless of how farcical her attempted would have seemed. It was probably force of habit for her, by now, given the constant scrutiny of a small, pigeon-toed town like Greentown.

Fortunately, Granny, in her age-old wisdom, cut her off with the wave of a bony, swollen hand. "You very much are, dear. And you always have been…and, I expect, you always will be, and the sooner you say it and own it and live it, the happier we'll all be."

Three Holloway heads turned to face her where she grinned, laptop folded up, feet just a rocking, Beats hanging loosely on her neck, like a DJ.

"What?" She shrugged, palms up in the air. "Did you think *I* didn't know?"

Atticus nodded because he had had no idea, himself, and the whole scene was beginning to feel quite surreal. Lincoln nodded, because the most risqué thing they'd ever heard Granny say was a good goddammit every now and again.

"No," Cara bit out.

"Oh, psh," Granny turned her gaze solely to the girl in her midst. "Little girl, I'm eighty-damn-three-years-old. I've seen more and done more in my lifetime than you could ever possibly imagine and I am no scholar. I am no prophet, but God don't make mistakes, honey. You're

200

gay. Be gay. Go get that woman and damn anyone who stands in your way."

"What woman?" Cara mouthed, incredulous, though it was impossible to deduce what was more unbelievable—Granny's progressive attitude regarding sexual orientation, or Granny's knowledge of Dre.

"Dre," Granny cursed. "Who else would I be talkin' about? The one woman who's been brave enough to put up with the likes of you and the likes of them." She thrust a finger out at Link and Atti. "And you two ought to be ashamed of yourselves, plotting to set her up with a stranger who wandered into town off the interstate and then shoutin' YOU'RE GAY at her in the middle of a damn farmer's market. There were better ways to have handled this, Atticus Caleb. And don't think you're off the hook, Lincoln Andrew."

Only then did it occur to Atti, for the first time of many, that his way had, almost assuredly, *not* been the most gentle, which he would later attribute to a knee-jerk reaction after hearing the raw pain in Andrea's voice over the telephone as she regaled him with her love of his incredibly stubborn, incredibly pig-headed sister.

Ever-so-slowly, an angry and slightly amused (but more angry) Cara Spencer turned to him, narrowing her eyes on him, black depths snapping fire, her gaze more scope than friendly. "You did *what* with a stranger who wandered into town off the interstate?!"

This was not good. At all.

Lincoln put his hands up and began to move quickly backward, toward the safety of the cab of his pickup truck. "It was a sweet gesture, really," he lied through clenched and anxious teeth. "We thought y'all'd make a cute couple is all. She seemed so nice and—"

"It was all Win's idea," Atticus added, sacrificing their absentee brother. "We didn't even want to help." The ludicrous vestiges of his fib were as obvious as the time of day, but he didn't care anymore. His sister was out. OUT! And he was reticent and scared, but elated.

She, however, was very clearly *none* of those things, and he had to stop and wonder, as she stalked off to her own truck and peeled out of the parking lot, whether she had the means, motive and know-how to build a bomb that could kill them all.

Time to Make a Change

Tristan had quickly, as the soon-to-be-parent of two, begun to miss her one-on-one time with friends. Specifically, she had begun to miss her one-on-one time with Dre, who had been keeping more to herself, of late, and become far more involved in the community outreach efforts Sam put together at the coffee shop where she worked. So, it was no surprise, that she was thrilled to receive a telephone call that requested her presence at a dive bar far from the central lesbian hub of South Waterton.

John's Bar, it was gracelessly named, with a plain, neon sign that hung out over the door, on the street. No drink specials, no rainbow stickers, no advertised political affiliations. Just a plain, brown, wooden bar, stools, and pool in a dusky, smoke-filled interior that must have been one of the last remaining hangs in South Waterton that hadn't gone strictly cigarette-free.

Breathing deeply as she strode inside, there was something that reminded Tris of college and the world outside her gay-friendly world there. Which was probably why Dre had selected the locale.

"Evening," someone greeted from the behind the bar, a hip, skinny young man with a Mumford beard and a gauged earring. His neck was covered in colorful artwork and when he smiled, three teeth were golden caps.

She nodded and scoured the scenery for her friend.

This is what real people do, she thought, moving forward, grateful that she had changed out of her embroidered school polo. Real people went out to bars with their friends and took in the world that existed outside—a world unencumbered by children's television shows and cloth diapers and

203

organic baby food thrown together in a pricey, stainless steel blender free of toxins that she had never, in her life, heard of. Real people—

"Sit down woman," Dre greeted, smiling. "You're lost in thought."

She was sitting, one leg propped on the other, on the swivel stool at the corner, drinking something in a green can that was unfamiliar to her, which wasn't saying much coming from a woman who was only rarely sans child and/or alcohol-free wife.

"Love where you've brought me," she laughed. "Is this where you bring all of your women?"

Andrea rolled her eyes and drank her beer. "Only the ones with wives at home."

There were very few patrons about, mostly older men in small clumps near the pool table in the corner, chain-smoking and drinking PBR in patriotic cans. No one looked up to acknowledge them, aside from the fidgeting bartender.

"Can I get you something?"

"Rum and Coke," Tris countered, feeling very twenty-one again.

"Slow your roll, captain," Dre teased, "I don't want to have to carry you home. It's barely five."

"Yeah, well," Tris said, sitting down. "It's been a long year."

"I can imagine. Pregnant wife, kid, job—"

"Bestie who's been actively avoiding me," she finished, accepting her drink from QuickDraw the Beverage Engineer.

"I haven't been *avoiding* you."

"I've barely seen you since you slunk back into town, and that was weeks ago." *Under cover of darkness*, she left hanging. It had taken three days for them to even realize that Dre was home. Her drapes stayed closed, her curtains stayed drawn, lights stayed off, and Buddy—God only knew what Buddy had been doing. Probably fending for himself, sustaining his strength using the dregs of her tears, both shed and unshed. Peeing in the sink.

And it was an awful feeling, to have known, all along, on some intrinsic level, that this bizarre romance with the elusive southern belle would only lead to torment. Not that she had ever voiced her opinion, or *would* ever voice her opinion. That secret she could keep for an eternity. There was no satisfaction to be had in her rightness, but she had been right all the same.

Southerners were whirlwinds, and Dre was not the whirlwind type.

"I had a lot to deal with," Dre mumbled, casually.

"You got dumped," Tris surmised. "Don't hide behind shame or embarrassment. Call it what it is. That bitch dumped you."

"She didn't *dump* me, we were never really together."

"You took her to meet your dad," Tris took a sip of her Rum and Coke and festered in her certainty. "That means you're a couple."

Dre's dad was her most protected asset. She only knew him because they had attended the same college and were roommates for a majority of that time. Parent Weekends being of such paramount significance to them (*Come look at how well I'm playing at being a grown-up, mom! See how I can boil water on my hot plate, Dad?*), it was only natural they would be introduced. Samantha, on the other hand, had only had the pleasure of Michael's acquaintance once, which solidified that if this southern dyke belle was allowed to meet him, they were something of a unit, regardless of whether or not Dre wanted to admit it out loud.

Tris drank from her glass again.

Jesus, rum is strong. When did rum get strong? Probably sometime after Sam got pregnant the first time.

"Yes, well, in hindsight, that wasn't a good idea."

"You know it's not your fault, right?" She felt compelled to mention. "The dumping part. You're amazing."

"I'm not amazing."

"You've got a great job, you're educated, you have all of your teeth, which I'm, like, ninety-percent sure cancels out most of her town…"

"Way to stereotype."

Someone turned on a radio and strains of classic rock filled the air.

"I'm just…seriously, Andrea." Tris only used the 'Andrea Tone' when she was conceivably preoccupied with an adult-sized sense of worry. "Tell me you're okay and I'll leave it all alone."

That part was only half true. Sam would peck her to death, a deranged harpy of gossip, if she did not at least bring home *some* details. In a sense, she needed Andrea to *not* be okay long enough to provide her with some intel to pass along to a wife who was already uncomfortably pregnant.

"I'm fine. I'm sad. I'm a bad gay, but I'm really fine. I'm not going to off myself or cry alone in a dark room." Dre waved to Hairy Hipster and ordered another beer.

"A bad gay? What does that even mean?" *A straight gay? A Republican gay?*

"Cara— *SHE*," Dre overcorrected sternly, seemingly afraid to put a name to her pain, "She was scared, to be a lesbian. She's gay. I know she's gay. Everyone knew she was gay, but she couldn't *be* gay, out in public, in any capacity that would have made a happy future for either of us."

"That doesn't make *you* a bad gay."

Honestly, it didn't make *her* a bad gay, either, whoever *Cara* was. Misguided, sure. Pitiable, of course. But not bad. Her ignorance did not undermine anything 'they' stood for. It didn't set them further back on the trail toward equality, both in marriage and in life. Her ignorance, instead, was what they were fighting *for*, to save women and men subjugated in the Bible Belt.

Christ, I sound too much like Sam's militant brigade.

She sounded like someone running for militant office, more like.

"I almost stayed with her, T," Dre said, quietly. "I almost…I think I would have stayed. Anyway. Like, hiding. If she had asked me to."

"Even though you think she couldn't *be* gay, in a public sense?"

She nodded a subdued *yeah* and focused on her drink for a time, listening to the pale melody of a propped up Who song. "I would have stayed, even though she couldn't be gay, really. Just to keep a piece of her. If she had let me, I would have."

"That still doesn't make you a bad gay."

"But it does. It invalidates me, us, everything we are. I would have been compromising myself, to hide with her. I would have been *nothing* like I am now, *here*." She gestured wildly with her arm. "And I realized, that's *not* what I want. That life, that woman—that's not what I need for my future."

Something in her cadence, in the mechanical lilt of her voice, was vaguely robotic, Tristan thought. Vaguely linear. Vaguely determined, in some sense, and she worried that her friend's definitive stance hinged too much on the cerebral and not at all on the less erudite faculties of love and affection. It was certainly possible that Dre could make up her mind to *not* care about this woman who was too afraid to be a lesbian, but that in no way indicated that her heart would heed the lesson. And that would have to be yet another secret that Tris kept only to herself. She could not, either for purposes of friendly compassion or civility, bring herself to ruin whatever fortifications Dre had constructed 'round the pain that must now dwell inside her.

"I feel like you've put a lot of thought into your future," she said, in lieu of telling her the absolute truth about her façade of psychological ramparts.

"I have. It's here."

"What's here? Your future?" Tris looked around, in jest. "Did I miss it?"

"My future is here, in South Waterton, where I am free to be who I am and I am embraced by my community. I need to be more active here. I need to *do* things here."

"You sound like you've been talking to Sam." All Sam ever wanted to talk about, when she was not immersed in Willow, nipple chafing, pregnancy symptoms, and lesbian documentaries on Netflix, was becoming involved and changing the world and mentoring youth and a thousand other causes that were founded on altruism and anti-complacency. Sitting back and enjoying the world, with all of its problems spinning around, was no better, according to Sam, than those who actively sought to make the world a worse place, filling it with hate and anger and injustice.

"I should be talking to Sam."

"Oh, God, no."

Sam was wonderful, nurturing…but was Sam was intense, and Sam had her own shortcomings that were unrelated to the cause of lesbian forward thinking.

"Sam, and women like Sam, are what I need in my life," Dre declared with certainty. "They're the change I told you about, the change that I have been looking for."

"I thought they were the sole reason you needed a change, in the first place." Hadn't that been why she'd run down to Florida? She wanted to get away from the pressure and the competition to be the gayest gay of all?

She shook her head, now, perhaps in retrospect. "I think I thought they were, but maybe life needed to teach me a lesson. Maybe life needed to wake me up and show me what I'm supposed to be doing with myself."

"You called me all the way out here, to a bar I've never even heard of, to tell me that you ran away from South Waterton because life needed to teach you to love South Waterton and become more engrossed in the lesbian political climate of South Waterton?" *Not that I didn't need an excuse to leave the house on an errand that did not involve grain-fed, free-range cravings and/or diapers. I should be grateful for that bit, at least.*

"Don't be ridiculous," Dre snickered. "I called you all the way out here to con you into introducing me to Dr. Gina P. Laudsdale."

At that, Tris spat Rum and what she had concluded was *Diet* Coke, all over her arm and the bar, like a fool. "You *what*?"

"I want you to introduce me to Dr. Gina P. Laudsdale."

"No, no. I heard that part. I think it's really stupid, but I heard it. I want to know why you think you need that."

Dr. Gina P. Laudsdale was one of the most pretentious women she had ever encountered, and the circle Sam kept at the coffee shop was the height of bougie pretention. Dr. Gina P. Laudsdale ate artificial salmon and brie on gluten-free bagels that were probably made of cardboard, and drank sustainable coffee from Colombia while claiming she could "taste the difference" between corporate roast and fair-trade blend. She wore espadrilles that were imported from the Peruvian mountains and only cotton fabrics locally produced and cast-off blazers from Goodwill that were ill-suited for her body shape. And none of those were contributing factors in her reputation as stilted and pompous; that bit she earned after criticizing everyone else around her for nearly everything they did, drank, smoked, ate or wore.

"I think we'd be good together."

"You think she fits in with this brilliant future plan." This absurd rationalization of never being hurt again, or never being made to feel homophobic pressure again.

"I think she'll fit in beautifully with my future plan, yes," Dre encapsulated, wearing an expression that was so serious it was downright shocking.

Empty Like a Used Capri Sun Pouch

Lincoln was not sure going to Cara Spencer's house without a weapon to defend himself was a good idea.

Scratch that.

Lincoln was not sure breathing in Cara Spencer's general direction without a weapon to defend himself was a good idea, but, like his brothers, he was fresh out of good ideas.

Dre had been a good idea. That one had been all his, in all of its glory.

Pushing her out of the closet had been a good idea. At least, to Atticus, who suffered all holy hell from his brothers once they were safely out of range of Hurricane Cara's deadly blows.

But those ideas, and the stupidity involved in their decision-making, had left them with one catastrophic consequence: the increased likelihood that Cara Spencer would never speak to any of them again.

That was the primary reason he chose *not* to knock on her back door. Knocking was too obvious. He knew she would not answer, and the sound would betray his position and leave him vulnerable to attack. Rather than the slow and painful death of being beaten past recognition by a feisty, one hundred and thirty pound woman, or being mauled by a dog with the guild of an elderly Chihuahua but the girth of a whale, he just used the spare key that had been left in Atticus's possession for emergencies. Lying in bed for two days while chickens crowed and goats whinnied constituted an emergency, he thought, as did rectifying the botched experiment he had somehow decided to enact on his sister's smoldering love life.

He could take no blame for Atti's brilliant idea to proclaim her homosexuality in the middle of the Greentown Farmer's Market, but he supposed had been there and had done very little to stop the show, so he had been deemed guilty by association and sentenced to a colossal apology—an apology the likes and size of which had never before been experienced within the Holloway clan.

"If we don't apologize, she'll never come around," Win had told him, all sage and big-brother-know-it-all-asshole. Like they hadn't already apologized to her a-thousand-and-one-times, in and around the apple stand, via phone call and voicemail and text, and smoke signal and messages laid out in the side yard with empty beer cans. He always did that, even when he knew full well he was also partly to blame. He dodged any personal culpability by mounting his high horse, putting the whole thing off on Atticus and Link, the condescending asshole.

Once, in the heat of an argument, Lincoln had screamed at him, "My father died in an airplane crash and I do not need another candidate for that position." Little good that did, as Win was just as ornery and just as patronizing as ever.

Head in the game, Lincoln.

Cautiously, he slid two feet into the back entryway of Cara Spencer's place and heard Greg Allman give a brief 'woo woo' from her bed by the stove (which was really just a tattered cushion from an old couch that his mother had donated to the Salvation Army). She was a gigantic sweetheart, especially to him, and he knew he had nothing to fear. It was the small one who could take him out.

In a blaze of growling, gnashing teeth, Grey Baby, a streak of half-black, half-white, and brown speckles, charged him, leaving a trail of saliva on the linoleum. Her eyes were white and, he swore, red, and sounds emanated from her body that were unnatural even in the feral animal kingdoms of Africa.

"God dammit!" he screeched, as her teeth landed in his leg, caught up in the pants he had (miraculously) the forethought to put on, anticipating the actions of the demon spawn. "Grey Baby, heel! Down! Stop eating me!"

But she would not listen, because she refused to listen to anyone aside from his sister, who clearly would not come to his aid.

"Grey Baby, no! Grey Baby, truce!"

There was solid logic behind the breed's ability to take down deer, cattle and horses, he realized. Solid logic in the Australian Cattle Dog's gumption and tenacity. Pushing her back for the fourth time, he yanked open the door and waited for her to charge again, this time using the precarious force of his shin to slide her right out onto the back screened porch, slamming the door in her angry, ferocious wake. She thumped against the wood, hard.

Greg Allman barely looked up in acknowledgement.

"Cara, dammit!" he called, sliding the key into his pocket as he caught his breath.

Outside, the heeler whinnied and scratched. "Cara Spence, I know you're in here! I just vanquished your stupid dog."

No sound met his inquiry, and he wondered, for a fleeting moment, if this would turn into some offbeat Dateline episode where he'd be confronted with overturned chairs, pictures torn from the wall and an empty bed, which was a really bizarre thought to even entertain, under the circumstances. Who could get close enough to kill her, with that mangy beast outside?

"You can't hide from me," he signaled, picking his way through the kitchen where, to his relief, he spotted empty popcorn bags littering the countertops and crusty cereal bowls in the sink. If nothing else, they were signs of recent life, so she wouldn't be well and truly dead. That was more comforting than it should have been.

He had not conceived, under normal circumstances, that he would miss the sound of her voice as much as he did, now that she fell silent. He had not conceived that he would miss her criticism or her laughter, her teasing and constant competition, either. There was no one to tell him how stupid he was being, the predominant factor in their botched romantic plans.

"Listen," he tiptoed into the hallway and wondered why the walls were still the puce green his grandmother had been such a fan of. "I know you're mad at us."

MAD?! Two shoes seemed to squeal, as they flew out of the master bedroom door and clanged against the opposite wall, rattling the Holloway clan kindergarten pictures, which had been standing guard in the same position for thirty plus years, as evidenced by the dancing rims of discolored paint. They were heavy shoes. Steel-toed work boots, he realized. Probably his, probably left in the yard on her back porch or down by the river.

They were all very much still living with one another, only in separate houses, which was probably considered weird in most of the rest of the civilized country. Win attributed it to the emotional state of orphaned semi-adults. Atticus had only wanted a free place to sleep and paint.

"Please don't throw my own shoes at me!"

This time a stapler came out, zinging past his frame to leave a giant ding in the wall.

Why would she have a stapler in the bedroom? Shoes were understandable, even though they were his, but a stapler? Was she catching up on office work? That was a stretch. He had never even seen her attempt any office work. And what office work would come, part and parcel, to a sad-ass farm with a tired cow that could barely muster the energy to moo most days?

"That's real mature, little sister."

Without waiting for a herald, a cable remote came out third, and it splintered into pieces with batteries rolling down to the floor and rubber buttons wafting like snow. Immediately, Link bent to retrieve them. He may have hated his sister's temperament at times, and he may have hated one of her dogs, but he really had a soft spot for Greg Allman and one thing he had picked up as dogsitter extraordinaire was that the Great Pyrenees would eat just about anything that was A) on the floor or B) very nearly on the floor. That would include chemical-heavy batteries.

"Can you at least take a break from your assault while I save your dog's life?"

The two Duracells rolled beneath the decorative, metal table that was buttressed against the paneled wall, no doubt to hold it into place when the adhesive grew too hot to adhere anymore. It held three burned down pillar candles and a boom box, and sat beneath one of Atticus's more vanguard artistic endeavors—an oil painting of a dog and a wave and a rose or some shit that barely made any sense. Too Salvador Dali for Lincoln, who leaned toward still life portraits of naked ladies.

"I would hate for Greg Allman to bite the big one, metaphorically speaking, because you're hell bent on breaking everything within reason and reach!"

An entire DVD player sailed out to make an appropriately timed exit just above his head.

Off-brand, at least, it was one they had picked up at the church yard sale about two months before for the low-low cost of one dollar, but still...

It could have caused major damage had it come into contract with something other than the wall. Something like his cranium.

"Alright, fine, I'll leave, but you'll still be gay as hell when I'm safe in my own house and you're moping about in this shit hole."

That oughta hit her below the belt, he thought, and he slowly counted backward from ten. If he knew anything about Cara Spencer Madeline Holloway, he knew she did not take kindly to criticism where her house was concerned. It had been her favorite place, even as a kid, somehow tying her to the generations of Holloways who had been before her.

At six, he heard, "This is not a shit hole. *This* was my grandmother's house."

Link put his hands on his hips, slipping the collected batteries into the pocket of his uncharacteristically long chinos with the fresh tear in the right leg. "Yeah, well, she's my grandmother, too, and I'm sure she'd appreciate it if you didn't leave tiny little dents in her walls when you have tantrums and throw shit."

"Well I'd appreciate it if you left me the hell alone!" Cara Spencer bit that statement out. "I didn't ask you to come here!"

He could hear the anguish in her voice, but she threw nothing else…at least, for the time being she threw nothing else.

"Have you exhausted your supply?" he called.

He knew she wanted him to leave. She wasn't the type of girl who said leave when she really meant stay or 'hold me, I'm scared' or 'hold me while I come to grips with my homosexuality and the fact that my idiot brother already told everyone about it.' She wasn't the type of girl to ask for a shovel when she needed to bury her own demons.

"You know I'm not really going to leave, Cara. I'll stand here all damn night if I have to. We need to talk, and you know it."

He wasn't entirely certain that was true. He could no more force her to open up to him than he could force her to go out and be a productive lesbian, and suggesting she do something that she was not ready to do would only make their current situation much, much worse. As if it could worsen, really.

Thankfully, she sighed. "Fine. Come in. I don't even care anymore."

Waiting for a split second, just for good measure, Lincoln figured his safety was more or less guaranteed when nothing else accosted him. He rounded the corner and looked around at the bedlam of the ordinarily messy room that his baby sister was stewing inside. There were clothes everywhere, but he assumed that was normal, if her high school bedroom had been any indication. Drawers were pulled out, but that too seemed par for the course. The covers were rumpled and she was swaddled in them, wearing an A.B.'s t-shirt that was stained with popcorn butter and cookie dough, and a pair of plaid pajama pants he had never seen before. Her hair was a hot mess barely tied in a neon pink rubber band and her face was raw and red and puffy. And she glared at him with menace, like a mama Cotton Mouth whose nest had been disturbed, but he didn't care.

"Move over," he instructed, nearing the bed that had become her feral hidey-hole habitat.

When she didn't reply forthwith, he repeated himself. "I told you, Cara S, I'm not leaving, so either I stand here and lecture you like you're a goddamn child, or you move over and we can talk like adults." *Adults lying in an unwashed bed in pajamas surrounded by crumbs and kernels and a spoon. And dog hair.*

With an exaggerated eye roll, she made space on the same bed she had been sleeping on for years, albeit swathed in everything from Lion King sheets to silk over the course of her life. It was the bed they had played

War in, using bent and torn playing cards from Granny's Bridge stack as giggling kids, the bed they made a giant fort beneath. It was the bed he had caught her crying in, years ago, though he did not know why back then.

"I don't have anything to say to you," she told him, curling tighter around herself, clutching the afghan and sheets and fluff to her chin like a baby. "I don't have anything to say to any of you." Her voice was hoarse from strain and hurt and her eyes were the deepest shade of brown, as she turned them to the comforter.

"Why? Because we knew you were gay and we didn't tell you?" Lincoln's theory of apology and rectification was predicated on his sister's ability to accept herself—the beautiful *self* that he and Win and Atti adored. He needed her to rise up, call things what they were, and move from the dwindling security that existed in the dregs of her own mind out into the open fields of newly acquired acceptance. He had come into her home, and into her bed, with the full awareness that he would have to be crass and mean and insulting in order to be nice (that was exactly why the task of redress had fallen on him and not the ever-soft Atticus who was still agonizing over whether he had done the right thing in shouting to the rafters that his sister had been set on an alternative path). Plus, lying to Cara Spencer had only set them further back, and he was beginning to tire of the outdated vestments she kept in her spiritual closet. "If that's a fucking crime, then sit here and be pissed, but we did what we did because we care about you and we wanted you to come to terms with *you* before we jumped into the business."

She mulled that over for a while, sheathed in the innocence of the blankets her grandmother had made during the time when they had nothing and no one save for the animals on the farm and the dirt of their land. "You should have said something. Like, *years* ago."

With a half-laugh, Link moved closer to her. "And what should I have said? *Hey sister, I can't help but notice that you've been eying the babysitter. Have you considered the fact that you may be a lesbian?* Come on."

"There were other words," she protested, and he knew that much was true. There were many other words, gestures, and acts of acceptance, but there hadn't been an excess of opportunity within which to voice them. There had never been a conversation. There had been no whispered agreement. They were boys, rough and tumble and ridiculous, and she was not and they had labored under the false assumption that there were some things they could not say to one another. And that had proved recklessly, and almost irreversibly, stupid.

"You never brought it up," he countered. "You never brought up dating, period."

"I never knew how." More than likely because they had been reared in a time and a place that adhered greatly to reinforced gender roles that had only slowly begun to change in recent years. Link had played football and gone hunting. Win had been a baseball prodigy. Atticus had been far more creative in his pursuits, but still held to the traditional archetype of masculinity. That left Cara Spencer with a dresser full of ribbons and bows and makeup and a closet full of gowns that she, apparently, had no interest in wearing—a fact that was enough to make Link physically sick to his stomach, just the notion that he and his siblings had been guided by some unspoken but understood dictate regarding the expected relationship between brothers and sisters.

"You know…it was awful," he pointed out, in a half-whisper. "It was awful watching you be so unhappy, with this thing inside of you that you couldn't seem to make peace with. For a long time, we didn't know what it was that troubled you so."

Cara Spencer sniffled, only a little, and wiped beneath her eyes with the blanket. She had cried so much, there were few tears left, and her skin, in those places, was red with irritation and raw hurt.

"How long have you known?" she wondered, aloud, twirling the worn corner of the blanket.

How many years had she fantasized about asking that very question, Lincoln wondered.

He ruffled her hair with his hand. "How long have *you* known?"

"Since the third grade," she blurted, like the dam inside her burst open and everything she had tried so hard to conceal poured out, words she felt but never voiced finally finding their sound at long last. "I have known that I was gay since I was nine."

"Then I've known since then, too."

"Really?" She was innocently dumbfounded.

"Really. You stared at all of my girlfriends."

"Dammit," she cursed. "I thought I was better at hiding it."

"You really weren't…" He wanted to laugh at the ludicrous words that he had been waiting a dozen years to say. And why had he waited so long, if it were this easy? Like a casual conversation between friends, which is what they were now, more than brother and sister. They were close because they chose to be, more so than because they were born of the same parents. "Did something happen? To tell you that you were different, I mean."

"Yes and no," she contemplated. "There was a girl in my class who fell off of the monkey bars. She had blonde hair and freckles and I caught myself wanting so badly to have caught her when she fell, to have saved her. All of my girlfriends were talking about boys and weddings and wearing makeup to middle school, and I just…I really wanted to sign that girl's cast first—she broke her arm in the fall—and I got really jealous when she let someone else have that honor. I told her I wanted to carry her bookbag around for her."

Lincoln was all but dumbfounded. Innocence had shown Cara Spencer that was not quite like everyone else.

"And you carried that secret around with you for the next twenty years? That you wanted to carry another girl's books to class?"

Cara Spencer nodded and wrinkled her nose. "I carried it everywhere. I spent four years in high school worrying about whether anyone else would notice. What if I looked at a girl for too long? What if I spent too much time in the locker room?"

Her honesty was the earthshattering kind, and the arrant tone of her voice was one that her brother had never heard before. He inched a little closer on the bed and hoped the dog wouldn't come in and ruin everything with a bellow, almost like their sudden closeness had become indescribably important to him, so precious and undeserved it was.

"I never really associated it with a name. I never knew I had a label. I didn't know there were other people like me."

"But there are gay people in Greentown."

"Not that we ever talked to," she laughed then, a staccato beat that started him a little. "No one was open about it. And Mom and Dad sure as hell never talked about it."

"Cara, Mom and Dad didn't really talk about anything." Nothing of any real importance to them, anyway. Maybe crop prices at market, or what they would plant in the North field come spring time, but not large, socio-romantic topics like homosexuality.

The Right Kind of Woman

"Back then, I was so obsessed with hiding it, I don't think I could have talked about it, honestly. I don't think anyone would have believed me. I didn't walk like a boy or dress like a boy and all of my friends were on the cheerleading squad. I thought I was this hybrid *thing*, not straight enough to be hetero, but not gay enough to be a lesbian."

"Is that a stereotype?"

"I'm sure it is, but that doesn't make it any less true. On the one hand, I didn't think I met any kind of gay standard of behavior, and on the other hand, I was terrified that, if I said anything, everyone would think I was contaminated, like they couldn't play with me anymore, or hang out at my house."

Her words at the haunting quality of something that had, at one time, been a huge thing that was nearly devastating, but whose effect was becoming less and less the central focus of her life. "Contagious?" Link clarified.

"Contagious, infected. Like I couldn't have any straight friends because they would all worry that I would be picturing them naked while we watched cartoons or no one would spend the night because they would think the gay parts would rub off on them."

"So you weren't straight enough to fit in, but you weren't gay enough to be gay?" That proved, beyond a shadow of a doubt, how very little they all knew about the gay community in podunk Greentown, South Carolina.

"Exactly," she surmised.

"And you never said anything?"

"I didn't know how to." Her feet shifted, beneath the covers, rubbing back and forth on the fitted sheet that was crusted with potato chips and food particles. "For a while, I thought I was bisexual. I really saw myself settling down with a man, so I convinced myself it must be just a phase or

222

just confusion. But then, time passed and I began to understand that it's not so simple as picking a gender to settle down with. I'm just attracted to women."

Lincoln rolled over on his side and faced her and speculated, discreetly, of course, whether she had been bushing her teeth regularly in her period of hetero-normative mourning. Clearly, there had been no brushing of the hair and very little changing of the clothes. "Can I ask you something?" he blurted, and then, without waiting for a response, "Why didn't you ever tell us? Why didn't you trust *us*? Maybe not the whole town, but *us*?"

Cara Spencer shrugged. "Every time I thought *I should tell them,* something would happen and I just couldn't find the words to do it. I would look at you and think, *he'll never look at me the same way again, if I tell him it's true.*"

"So you knew we had an idea?" *Idea* sounded like a much better word for what they felt than *suspicion*. People were picked up for *suspicion* of criminal activity.

"I knew that Greentown is tiny and people talk, like they always have. I knew there was the probability that someone would have said something in your presence, but I never wanted to put you into the position where you had to defend me."

"I've only been defending you since I was four years old."

She shoved an elbow into his side. "You know what I mean. People are horrible about it sometimes."

People were horrible about it, sometimes. Seeing the hell that Cara Spencer had gone through, though, had cured the Holloways of any such sentiment. It had been a hell they had all been privy to, one they could all name as an intensely personal experience to witness and by unable to change, and, regardless of their personal connections, they had not been raised that way—in the way of judgment and ugliness. They had been raised a good and loving people, by good and loving parents, no matter how detached they had become in the years leading up to their untimely deaths. They had been instructed to treat everyone around them as they would want to be treated rather than withhold services and the grace of polite society when confronted with those who followed a separate path.

"You know we don't care, Cara Spencer. I have gay friends."

She snorted. "You know approximately one gay person, Link, and she worked at the restaurant two years ago. That does not constitute *gay friends*."

"Did she know?" *Shit, that was a stupid question.* Sue Redding had been the Kitchen Manager at A.B.'s for about six months before blowing town to head for the greener pastures of Myrtle Beach.

"Did she know about *me*?" Cara Spender clarified. "I think I've been so wrapped up in my own hiding, I never really thought about it."

"Y'all never talked about…about, like, being gay?"

"Are you asking me if I slept with Sue?"

"No," he responded, a little too quickly.

Sue had been smart, funny, and extremely capable. Cara could have done a lot worse—

"Yes, you are. You are totally asking me if I slept with Sue Redding."

"I liked Sue Redding."

"I am not discussing my sex life with you, one, and two, I am not attracted to all lesbians, just like you are not attracted to all straight women."

"I am pretty much attracted to all straight women."

"You are pretty much an asshole."

224

In this, he knew he needed to own that summation. "I'll take that, because I had no business getting involved in anything that you had going on. But I would like to point out that Dre was awesome. She was insane smart, she knew everything about beer, she had a good job, she loved her dog—"

The haunted look came back to Cara's expression. "Lincoln, stop."

"*And* you were feeling her, I know you were."

Cara covered her face with the afghans and the sheets and the blankets and the mass that was formerly her body nodded.

"And she was feeling you, we could all see it."

The mass nodded a second time, and sniffled. Greg Allman wandered in from the kitchen and made another bed on the pallet of clothes that spilled forth from the master closet without so much as a glance toward the bed. That was what made her such an amazing pet. She needed absolutely nothing, aside from food stuffs. Conversely, Grey Baby, the self-appointed and ever-vigilant one-dog Queen's Guard, was still no doubt foaming at the mouth on the screened porch, tearing gouges into the doorframe, awaiting her revenge, and (secretly, though) Link had to semi-respect her tenacity. Grey Baby was the most formidable canine he had ever encountered.

"So…what happened? If you were attracted to her and she was attracted to you?"

"I don't know," mumbled Cara Spencer. "I just… I don't know what happened."

He yanked on the blankets. "You don't know? Cara, that's a copout. When you left for Florida, you were ecstatic. When you came back—after Atticus *came to get you*—you were a fucking mess."

"I said I don't know." She poked her head out and pushed at a clump of waves that fell over her eyes in a tangled mat. "It just didn't... It didn't work, like it was supposed to. I don't know how to explain it. It just didn't work."

"She's not a car or a toy, Cara. She's a person. You can't just say *it didn't work*, that could mean any number of things."

"It means," Cara heaved a great sigh as she spoke and shielded her own face with her hand, "it means that things were fun, and they were fine and they were cool and they were...whatever...and then I heard her—she had this long talk with her dad—and she said she wanted a future with me, like a *real* future, with a marriage and living together and having kids maybe and... I don't know."

Taking a massive leap, her brother reached out to her. "Things got too serious. And you got scared because you knew that you would have to come home and explain to it to us and you didn't think anyone in Greentown could handle the fact that you're a gay woman who wants to spend her life with another, equally awesome, gay woman."

All along, he and Atticus and Win had figured it was something like that, their suspicions confirmed when they finally broke through to Dre. There had been love between them—newfound, certainly, but present even now. There had been something much deeper growing than any of the brothers could possibly have predicted.

"I really, really love her," Dre had said to Atti on the phone. And love never went away. Not real love, not really.

There had been understanding and attraction and fun, and future possibilities, and Cara Spencer's own fears had squashed them all, leaving one woman scared and hurt and confused in Massachusetts, and one woman two inches from a zombie, hibernating in her own filth in South

Carolina, with one dog who was beside herself with hunger and one dog who was beside herself in blind rage.

"Seriously, like we'd run you out of town or fire you or disown you? Or did you think people would walk down the road beside you and spit on you?" When Cara did not respond post haste, Link knew he had hit his mark.

Taking a cue from the blustering Atticus, who had only recently found his spirit of meddlesome disturbance, he stood from the bed and yanked, quickly, all of the blankets, which scattered against him and landed in a much heavier weight than expected on the thin, pilling carpet. "Get up. I think you should go get her."

Horribly hairy-legged, with her pajama pants having ridden up like shorts, Cara burrowed beneath the mountain of pillows and shook her head, vehemently. "No!" she screeched, akin to a barn owl's cry. "What are you doing? No!"

"I'm serious. You need to go and get that woman. You've wallowed enough. Your hair is a mess."

"I'm not driving to Massachusetts, Lincoln. It's over. I walked out on her. I literally left her standing in her own father's backyard and got into a cab."

"Then you should definitely start with an apology. *When you get to Massachusetts.*"

Cara Spencer had been an emotional runner since the day she was born. When shit got heavy, when things needed attention and care and serious discussion, she was out like a light. And it was high time she faced up to what she had done. Lincoln could only assume Dre felt something of the same, felt a shared guilt in the demise of whatever beauty that had bloomed between them, and had been going through her own version of

227

breakup hell. He didn't want her to blame herself for a problem that he had helped to create, and he wanted to fix things the only way he knew how: through drastic, soul-bearing action.

"Get up, take a fucking shower, put on some clothes. I'm going to put gas in Atti's truck."

"Link, really—"

He stared down at her and knew that this was the single dumbest plan he had ever come up with in his entire life—far dumber than their initial plan to set her up with a charmingly lesbian stranger—but it was only by a dumb plan could he rectify the ruins of his other almost-equally-as-dumb plan. "Really, sister. You get one shot at life. You get one shot at Dre. If you love her, if you miss her, if you need her, you will get your smelly ass in the shower and knock the funk off because you're driving up to meet her. And it may end badly. She may slam her door in your face, but…that's life. You cannot live the rest of your days knowing that you didn't have the wherewithal to apologize for the mess you made and tell her how you really feel."

His heart was racing and indecision cloaked the two of them, with Greg Allman's head popping up from her hole.

How had they gotten here in just a few short minutes?

How had he gone from *I'm sorry, I'm sorry, I'm sorry* to *GET YOUR ASS UP, WE'RE GOING TO MASSACHUSETTS*?

Win and Atticus would never believe this. Win and Atticus would barely believe that she had permitted him entry to her home.

"He's right, you know," came a familiar voice from the doorway. "And it pains me more than you can understand to have to admit that…We really liked Dre, and you may be able to live the rest of your life knowing you were a huge bitch to her, but we owe her an apology as well."

Win strode in, still in his work uniform, but already drinking, wearing a ball cap and a pair of sunglasses that gave him the impression of a man so busy he hadn't had time to take them off in the car. Behind him, Atticus was a bit more meager (given that he had outed her to the entire town), but still filled with utter conviction. "I third this motion. Put on some clothes. Let's do this."

"She really needs to take a shower, first," Link interjected, and then looked at his brothers with an expression of *If you guys were coming in as backup, why couldn't you have helped when the dog attacked me?* Neither of them appeared remorseful. It was the nature of brotherhood.

"This is beyond stupid. I do not even know where she lives," Cara started to protest, but they all knew she was about to cave and bathe. "I don't know anything except the name of the town."

"We'll figure that part out." Win was stone somber and stone serious.

"I need to pack."

"We can do that, too," Link told her, but wondered if there were any clean clothes to be found in the entirety of the house.

"I don't know what to say when I get there."

"I'll make you some notes," Atticus grinned.

And then they all stared at her in expectation, frozen and awkwardly so. It would be another of those moments that would come up again and again, in the future.

"Fine," she stuttered, after an hour, or three minutes. "Fine. I'll go."

Appeteasers

"Would you care for any appetizers?" questioned a waiter in a trim pair of black slacks and a white button-down with a plaid bow-tie. "Poached asparagus? Steamed clams? Calamari?" Her voice drifted into oblivion as Dre stared down at the leather-bound menu in her lap.

Her palms were sweaty. She was wearing a plain, matte silver band on her right middle finger. Her cuticles were trimmed.

"I think I'll have the calamari," she forced a smile, ordering enough to split with Dr. Gina P. Laudsdale, who was perched opposite her in a crowded, but *tres* chic, grass-fed Italian eatery just down the block from the apartment in South Waterton. It was their first, *official* date, though they had corresponded briefly via text message after Samantha had been kind enough to make the initial introduction on Dre's behalf.

"Go into it with an open heart," she had whispered with finality, passing a slip of paper with the number scrawled across it. "I can only hope for the best."

That had been somewhat sage advice.

"And for you, ma'am?" the waiter inquired, innocently, directing her stare to the professor. "Would you like anything?"

"Please, call me Doctor, *ma'am* is so…patriarchal," came a delicately sharp reply. "And I'll have the poached asparagus." Her voice was as confident as her side-shaved, pageboy haircut and the tweed sport coat she wore. There were no tentative undertones to her movements, no hesitation present in her eyes. She was educated, accomplished and clearly a woman who was comfortable with her own sexual preferences, reveled in them, actually. But she was not the least bit sexy. Not to Dre.

She was the exact opposite of Cara Spencer Holloway, and that should have been refreshing. Only it wasn't.

When the waiter, a clean-cut girl in her early twenties, disappeared, she reached across the space of the small, linen-covered table and took Dre's hand in hers. Leaning in, she rubbed her fingers over Dre's knuckles. "I'm a strict vegetarian," she said, tracing the crossed patterns of skin. "I cannot condone the senseless slaughter of our earth's animal population, not when there are so many delicious alternatives. It just reminds me of all of those people with big, natural animals—like even large dog breeds—cramped up in apartments. So very wrong. So selfish."

On her best, and fanciest, behavior, Dre was now at peace with her decision to have Dr. Gina P. Laudsdale meet her at the restaurant. There was no telling what she would have mentioned, after watching Buddy 'cramped' up in the apartment. Also, Italian would not have been the best option for a strict vegetarian and she could not see why that divining fact had gone unmentioned in their lively, text-based political discussions. But whatever. There was no point in dwelling on things that were not to be changed. Buddy had been kind enough to keep a miserably first-trimester Sam company while she and Willow napped and Tris went out for dinner and groceries, and they were already seated in comfort, so they would muddle through the meat-heavy dinner as best as they could.

Wearing black dress pants (after being told she could absolutely, positively not wear the skinny jeans for one more minute by a hormonal version of Sam), and a white button-down with a grey, tuxedo vest, Dre wondered if she would be confused for a member of the wait staff. Her hair had gotten shaggier, and she'd gone in for a trim that afternoon, opting for something that resembled a pompadour.

"I make the most wonderful eggplant parmesan," Dr. Gina P. Laudsdale smiled and continued to talk, pleased with the sound of her own voice. "I'd love to make it for you someday."

Her mannerisms came off with a brusque illegitimacy, though Dre did not doubt her words. It was only that everything she said and everything she did gave the impression of somehow being overdone, which was calling into question the feasibility of her long term plan.

"I can't say that I've ever had a *wonderful* eggplant parmesan," she responded, which was not technically a lie. She just omitted the entire section that detailed how much she detested the taste of eggplant.

"My mother made it all the time. She said, after teaching all day, cooking gave her real purpose in life."

Andrea reached for her wine. "My father was a baker. He didn't seem to cook much when he came home. I suspect he was quite tired of being in the kitchen."

The Doctor opened her ebony napkin and dabbed at the corners of her mouth in a distinctly Victorian gesture, despite the fact that nothing about her was dirty. She had immaculate table manners and was drinking a deep, red wine that no one outside of France could pronounce appropriately. "Is he a baker still? That's such a beautiful thing, maintaining a blue collar job like that, like the jobs of our communal ancestors."

Funny, Dre had never considered owning a successful bakery to be the "blue collar job" of her "communal" ancestors. And she had never considered the possibility that dinner with Dr. Gina P. Laudsdale would be anything short of amazing. On paper, the woman was astounding. She was driven, she was articulate, she was educated and proper and she was overwhelmingly lesbian. She never wore a bra, she orchestrated marches for parity on multiple counts. The brunt of the coursework she assigned pertained to the perpetuation of the feminine icon in various and sundry fairy tales and even modern animated films. Her dissertation had been published by three different homo-relevant magazines. Even in circles that existed far and outside South Waterton, it was acceptable to compare her to Gloria Steinem.

For fuck's sake, she was the living, breathing apotheosis of what a well-respected lesbian was. She was a good gay. She liked the Indigo Girls. But she wasn't doing anything for Dre. Not a raised pulse, not a quickened heartbeat.

She was...vanilla, but maybe vanilla wasn't the worst of choices, Dre thought, as she sipped her own house blend cab and stared out at the setting sun and the traffic on the main road that rounded the fountain downtown and came to a stop very close to her apartment parking deck. Loads of people enjoyed the scent of vanilla and the texture of vanilla. Loads of people lived whole lifetimes ensconced in vanilla.

Seventeen Hours Later

For her first time in Massachusetts, her first time up North, period, actually, Cara Spencer felt she had performed swimmingly, maneuvering her brother's Ford pickup in and out of congested interstate traffic like it weighed no more than a feather, like it were a veritable Smart Car, which it decidedly *wasn't*. It was a gas-guzzler. But, he had insisted that she drive it. They all had, really, terrified the Apache would strand her just inside Virginia, if it even got that far, which she felt was a stereotypical assumption because it had only done that one time before.

They had all been insistent that she drive Atti's truck, all insistent that she go and do this. They had packed her bags and forced her out of the door while Grey Baby and Greg Allman could only watch in disbelief, along with the goats they promised to feed and the chickens they promised to feed and Erin Andrews, whom they collectively promised, especially, to look after and not make steaks out of. They were insistent she apologize, on their behalf and her own, and endeavor to win back the affections of their combined lady love.

"But what if she's moved on? It's not like I've called." That had been the most legitimate of her last-ditch points. Dre was, after all, far more of a catch than she was. She was a neurotic belle surrounded by affable idiots.

"Moved on?" Win banished the thought. "Moved on to what? Who wants vanilla when they can have coconut?"

Coconuts, is right, she told herself. This entire plan was flat-out nuts. Bonkers. Yet, here she was, pulling into the parking garage for the London Swells Apartment Complex, hoping like all hell she was in the right place, even though Link said Dre's father swore to him it was the right place *and*

234

she had recognized the designs on the exterior from one of Dre's idle napkin doodles.

"How did you find her dad?" That had been one of the last things she had asked, before they practically shoved her into the cab of the truck and threw wads of cash in her direction. "How did you even know his name?"

Lincoln shrugged. "Turns out, there aren't that many bakeries in Saint Augustine."

"We called, like, six. Link just kept asking if they had a gay daughter named Andrea-Dre," Atticus supplied. "Finally someone said yes."

"And he knew who you were immediately. Said he really liked you."

"Well… That was his probably his opinion before I drove off in a taxi and left his daughter stranded in the driveway."

"He may have mentioned that part." Atti had never been one to withhold. Although, that wasn't really true, was it? He'd been withholding in regard to his knowledge about her 'lifestyle' for close to twenty years.

Still, knowing which apartment building to go to didn't negate the fact that this entire plan could be a colossal mistake, and being mistaken thirteen hours from home was the stuff of nightmares without factoring in her distinct lack of cell phone, on account of her brothers' maniacally thoughtless plan of action. Three hours had gone by before she even realized it was missing. By that point, she figured if the pilgrims could make it to America without Verizon, she could make it to Massachusetts.

"I am such an idiot," she said, flipping off the A/C. *And that's what I get for listening to any of them and for running out of the house in a big damn hurry, like me speeding to get here would make a difference.* She probably had no underwear packed and the location of her wallet was a guess. "Here's to hoping I won't need a hotel room."

She pulled the vehicle deftly into a tight spot that said Compact Cars Only, though she didn't give a damn, and overshot it on the first two attempts. Her nerves were a soggy, wet, frayed mess, after being left alone with her thoughts for approximately one million hours and forty-eight minutes.

She had no idea what she would say to Dre.

She had no idea if Dre would even open the door, or even agree to hear her out.

She had no idea if Dre was home. What if she had gone back to Florida?

I'm sure her father would have mentioned that to Link on the telephone. Unless he's harboring a grudge because I'm such a fucking asshole.

In the first of her Worst Case Scenario predictions, Dre would be slamming a door amidst a flurry of curse words aimed at sending her right back to the backwoods. In the second, she would be sent on an even longer drive down to Florida, to seek out the love of her life. Conversely, her Best Case Scenario involved hugs and kisses and sex on the floor.

They were equal parts of a very unique whole and multiple ends to a tumultuous spectrum.

But she had to admit, Lincoln had been right to make her do this, as had James Winter and Atti. She could not live the rest of her life without at least explaining what she had done in Florida. Dre deserved that much, and maybe a lifetime of atonement.

With a wink and prayer, she made the parking spot on the third try. Garages always made her nervous. It was definitely the pylons. They seemed so severe.

The Right Kind of Woman

Stop thinking of reasons to stay in the car. Get out, she told herself. This had the makings of a NOW OR NEVER kind of a situation. Yet she was wearing what most people considered workout clothes.

Whatever, just do it. She slid from the driver's side door and out onto the tidy concrete walkway of the parking deck, straightening her Led Zeppelin shirt. There was absolutely no saving her ensemble. She looked like hammered shit. She had just spent an entire workday behind the wheel of a truck that wasn't hers, mainlining caffeine and listening to sad love songs from her brother's plugged in iPod because she could not figure out how to disconnect it. Her leggings had lost elasticity two states back, her hair was a rat's nest (not that that was far left of her normal) and she ditched her more traditional sneakers while pulling out of the driveway, in favor of driving barefoot so her toes could breathe.

"Shit, shoes!" She needed shoes if she were about to confess her love to Andrea-Dre. Confessions of love required decent footwear. Or footwear at all.

She returned to the truck and rummaged around in the miniscule space behind her seat, tossing aside Link's empty burger containers and drained cans of Diet Mountain Dew. Her Rainbow-brand flip-flops were down there somewhere, covered over in the floorboard, beside the suitcase that she may never need because any idiot would slam the door in her face when she tried to lay out all of the reasons that they would be perfect together and could make a future, despite her previous life in the closet and her reticence to commit to anything back in Saint Augustine.

Oh, Jesus. This was bad.

To keep her blood pressure on a level playing field, she recited her reasons for the seven millionth time since her departure from Greentown, watching her brothers wave at her in the back glass.

Reason Number One Sexual Chemistry: She and Dre had electric sexual chemistry. They had been intimate on a tree, in a bathroom, on a beach. Dre had done things to her body that made Cara Spencer feel as if their souls were entwined, as if that were her only reason for breathing, and she had shared with Dre parts of herself that she had never shared with another living being.

Reason Number Two Dogs: They both loved dogs. And Grey Baby was a mess without Buddy. She disappeared for hours on end, roaming through the forests. Greg Allman was sad, too, but she leaned toward eating her feelings by way of three additional bags of dogfood.

Reason Number Three Compatibility: Regardless of the story told by the circle of their relationship, they were horribly compatible. Dre was infinitely patient. Cara Spencer was infinitely crazy. There was a tremendous amount of comfort in the universal balance provided in that arrangement, but more so, Cara needed patient and Dre enjoyed the crazy and the chaos, not that she would ever have said as much aloud.

Reason Number Four Love: Cara Spencer was a horrible, sopping, bereft mess without Dre.

And those four things would have to be enough.

They would be enough, because she had no idea what she would do if this venture proved futile.

* * *

That woman has the biggest hair I have ever seen, Tristan Alexander thought, climbing the ever-lovingly monotonous stairway that led to her blasted apartment, arms laden with organic groceries that made her feel like she belonged on a commune covered in dirt and sweat and horse shit. *That woman's hair is absolutely ridiculous. It's a wig.*

Also, it registered on some level that she had never seen that woman before, and that that woman was very obviously *not* from South Waterton. That woman's skin was a golden tan, like an *I've-worked-summers-in-a-field-tan.* That woman's fingernails were painted and her eyes were rimmed in deep brown. Her lashes were long, but smudged. Her flip-flops were half-chewed, half-encrusted in muddy clump soil, and her leggings had seen better days. And, alert of all alerts, she was wearing a long-sleeved denim chambray shirt with bleach spots down one of the arms, over a soft Led Zeppelin tee that almost seemed like legitimate concert swag.

That woman was most definitely a stranger, and she was sitting on the flat space created by a slight break in the stairs, by the third floor door, where Dre lived with a smattering of other tenants who were all young and "lesbian" and single, but in a trendy way. She was not trendy, Tris almost said with her eyes. Trendy was sundresses over jeans and fedora hats, not… Whatever that woman was wearing.

Not knowing quite what to do, but knowing that if she didn't make a sound the big-haired woman would continue to block her path up the stairs, Tristan gave out a concise, fake-cough and shifted the brown paper sacks (no plastic, only paper) in her arms. Of all of the days Sam had to have a craving, she picked the one day her partner was absolutely run-ragged and exhausted, overwhelmed, to put it mildly, with state testing and teacher observations and the responsibilities of her new job as a department head, which amounted to two-hundred dollars more per month that was desperately needed with Sam sitting at home and dreaming of a life in the country with cloth diapers and Kerouac and soy burgers, all on a processed, McDonald's Value Menu budget. Her feet were throbbing and she felt like she hadn't seen Willow in ages.

Well, she had seen the kid, she just hadn't *connected* with the kid, and being the mom whose uterus had not been used for growth sometimes made her feel like she had started the race of parenthood a full lap behind.

And Dre was out on a date with Dr. VAGINA P. Laudsdale and she really had not made her peace with that idea and the looming idea of this perfect long term, super lesbian and gay life plan, but that was an entirely different set of problems she couldn't muster the energy to face. Right now, the only thing she could face was the lump of reddish-blondey-brown curls in her path up the stairs.

"Can you move?" she blurted, more short than she intended. But come on, she was standing with, like, four bags of groceries.

"O.M.G., am I in your way?" the mystery woman burbled, the heavy wool coat of her accent almost overcompensating for her use of the acronym rather than the expression. Sugar sweet tea nearly dripped from her exclamation. "Of course I am. I'm so sorry."

Without waiting for confirmation, she leapt up, brushing her ass off with manicured hands, a set of keys on a Grateful Dead ring jingling by her side. "I didn't even hear you come up."

From a standing position, it was obvious to Tristan that the woman opposite her was built more like Marilyn Monroe than even the best trans impersonators down in Boston. Her hips were full and round, her body sliding into an hourglass that seemed nearly unbelievable in an area predicated upon vegetarian tacos. And she was wholly at ease with the sex-kitten thing, nearly nonchalant about it, accepting the illusion of her shape with a deprecating confidence that was apparent in her languid motions.

"It's really fine," Tris conceded, because it seemed like the appropriate thing to say to a woman who was more Anna Nicole Smith than Anna Nicole Smith. "Are you lost?" It wasn't everyday Dolly Parton made an appearance.

"Ah, no…" Southern Barbie said, but her voice said otherwise. "I'm waiting for someone."

"In the stairwell?"

The stranger flinched. "I, ah… I don't know the apartment number. Or the right floor. My brother told me and I wrote them down somewhere and now I can't remember where I put the note and I left my phone back home because I'm an idiot."

The unselfconsciousness of her words was refreshing. All day long, Tristan felt like people said only what they anticipated she wanted to hear.

"I leave my phone at home all the time. I can never remember to put it in my bag."

"Do you drive thirteen states away after you do it?"

"Um, no. Usually I just drive to work and make my partner bring it to me."

"Yeah…"

Shit. She wanted to leave and put her feet up and drink wine and play with her daughter and forget that more than half of the kids on her roster more than likely wouldn't pass the stupid upcoming ACT. She wanted to forget that her back was sore and her brain was mush and her partner wanted a jersey cow and a backyard that was fit for a jersey cow and they were operating with finances that didn't even meet the prerequisites for a degree in shoestring.

But, she didn't. Because, at her core, she was a good person and good people would always and unfailingly do what needed to be done, even if that meant teetering on sore heels with multiple bags of food and melting ice cream while sorting out the private affairs of a country singer with no phone.

"Well, who are you looking for? Maybe I can help. I know just about everyone in the building." *And you really don't look like an axe murderer, unless Axe Murderer is the name you use at the strip club two towns away.*

Barbie looked so relieved Tris wondered if she were about to reply with *I could always depend on the kindness of strangers* in Scarlet O'Hara's voice, but that was stereotypical and being stereotypical was wrong. Wasn't it?

"You are too nice," she said, emphasizing the long-i sound. "I thought I'd be sittin' out here all night waitin' on Dre."

Suddenly, Tris was suddenly not bothered at all by the melting and the weight and the stiffness and everything else that five minutes before threatened to close in around her.

Suddenly, Tris was suddenly not bothered at all by the Dudley Do-Right outlook that led her to lend a helping hand in the first place.

"D-Dre?" She sputtered.

"Um, Andrea? Martin? About yay tall?" Twang put her arm out. "Black hair and a big, brown dog?"

You mean the black-haired woman my wife just sent out on a date with the most annoying woman in the world and her dog, the big brown lump that's probably asleep on my couch at the moment?

"Dre?" she said again, like an idiot.

"Right, Dre," Mystery Lady seemed reluctant now. "I'm Cara Spencer Holloway. I'm from South Carolina." She stuck her hand out in a friendly, if hesitant, salutation. "I should have led with that, I guess."

Well, shit, what a wonderful place the world is...

"You know," Tris had to laugh a little. "I don't think I would have believed it if you had."

Trying to Like Vanilla

Dr. Gina P. Laudsdale had monopolized the majority of the conversation all throughout dinner; a veritable fount of lesbian statistics and little known facts and history and political knowledge, was she. She knew everyone important in South Waterton—all of the most prestigious people, all of the *right* members of the community. She was a tenured professor at a local university, teaching entry-level writing skills as well as three gender studies courses that examined the patriarchal undertones of modern socio-economic media and communication. She had a cat, named Cersei, but Cersei Lannister was a rescued Siamese, which fit in well with her ideals of humane animal "ownership," vegetarianism, gender-neutrality, and a thousand other things that Dre could not possibly be bothered to keep up track of.

She hated the sexual violence of the newest season of *Game of Thrones*, but kept up with the program due to her deep-rooted distaste for current, "network" scripted dramas, on Sundays she had brunch at an organic deli down the block from her standalone house painted in all shades of lilac and blue, and she bought used books from a consignment shop because she lusted after the sensation of turning "actual pages" with the pads of her uber sensitive fingers. She had three sisters and two nieces, named Loki and Wren. Her Subaru was always laden with burlap shopping bags and she donated time and money to the same center Sam volunteered through, choosing to spend time with LGBTQ youth, who were both "appallingly disenchanted with hetero-normativity" and "disenfranchised by our obsessively materialistic culture."

The Right Kind of Woman

Dre was reasonably certain that the LGBTQ youth of America knew very few of those superfluous words.

"I just can't get over the repeated rape of our natural resources on the part of the large-scale bottling corporations. One dollar and ninety-nine cents for water, the free and beautiful bounty that is the product of Mother Nature, wrapped up in a plastic bottle and peddled by every gas station from here to South Carolina…" She was in the middle of professoring, three glasses of wine into their after-meal chat, which was beginning to encroach upon the excruciating, usurping all of the air in the room, and all of the fun in the room as well.

This is not fucking vanilla, this is horse excrement. That was an awful thing to think, unbidden and unfounded. Dr. Gina P. Laudsdale was well-read, witty and incredibly insightful, where the ways of the modern world were concerned. She was just…intense? Was intense the right way to describe it? Intense was certainly one way to describe it. The Doctor was severe and harsh and chose to examine the current state of the world and criticize, rather than build up or encourage, and that was a heavy load to push off over veggie lasagna and tortellini in the dim lighting of a trendy, two-year restaurant.

That was a heavy load to push off over the Irish potato famine.

"It's just appalling how they treat the earth, our mother. I cannot… Oh, I've gotten carried away again, haven't I?" Dr. Gina laughed and pushed a sliver of hair behind her ear, which was a rather girlish movement for someone so ill at ease with her rigidly repressed girlishness. "The time has gotten away from us, hasn't it?"

Dre nodded, but she didn't mean it. It wasn't late, not by a long shot, yet she sincerely wanted the awkwardness of this tryst to be over. She now felt guilty about having a dog in an apartment, eating calamari (which "had

245

a depth of feeling, to some extent"), eating meat sauce, drinking bottled water and sometimes forgetting to dump out the recycling in the right bin. On top of that, she didn't really deserve the title of lesbian anymore because she wore bras and, on occasion, shaved her legs because it helped in managing her winter eczema. She also didn't hate makeup, she just chose not to wear it. Makeup, she assumed, was like a shield, or a cloak, encouraging women who may feel invalid for whatever reason, to man up and take back their positions within the patriarchy. Who was she to say that was wrong?

"Would you care for a nightcap?"

"I'm sorry?" She could not have heard that correctly. The Doctor was coming on to her? That somehow seemed at odds with her high-brow persona, inviting a first date in for a night cap.

But Dr. Gina P. Laudsdale chuckled. "Would you care to come to my house and put that tongue to good use?"

* * *

"I'm sorry?" Little Miss Can't Be Wrong was gawking in the stairwell.

"It's a long story," Tris told her, shrugged. "Listen, why don't you follow me up to my apartment and I'll tell you all about it." Sam, the World's Biggest Romance Novel Enthusiast, needed to see this with her own eyes, and Dre was out with Dr. Vagina Monologues, anyway. They had some time to kill.

"Shouldn't we find Dre first? That's kinda the reason I'm here."

246

"No," the bags had become inhumanly heavy. "She's out, at the moment, and I'd hate the idea of you sitting out here for hours when I know Dre will be coming up to my apartment as soon as she gets back."

Tristan entertained no illusions when it came to Dre and Dr. Gina P. Laudsdale hitting it off. She had not been a fan of this match from its inception. They were literally nothing alike, and not in the cutesy, *opposites attract* kind of a way. VAGINA was egocentric and elitist and pretentious. She, and women like her, were the reason Dre fled South. They were the lesbian ideal and they led the lesbian scene in clusters like South Waterton, making it their lesbian duty to educate the unsuspecting public on the finer points of the gay agenda, and that was beautiful and amazing, but it wasn't for Dre, not even the New Dre with her fancy life path and her recondite thought pattern.

Dre just wanted to be accepted and loved, not indoctrinated. She wasn't trying to be anything but herself. Ironically, that was what drew people to her.

"I'm Tristan, by the way. Dre's a really good friend of mine." She led the way onwards and upwards. "And I'm married, with a kid. It's perfectly safe to follow me. I'm not a serial killer."

"I'll bet that's what all serial killers say."

"Well, if you're not grain-fed and free-range, there'd be no point in harvesting your meat anyway. My partner won't touch you." That, at least, made this Cara Spencer person laugh, no matter how many dollar signs accumulated in the grocery cart down at Whole Foods.

"I promise y'all don't want me, then. Although I do raise my own chickens."

Tristan could not determine which fact she found more interesting—the bit about "raising my own chickens" or the fact that she used the colloquialism "y'all." She went with the latter.

"I've never heard anyone say *y'all* before." It was an urban myth, something seen on the late night episodes of *The Chrisleys* when there was literally nothing else on television in the middle of the night and Willow refused to entertain the notion of sleep.

Just a few more steps and they would be on the right floor.

"Well, I've never met a gay family before."

* * *

Cara Spencer figured that the present was as good a time as any to get her head out of her ass and start being earnest in the world. There was a lot she did not know, and a lot she probably needed to learn if she were serious about having a future with Dre. Or anyone, given that Dre owned the right to shut her out completely if she chose to.

"There are gay families in the South," Tristan told her, shifting the weight of the brown sacks in her grasp. "Sam is really active with the Gay Southern Alliance, online."

That sounded vaguely like a Facebook group, but Facebook had never been something that took up much of Cara's time on her fledgling farm, aside from manning the A.B.'s advertising link when she was forced to and buying a cow that time.

"There are not gay families in Greentown, South Carolina."

"Then that's a shame. We're not that weird." The flippant and casual way Tristan dealt with her naiveté was reassuring and she had instantly liked the other woman, appealingly informal in her khaki pants and her crimson polo shirt. She was patient and calm and empathetic. It was easy to see what drew her to Dre, and vice versa.

"How old is your kid?"

They stepped through an oak door and into a narrow hallway lined in green wallpaper with yellow carpet. "Her name is Willow. She's about eighteen months, but I don't know why people measure it in months when you can just say a year and a half."

"I wouldn't know. There are no kids in my family. My brothers are single and childless, which is probably for the benefit of mankind. I can't imagine that procreation." The goats and the chickens and the cow and the dogs were more than enough for her to take care of. Grey Baby alone was the equivalent of ten crying children, on her best day.

Tris rounded up to a door and knocked with her foot. Inside, a dog bellowed.

"It's the most amazing thing Sam has ever convinced me to do. I sure as hell never saw myself doing it. I guess that's what happens when you find someone to love. They change you and you don't really realize it."

Cara Spencer opened her mouth to respond to the prophetic tone of her words, but the door flew open, exposing a lovely, willowy woman with straight blonde hair that fell to her waist, parted in the middle, with a baby on her hip offering up gooey, baby hands, and a small, pregnant belly that was nearly indistinguishable. She was wearing a rustic, eggplant purple tunic that clung to her midsection and soft, brown leggings, with large, golden earrings that swung with her movements. When her pale green eyes met Cara's, she stepped back in unveiled confusion.

"I send you for ice cream and you come back with another woman?"

Willow—supposedly Willow—grinned, brandishing two small, pearly white bottom teeth. She reached for Tris, and Tris cooed. "Sam, my love,

249

this is Cara Spencer. I found her waiting on the third floor stairwell. She's from South Carolina."

They moved inside and Cara Spencer felt herself relax as she came within the confines of their airy and peaceful living room, all done in tones of cream and chocolate and aubergine with pale aqua accents. Immediately, Buddy bounded out of the kitchen and nearly bowled her over with affectionate grunts. His tail nearly propelled from his narrow body and he yelped in excitement as Tris stepped around him and made her way into the stainless wild of her kitchen.

"Hey there, boy! Hey, Buddy!" Cara giggled, leaning over to let him lick her face. "Did you miss me this much?"

Sliding Willow happily to the floor, Sam put her hands on her burgeoning hips. "How do you know Buddy? Tris," she turned around. "Tristan, how does she know Buddy?"

In the other room, Tris whistled. "She's from South Carolina, babe. Remember that trip Dre went on?"

"Well, of course I do."

"And remember that woman she met while she was there?"

Sam seemed to wobble on her feet and reached backward for a door or a table or a life raft. Momentarily, Cara Spencer wondered if the woman would fall over, and wondered what she should do in that eventuality, but Sam seemed to catch her bearings and push the hair from her face, inadvertently jiggling her gypsy-style earrings. "You're the woman from South Carolina?" she hissed in a hushed tone. "*You're* the woman from South Carolina? And you're here? *Now*?!"

"She's the woman from South Carolina," Tris agreed, coolly, almost as if she had known the outburst would come in due time.

The Right Kind of Woman

From her low vantage point on the faux shag rug, more cotton ball than fabric, Willow gurgled and slapped her tiny hands together, formulating some secret plan of her own. Obligingly, Buddy sauntered to her side and flopped down like a lumbering sack of anvils.

"I'm the woman from South Carolina," Cara Spencer nodded. "My name is Cara—"

"Spencer, I heard you, double name, South Carolina." Sam stammered, still dazed and a bit dumbfounded. "You're the woman."

Suddenly, the sound of groceries being put away was all they could hear, cabinets opening and the refrigerator groaning, drawers squeaking. It all seemed so regulatory, so normal. Like it happened every day, which was comical, because every day Cara Spencer didn't drive 12.75 hours to tell another woman that she was hopelessly, blindly, forever in love with her.

"Have a seat. Come in. You don't have to stand in the doorway," Tristan hollered. "Babe, be civilized," she chastised, without showing her face through the doorway.

Sam's eyes flashed to attention. "But she's on a date."

"Who's on a date?" Cara Spencer questioned.

"Baby." Tristan's voice was thick with warning.

"Dre," the barely pregnant woman clarified, rubbing the side of her belly. "Dre's on a date. Right now."

Thankfully, Tristan chose that moment to walk back into the living room with two beers in her hand. Wiggling her eyebrow, she offered one to her guest. They were frosty cold and brown and, for the first time since she had come home from Florida, Cara Spencer felt like she was in the right place for an IPA.

251

Namely, she was not surrounded by her Nosy Nellie brothers and their Nosy Nellie tendencies, she was in Massachusetts, with people she did not know, and she had just been informed that he woman she had driven all this way to see, the woman she was ready to give up her life to be with, was out on a date without someone else. Who wasn't her. And that was just plain shitty.

"I'd love a beer," she stated, blankly. "I'd love a beer after driving all damn day to see Dre who is obviously totally not bothered by how we left things in Florida and has moved on to someone else."

* * *

Why am I doing this?

Dre's sense of reason, her internal leader—the cortex of rationality and precisely measure thought—threatened to send her running for the hills.

Why was she here?

This was a bad idea.

This was one of the worst ideas in the history of ideas.

This was worse than spending the night in freaking South Carolina, of all of the places to stop in the world.

This was sex with Dr. Gina P. Laudsdale, in her inner sanctum. And, when she reached deep down to inspect the more contemplative sections of her consciousness, it was clear she did not want to be within ten feet of Dr. Gina P. Laudsdale's *inner sanctum.* She was not the least bit attracted to this woman, although she could concede why other women would be. Closely shorn and more masculine than most, the Doctor was as hard-bodied as she was. Muscular. Athletic.

The trouble lied in the fact the she had no desire to feel that hard body pressed against her own. She wanted softness and curves, rounded edges, she wanted hair fisted in her hands, and hips grinding into hers and lips that spread open and parted with a necessity that bordered on madness. Which did not describe any of this.

"The bedroom is this way," Dr. Gina P. Laudsdale told her, which, in another life, would have been beckoning, or quite possibly enticing. "There are things I can't wait to show you."

* * *

Tristan was not happy that Sam had blown the cover of Dre's date. She would have been in favor of a more tactful approach, not a free for all slide down the hill of a blurt, but it was all out in the open now and there was no taking it back.

"It's not serious," she pacified, because she was nothing if not level-headed in even the swirling winds of a crises. "It's not serious even a little."

Sam nodded vigorously—it was really the *least* she could do, given that this was all her fault—and came around to sit on the couch, with Willow between the knees of her stretchy leggings. Her feet were bare and her toenails were unpainted. Tris wondered if Cara Spencer thought that was strange. She seemed like a woman who took her feminine upkeep seriously, clashing wildly with Dre's low maintenance outlook on life. Not that Andrea wasn't hygienic. She was painfully hygienic. She flossed twice a day, every day. But this? This was a real girl. Her toenails were red and glossy, her skin was pale and soft and moisturized, which made it hard to reconcile her physical form with what Tristan and Samantha had been told about her. Farm. Apple stand. Goats. Outdoors.

"It won't work out," Sam continued. "It was a whim, someone we tried to introduce her to *before* she left for South Carolina."

"Someone *you* tried to set her up with," Tris accused. "I don't care for Gina."

Sinking down, she nestled into place by her partner's side, inviting Cara Spencer to sit opposite them, on a loveseat the color of an olive that had not yet reached maturity, draped with a throw in the pattern of a cow. "My partner is horrible with blind dates. She loves to set people up, but they never work out."

"They sometimes work out," Sam supplied, but then reconsidered her statement and shrugged. She shifted, gracelessly, uncomfortable and not even yet grossly pregnant.

"Dre's on a date," Cara Spencer repeated, feeling the words form in her mouth. "Dre's on a date right now."

"Yea, but it's a sad, boring date with a woman that will not interest her in the least."

* * *

"Don't tell me you're shy," Dr. Gina P. Laudsdale shrugged out of her blazer and left it on an overstuffed chair by the door.

Her boudoir was a wash of colors that were infinitely dark and infinitely rich, but infinitely sterile. Her bed was small. Her headboard was painted with shiny sheets of gold.

"I don't think I'm shy."

"You're not moving."

The Right Kind of Woman

"I'm not..." *I'm not what? That kind of girl?* Was it 1954? A month before, Dre had no qualms about slipping her fingers into a stranger propped up on a tree. What was wrong with her? This was what she wanted. It was the first step in her long-term plan. She wanted to share her life with a woman like Dr. Gina P. Laudsdale, with *like* apparently being the operative word.

It All Comes Down to This

Two beers into her (at first painfully) awkward visit, Cara Spencer had honestly begun to care for Dre's friends and the easy simplicity of their lives in South Waterton, where they were considered just as normal as everyone else. Samantha, who went by the generic *Sam*, was quick-witted and silly and a natural parent, her needs solely in tune with those of her daughter, who was fat and happy and playful and filled with the joy than can only come from being surrounded by a loving family. Tristan, who went by *Tris* because she resisted the impulse to compare herself to the Arthurian legend, was mellow and steady and served as the voice of reason in her home, her every motivation that of an equal partner and mother. Rather than concoct a meal for herself, she first served her child. Rather than stretch out and relax after a day at work, she ensured her wife's comfort, even though her eyes were exhausted and her shoulders carried the weight of more responsibility than she had ever bargained for.

Having changed out of her school uniform and into a more comfortable outfit of joggers and a vintage Indiana Jones tee-shirt, she was in the middle of a laugh, with her arm thrown lazily around her partner's shoulder. "I think the world of Dre, don't get me wrong. I've known her since college. But I cannot picture her in a goat pen, *feeding* goats. She just takes herself too seriously for that."

Over her ice water, Sam shook her head and giggled. "Remember when Stephanie took her to the zoo? She was absolutely repulsed by the petting area. Wouldn't go near it."

Though disinterested in hearing anything about Dre's former relationships—if this *Stephanie* person had been a former relationship—

The Right Kind of Woman

Cara Spencer had to laugh along with them. She had no concept of what Dre was really like, away from her.

"Did she really get in and touch them? Like, touch the actual goats?" Tris pressed.

"She really did. I have two babies, they're only a few months old. She seemed very taken with them."

"Taken with a *goat*?" Sam smirked.

"Taken with a *baby* goat?" Tris quipped. "She must really have feelings for you, then."

"And you really do love her, huh?" Samantha was clearly the more romantic of the two. She was lying on the sofa, her puffy pink feet over Tris's legs, her arms and her belly hanging limply from her lithe frame in a position that would really only seem comfortable to a walrus, or a woman in the family way. "Enough to drive all the way here and wait to profess your love?"

Cara Spencer said she was. She was more than ready to profess her love and find her answer, whatever the hell her answer would be. Either way, it would pave the meandering road of her future. Either way, her life would never be the same again. Her life *could* never be the same again, not after she had been given a taste of what it was like to live in union with another woman and seek happiness and acceptance and feel loved and understood.

Not after she had made her peace with the restless lesbian spirit she had always sought to ignore.

"I really love her. Even if I have to drive all the way home tonight, and spend thirteen more hours in the car, it would be worth it just to know that I gave it everything I had to apologize for what I've done." Technically, those were Atticus's words, but no one ever need know.

257

Sam sniffled, and swatted at her partner with a quilted chocolate throw pillow. "Why can't you be that romantic?" she cried, fanning her long lashes. "You've never driven anywhere, never done anything."

"I went out after work, stood around on sore feet, fucking exhausted, and bought you dairy free peanut butter and banana ice cream. It was eleven dollars. That's enough."

"That only took fifteen minutes."

Ripping them from their frivolity, three knocks rang against the apartment door.

Three knocks and Cara Spencer knew it was now or never.

***

A nightcap?

Let's put that tongue to use?

You seem shy?

There are things I can't wait to show you?

First of all, who said "nightcap" anymore?

Second of all, they only just met. Even militant lesbians must have standards, but the Doctor wanted a tongue-bath nightcap on the first date? Despite the increasing void where any attraction would have been?

It had not taken one date with Cara Spencer. It had not even taken ten minutes with Cara Spencer. That had been wildly different, though. That had been Cara Spencer. And Cara Spencer was inherently and forever the polar opposite of every woman ever to saunter over the cultivated face of the earth. Cara Spencer was salt and wind and unadulterated power, and that put the future of Dre's romantic life into pretty fine perspective.

I'll die miserable and alone.

258

The Right Kind of Woman

Feeling for the keys in the pockets of her dress pants, Dre wondered if she had even remembered to bring Tris's apartment key with her. Nothing fit in the pocket of her stupid dress pants. Nothing of any value, at least. That was why she always wore skinny jeans. Skinny jeans were littered with pockets.

She pounded again on the door and hoped they were still awake. What time was it? Nine. They went to bed so early she could never be sure precisely when they retired. She simply assumed that when the sun went down, they turned in and watched too many episodes of *A Baby Story* on The Learning Channel.

"Come on, guys!" she called, trying not to be loud enough to wake a baby while somehow being loud enough to rouse two unsuspecting women and an incubating fetus, and a Labrador. "I need my dog!"

He would have been fine to stay overnight, but she was not too proud to admit that she wanted the company. Without Buddy, she may as well have no purpose in this life.

"Come on, guys! Seriously!"

Tris unbolted the locks and cracked the panel, if only a smidge. There was an unfamiliar twinkle in her eye and Dre couldn't hazard a guess as to the cause. She was simply too tired, too worn down from the hope and then lack of hope relating to her date, and, in a sense, to her agonizing life plan, which could now never include a real relationship with a real lesbian woman, because no one else would ever bring her to the brink of attraction again.

Seriously, I'll die miserable and alone. With no one except Buddy.

What would happen to her now?

"Don't ask any questions," she said, in a more callous tone than she would ever intend toward her oldest friend. "I'm sorry. I didn't mean it."

"It's fine. I wasn't going to," her friend dodged.

"I just want my dog and I'll be out of your hair."

"About that."

Dre cut her eyes. "T, I'm serious. Just give me Buddy and I'll call you in the morning and fill you in on Dr. G."

"You really don't need to," Tris said quickly. "It's not something we had any hope in. Well, it's not something *I* had any hope in. Sam hopes for every damn thing."

Didn't that just take the sting right out of the ant bite? "You had no hope in it?"

"Right. I didn't expect it to work out. Gina's awful for you. I tried to tell you. At least, I thought I tried to tell you, but I might not have tried that hard. You were in a weird place and I didn't know how much honesty you wanted to hear. I just knew she wasn't right for you."

"And how the hell would you know what's right for me?" Besides the fact that the two of them had been friends since God was a boy.

At that, Tris kicked open the door and exposed the full scale of her living room; Willow, sleeping in the chair, wrapped in a soft, fleece blanket, Sam sprawled out with her feet and her arms dangling at odd angles, her eyes the size of tea saucers, and Cara Spencer Madeline Holloway, sitting on the loveseat wearing a dazed expression.

Cara Spencer?

Cara Spencer.

Shit. There she was.

There was Dre.

In black slacks and a white shirt, a vest, black Converses. When had she developed a taste for Converses? Why wasn't she in those damn skinny jeans that Cara had been picturing for weeks? The ones that hugged her ass in all of the right places?

Because she came from a date. She had been on a date. With another woman. And she had wanted to impress the other woman, who wasn't remotely Cara Spencer Holloway.

Fuck, she was staring. She was staring and she needed to stop. She needed to say something. She needed to say that she had driven all of this way to tell Dre that she loved her and couldn't think of being without her for one more second and that she would give it all up—the goats and the chickens and the cow and the dogs, no, not the dogs—to make her happy. She would give up her family, not that she needed to. They already loved Dre just as much as she did, and there was an increased likelihood that wherever they ended up in their Happily Ever After, Link and Atticus and Win would come along for the ride.

But "um" was all that came out when she opened her mouth. "Um...Dre...Hey."

"Hey?" Dre may have been confused, but that passed in the blink of an eye. "Why are you here? What are you doing here? In my best friend's house? In my apartment building? In Massachusetts?"

In an effort to divert attention, Tris set her beer down and stuck her hands in the pockets of her grey joggers. "Listen, Dre, I found her in the stairwell. She was lost, she had been waiting for you. I brought her here so she wouldn't have to wait in the hallway."

"And we like her," Sam pointed out, shoving herself up from the couch to balance halfway, as if this were her dying declaration and required only the best posture. "She's smart and funny, and she raises chickens and goats."

"And she left me, standing in my father's fucking driveway, in Saint Augustine, Florida."

Ouch.

"I think you two need to talk," Tris sheepishly suggested.

They had not intended to like her very much, Cara Spencer knew that much. She was not their usual choice of woman. She was not like the other women in South Waterton. She was not earthy or low key. She was, in reverse, womanly. Not that Cara Spencer really understood what that term meant, in the context of a cosmopolitan area without cows shitting in the yard or drunk brothers meandering the property, stumbling home at all hours of the night with girls from the cosmetology program at the local technical school. But they had decided to like her, all the same. They had decided she deserved a chance to tell them her side of the story, and they had decided to help her.

"I do think we need to talk," she agreed, because it seemed like the thing to say and there was no other phrase to express the same sentiment, despite what William Shakespeare may have said in that exact moment.

They needed to talk, and not in front of an audience, no matter how well-meaning. Things needed to be said and considered and worked through or worked out. Only her body wouldn't—*couldn't*—move from the couch, and her mouth was curiously dry and her brain was a hunk of muddled information and mush and phrases like *I love you, I'm sorry, Please take me back, I'll never hurt you again, I swear it.*

"I have nothing to say to you," Dre muttered, turning away as if she were about to leave, but then she didn't. "There is nothing I have not already said. You are who you are and I am who I am and we are not meant to be."

The Right Kind of Woman

"Yes, we are," Cara Spencer declared, because she knew that with a total conviction on top of which she had mapped out the entire trip to Massachusetts.

From the sidelines, Tris and Sam, now cradling their toddler to her chest, watched, as if a tennis match were about to unfold.

263

Things That Needed to Be Said

"I really don't have anything to say to you, Cara. I wasn't joking," Dre reiterated, once they were alone together, which had taken an act of congress to get her to consent to. Three people, in fact, all plying her with doe eyes and reason.

And why should she consent? What purpose would this serve? She had already been let down, like a thrill-seeker falling from a rocky outcrop of mountain, and she had no inclination to do it again in the same evening.

But they had retreated to her apartment; her tiny, metropolitan apartment that had seemed like home before, when Cara Spencer had not been standing in it, but now it felt hollow. Or suffocating. Or blank. Or empty and full all at once.

"I don't know why you drove here."

"I drove here because I love you."

"You love me?!" God, that was laughable. Farcical, stupid, childish. "You can't love me. You're not gay, remember?"

Cara Spencer winced and turned her eyes to the floor, which gave Dre a perverse sense of recompense that, in turn, made her feel incredibly guilty. "Remember what you said? Remember your holy secret? All of your hiding? How people will talk about you?" That had been the most painfully one-sided conversation of her life, having fallen so deeply in love despite the potential for consequence and pain. She had allowed Cara Spencer into her life and into her heart, and shared parts of her soul with the other woman that she could never reclaim. All to be left, bleeding and broken, on her father's back lawn, like a jilted prom date with too much time on her hands.

The Right Kind of Woman

"Of course I remember."

"Then you can't possibly love me." The words were soaked in grief as they rolled forth, driven by anger and fear and confusion and doubt. "You don't get the right to love me. Not you. Not when you're so afraid of it, not when you'd only make me hide." Tears sprang from her guarded gaze and she felt herself begin to cry, shattered and unrepentant.

She had not cried for weeks. She had not fallen into the pits of classically feminine emotion. Her heart had been smashed, eviscerated, destroyed. But she had not cried, not after finding the strength to crawl out of her Explorer, until she stood now facing Cara Spencer, the smasher, eviscerater, and destroyer of her hopes and future dreams of happiness. "I can't hide. I can't pretend. I can't be someone I'm not. And I can't be with a woman who wants that for me."

"I don't want that for you," Cara responded. "I don't want you to hide."

"But you do. You want secrecy, code words, roommate titles. You want passivity to the inequality around you."

"I just want you." Her words were simple, and they infuriated Dre.

"How can you want me?" She shrieked, as the tears fell in earnest now. "Or should I say, *when* do you want me? At night? In the dark? Hidden away? Between your legs where no one can see me? Where you brothers won't see me? Where I can hide from your little fucking town and your little fucking responsibilities?"

"Please stop."

"Why? Why should I stop, Cara? Am I making you uncomfortable?" Dre put her hands on her hips, then jerked them roughly through her own hair. "Am I being too gay for you? Too fucking queer?"

"No."

265

"Not gay enough, then?" Hysterically, she grabbed at her own crotch, forcefully and angrily. She was lost in a tidal wave of suffering, angry at God and Dr. Gina P. Laudsdale and everyone else for being happy while she wasn't good enough. "Come here, baby," she purred. "Let me show you what you've been missing."

Undulating her lower body, she bit her bottom lip, knowing it would seem more obscene than seductive. If she had been brave enough to examine the truth of her own actions, she would have seen a woman derailed, whose bitterness had taken full hold. It was hard to even see what she was mad at. Cara Spencer, society, her own sexual identity, God, Tristan and Sam, for being so in love, Dr. Gina P. Laudsdale for being so wrong for her, South Waterton, for setting the bar so high, South Carolina, for pushing it back down, her father, for being so supportive, her mother, for dying, Buddy, for shredding a couch cushion the week before (which he had never ever done before in his life)… No, not Buddy. She could never be mad at Buddy. That much was clear. But everything else, maybe.

"I love you, Andrea Martin."

"Yeah, well. If that's all you came up here to say, you can go on home now." She was fine when she was alone. More than fine. She was fucking perfect when she was alone. Self-fucking-reliant. She was Ralph-Fucking-Waldo-Emerson. She was Henry-Fucking—

"It's not," Cara Spencer sighed. "What I came here to tell you…I love you, I mean, I love you. I just didn't drive the length of the East Coast to tell you that, like, by itself."

Well, shit. "Fine." She tried to breathe normally and felt pretty stupid doing it. She was sniffling and sniffles were for children, or crazy women in the heavy throes of drastic theatrics. "Say what you have to say, then."

If Cara Spencer had come on the false hope she would get more of an invitation than that, she was in the wrong place. Forced sanity happened to be as much as Dre could muster, at the moment.

"I, um," Cara searched for the words she had outlined in the solitude on the long drive up. She searched for the words she had planned and prayed for at night in her bed. She searched for the images, the movies of her heart. She searched for the inner strength to give them life and, in doing so, bring peace to the fractured woman before her, whose soul fit so neatly next to hers in bed at night.

Then, she took a deep breath and leapt.

* * *

"I told everyone, about the gay thing. Actually, Atticus told everyone and then the town—like, the whole town—found out because he sort of yelled it out in the middle of the farmer's market. So, the cat's out of the bag on that one, not that I'd been hiding it as well as I thought I had. Turns out, they all pretty much knew. Even Granny, who was pretty cool about it, after the fact. And I'm okay with everybody knowing. It's weird, but I never realized how heavy it was to carry that around. The shame and the pain, not that I had anything, really, to be ashamed of. I'm not an axe murderer."

Holy... Just...

"I had a few days where I didn't handle it well," she continued. "I laid up for a while, until Link couldn't take it anymore."

Dre wondered just what he had done to rouse her from her wallow. On top of that, she wondered just how things had gone down in that farmer's market confessional.

"He told me the biggest mistake of my life wasn't hiding the gay thing," she looked up and stared right into Dre. "It was losing you—giving you up, because I wasn't brave enough to be myself. I didn't value you enough to put you in a higher place than that."

A bomb could have gone off in the silent aftermath of her announcement. She was out, maybe not proud yet, but out, and she had driven over a dozen hours to give breath to her love, the love they both had known was unfailingly present.

"He was right. You're so much better than that. You *deserve* so much better that. And I know I'm not a catch, not here, where you could have your pick of the well-adjusted lesbians who don't come with dogs and brothers and goats and a shitload of baggage..."

And a lame ass cow that only takes up space.

"And a cow who only takes up space, but I fucking love you. More than I ever knew love was possible in this world. More than I ever expected to find, more than I deserve to have with anyone. I love you, and I know I don't deserve you."

"You don't," Dre agreed, but she moved two steps closer because she could no longer stand it. "You really do not deserve me. Not even for a moment. Not even for a single, solitary second do you deserve me."

"I really don't, but I'll try to everyday, good and bad, Massachusetts or Greentown, for the rest of my life, if you'll let me."

Her words were sincere, Dre could tell as much from her tone. Her eyes were wide with fearful honesty, and her hand trembled a little, giving the impression of an anticipated caress, or a living flesh memory. She was nothing like that furtive Floridian version of herself, nothing like that scared and shaking girl too used to hiding in the dim light of her self-imposed prison to walk out into the sun. But still...

The Right Kind of Woman

"Hold my hand in public?" she desperately wanted to know. "Be a couple with me? No different from anyone else? No telling people we're roommates? No saying we're friends?" she spelled out each occasion, each trick and flippant deception. She left no room for trickery, because she could bear none.

To open her heart again, to fully love the ragged, wild woman before her, to be fully loved in return, she needed to know these things. To put her future in this tenuous basket, she needed to know. "No more hiding?"

All of her, her life before, the change in her soul, the feeling of helplessness and *un*belonging, of being left out and invalid, the journey, the searching, had all culminated in this one, precise moment. This one pivotal, seemingly inconsequential, randomly assigned moment in which she returned from a lackluster blind date to find the woman she loved standing in her best friend's apartment. Her trip had brought her here; out into the open, onto a beach, traipsing through hell and now tentatively staring toward freedom and happiness and love and acceptance.

"No more hiding," Cara Spencer whispered in response.

In the Spaces After

In the husky time that followed, wrapped in love and hapless, contented wonder, there had been no talk of future plans or moving or the combining of two households, or the map of the future. There had been no soulful discussions, no deep mental connections made. There had been only peace, and not the kind of frivolous peace derived from passing fancy, but the spiritual peace that could be born of lazy Sunday afternoons spent entwined with the only person necessary for breathing.

Early Monday morning, in the grey-streaked hours before dawn, wearing only the thin Led Zeppelin shirt she had come up in, Cara Spencer shivered under Dre's feather light touch, her skin rising to meet its one true owner. Buddy's snores drowned out the sounds of South Waterton's early morning commute into the larger city of Boston, and the refrigerator hummed in an odd and unexpected whinny.

"Baby…" she mumbled, drowsily, stretching like a cat while thick fingers traced her rib cage.

It was early, even for her, and especially early under Dre's strictly enforced DON'T WAKE ME BEFORE EIGHT policy.

"You okay?"

"I'm happy." Hands found her soft hips, tight breasts against the blades of her shoulders. Andrea wore a white, ribbed tank and a faded pair of boxer shorts, low slung on her waist. Cara could feel the material against her bare ass.

"Happy?"

"Happy…" Dre grabbed the rounded skin of her belly, fingertips dipping low into tendrils of soft brown. The answering flood of willing seduction made her giggle with throaty possession. "You want to make me happy, don't you?"

A low moan escaped and Cara Spencer felt her body go liquid, all heat and molten need. This was more than physical—more than carnal satisfaction, more than the simple, primal act of sex—this was a union, two independent beings with two sets of wants and needs and goals, coming together to make a life. She would be alive without Dre, but not truly. She would see without Dre, but not in the colors of the world. She would laugh and cry and feel without Dre, but not with her heart.

Reveling in the closeness of their shared heat, she locked fingers with Dre's free arm, the one beneath her neck, always pulling her closer, needing her constant nearness even as they slept. Seeking the warmth, she pushed further backwards with her rear and spread her thighs, only slightly and with painstaking slowness. Her lover's sharp intake of breath as fingers danced in the hot sting of wet desire thrilled her. Coaxed her. Soothed the still-shadowed parts of her that were as yet uncertain.

"Good girl," Andrea heaved in her ear, her voice torn and ragged, exposed, as she masterfully entered Cara spencer from behind. She was filled and driven to the brink again, just as she had been in the night before—in the hours before. Her whims and fantasies had been tempted from her, nurtured and worshipped.

"Tell me you want me."

"I want you," her hips began to rock of their volition. "Oh, how I want you, Dre."

Feeling her hips throbbing and wet, she struggled and wriggled but Andrea held her still, kept her close. Impatiently, she threw one leg over Dre's hip, only slightly behind her, urging her partner deeper and begging for more. "Please…"

"Open for me," was the revered response.

Obediently, she opened, stretching, reaching the orgasm of crescendo as Dre penetrated with most of her hand. As she opened her mouth to cry out, Dre captured it and all she could see and all she could feel and all she could taste was Dre. Dre's lips on hers and Dre's body against hers and Dre inside of her. Fireworks erupted, a symphony rang out and her back arched, breaking free.

It was the most intensely erotic experience of her life, made even more so when she opened her eyes after an eternity and saw Andrea smiling down at her, propped up on an elbow. Sweetly, she rubbed her thumb against Cara's hand and nuzzled in her hair.

"I think I like mornings," she whispered, sliding her fingers out to finger a sensuously wet pattern on her lover's thigh, burrowing further down, draping the cream-toned Ikea duvet over them both.

"It's not so much morning as it is the middle of the night."

"I'm with you."

"You *are* with me." And they were happy. And they were together. In South Waterton, Massachusetts. And that was fine. Aside from one thousand pitiful text messages sent to Dre on the daily (including mopey still shorts of Grey Baby and Greg Allman) with origins three deep in the Holloway clan, life up North wasn't so bad. Granted, it had only been a handful of days, but life up North had been oddly liberating.

Then why do I feel like part of me is missing?

"So I've been thinking." Dre flopped over on her back, and ran her hands through her hair, her silhouette illuminated in the smoky tendrils of waxing daylight, all harsh ridges and high tight peaks. All the masculine femininity that Cara Spencer could not seem to get her fill of.

Yawning, she rubbed her nose. "You've been thinking *and* you're up before eight. Who are you?"

"Yeah, well. What can I say? You've had a profound effect on me."

"Next thing you know, you'll be driving a beat up old truck and leaving laundry in a heap on the floor." That was an infinitely ridiculous notion. Andrea Martin would sprout wings and alight before she left anything in a heap on the floor. Not even the floor was left on the floor most of the time, and when it was, it was superbly clean.

"I miss your beat up old truck."

What an odd thing to say, especially when no one else in her family missed that damn truck and it was sitting, pretty as a picture, on their property at the moment.

"It doesn't even run most of the time."

"I miss the pole shed it sits under, then."

"I'll be sure to give it your regards." *When I go on back home.*

Am I going home? When am I going home? Is this home? Link and Atti and Win were all fine. Scratch that, they were a discombobulated mess, but they would be fine. They had one another and Granny, if the sky truly fell in. They were feeding the goats and the chickens and the cow, begrudgingly—most begrudgingly the cow, of course, because, as Win put it, "she's just a drain, man, and she contributes nothing." Atticus didn't much mind the absence of his truck. With two dead parents, they were two perfectly good vehicles in the enclosed garage at the Holloway main house.

Cara Spencer's breath caught for a moment. She had not really thought of her parents in ages, almost so that they had become tertiary players on the plane of her life, though not via malicious design or interpretation. Their journey had simply taken them so far from Greentown, and Greentown was home. Wasn't it?

Greentown had always been her home. She had been born there, had gone to school there, had come up along the banks of the river her family owned, worked in the fields her father farmed. Everything she knew was there, but suddenly, that didn't feel like her world anymore.

Dre felt like her world. Dre had already felt like her world, if she considered it.

"I don't want you to go home."

I don't want to go home, Cara almost said. Home didn't seem to mean home anymore. Not the physical address. Home was Dre. She knew it just as sure as she had known the sun would come up. She would need to arrange for the dogs, of course. They were as good as children to her, but Link and Atticus could drive them up and the farm could stay behind. Luxury, cosmopolitan apartments were no place for livestock.

"I want to move—" she began to say, but Dre cut her off, unintentionally.

"I want to go with you."

Cara Spencer felt her jaw drop, and she stiffened, imperceptibly.

"Hear me out," Dre reasoned with her, breathing in heavily.

It was so silly that they were both awake, the hour lost between them as hearts spoke.

"I'm a web designer. I can work anywhere there's a web. I have no family here—Greentown is actually much closer to my father and my brothers than I am right now, and I have no roots to speak of."

"But you have Tris and Sam."

Dre nodded. "And I'll always have Tris and Sam, but they are not to me what Link and Win and Atticus are to you." Link and Win and Atticus, who had come to be so close to her, as well, the trickle of unreturned correspondence opening like a floodgate of daily jokes and farm updates.

Now their group text messages were sent to five, rather than the original Holloway Four.

"But South Waterton is so…"

"Gay-friendly, I know. It's the lesbian capital of North America."

"And South Carolina is not that." South Carolina was deeply and presumably irrevocably Republican, conservative and slow to change, albeit quite scenic. For its residents and snowbird tourists, it had become all too easy to forget the festering socio-political climate when ones toes were in the sand, and one could breathe in the good, salt air eight months of the year while other states suffered under the thick blanket of perpetual winter. But life there would be no walk in the park.

"Cara, my being in Greentown will not make me any less gay, or any less proud to be gay."

Dre's being in Greentown wouldn't make her any less gay, but it stood to make Cara Spencer way more gay, and that she did fear a little. While it was one thing to be "out" in theory, it was an entirely different beast to be "out" in public. What would people say?

Hold my hand in public?

No more hiding?

"No more hiding," she said softly.

"Hmm?"

"I'd love it," she gave her answer, with no hesitation. "I'd love it if you would move with me to Greentown, but only if you want to, and only if this is serious."

"Was this ever *not* serious? You drove all the way here." Dre laughed, but Cara Spencer narrowed her eyes.

"I'm serious. I only want you to come home with me, if *you* want to come and make a home with me. I can't ask you to do this."

"Oh, baby," Dre reached again for her. "Believe me, I want to."

* * *

Watching Cara Spencer Holloway mount her would forever be the stuff of fantasy for Dre. Ever seductive, ever curious, her lover had proven a quick study, just as dedicated to pleasing as she was. Warm. Soft.

Splitting her thigh, Cara straddled her just below the hips, the wetness of her groin tantalizing through the thin boxers she wore. This was not a gender neutral pronoun. Not that there was anything egregiously wrong with a gender neutral pronoun. This was all woman. This was wide, swinging hips and heavy breasts that swayed beneath her shirt.

"Lose it," she scratched, because she wanted to see what was hers, the weight and the contour and the taut nipples in deep ink and peach. "Lose the shirt."

"Lose the pants," she instructed.

Shucking them, her pulse raced. This woman was her life, her future, her dreams and her purpose. Happy, shitty, tired or hung over, she wanted it all, and she would have it wherever they ended up. No one, no government, no law and no Bible could, or would, stand in the way of her spending the rest of her days tied to this woman.

"Marry me," she moaned, as Cara bared her cleft and shimmied to the end of the bed on her knees.

"I already am," she heard, as her partner split her muscular thighs and crawled up into the hollow between them, smelling of roses and outside and lilies and happiness.

I already am.

The Right Kind of Woman

The brush of her sweet tongue had Dre straining, her body in a jack knife off of the bed. Her heels dug into the mattress. Gingerly, Cara Spencer moved in and out, the sweet proof of her arousal dripping down onto the sheet.

I already am.

Reaching, grasping, clutching, she fisted her hands in hair, in the wild mane of brown and auburn and blonde. She felt her body tighten and release, felt Cara swimming in her secret skin, her lips a brilliant breath of hot and cold.

I already am.

Rivulets of sweat, fine beads of moisture, broke out on her arms and the muscles of her stomach, barely concealed by fabric, rippled and twisted. The sensations were unrelenting. Cara Spencer's mouth. Cara Spencer's cheek. Cara Spencer's teeth. Cara Spencer's gentle sucking. Cara Spencer was in her.

I already am.

Forcing her eyes open, Dre stared down, lifted the hair from Cara's face and watched as her lover lapped at her, awash in love and feeling. When she met her release, she would do it just like this, staring at the woman she could not live without.

It would never matter where they were, what state they chose, what life they built. It would never matter if people stared. It would never matter the title given to the relationship that had grown and blossomed and spread between them.

What *would* matter, for the orphan with no roots and a long-term plan mapped out on a spreadsheet, was that she was home.

Epilogue

Approximately thirty seconds after Dre's arrival in Greentown (the second and final arrival, not the first dimwitted attempt), she realized a litany of changes would be in order if she were to set up house with the woman of her dream, who was, in actuality, a complete slob. Practical changes, not changes of the spiritual variety, of course, although those would come along later, as they bricked a path toward forever.

Her work necessitated an office space, for one. Her car required a garage, for two, in order to protect the paint from incalculable amounts of bird shit. Not to mention, the sagging roof and dilapidated porch of the farm house, whose foundation would never stand any modifications without some serious structural patches.

Not surprisingly, it had taken all four of them—three local Holloways and one determined Yankee—to rankle any sense into Cara Spencer where the dreaded "change" was concerned. For days, she sulked and stomped and avoided and wouldn't speak to any of them; she only pouted on the porch and spent all of her time with the speckled Tasmanian Devil and the mountain lion she thought of as house pets. Until the day the construction crew drove up into the front yard, replete with a backhoe and a bucket loader, she had simply refused to acknowledge the great wave of change that was rising around her.

"Great wave of change, my ass," she would snark at Link's catchy nickname, meant to solicit smiles rather than grimaces. "There was nothing wrong with it the way that it was."

278

The Right Kind of Woman

Except the rats and the termite damage and the leak in the roof and the generally understood fact that it was roughly one hundred years old and had never been fully renovated or fixed up by licensed professionals.

Six months later, with the moving and the shaking and the sanding and the painting completed, Dre did not have to wonder if her partner had changed her tune. Cara Spencer was a new woman.

Naturally, she still rose before God showed his ass, and Dre still tried to rise at the more appropriate hour of eight. She also insisted on making the bed daily, but gone was the dank, age-old bedroom. In its stead, she cracked her lids in a seashell of pale green and cream, with a brand new master bath done in earthy tile of brown and grey, but a tawny woman who operated an entire custom-tile outfit called "RepTile."

The kitchen was larger, too, extended out over the tattered screened-in porch, which was now closer to the freshly fenced field. They had high-speed Wi-Fi, Dre's couch, and a gas range, and the lackluster Facebook bovine had been successfully relocated to a brand new barn with more space, more hay and a working light.

But the best part, the part that warmed something in them both, was the space custom-created to house guests on a semi-regular basis. Slightly detached from the home, and styled much like the Martin's beloved guest house in Saint Augustine, Dre and Cara Spencer had erected a beautiful, three-room bungalow with an adjoining bathroom and small kitchenette, "you know, in case my dad wants to bake a little when he visits, or Ami wants to bring those scones you like so much," Dre said, in justification of the exorbitant purchase funded entirely using her nest egg, because combining two lives was cause for celebration and if nest eggs couldn't be used for celebration, then what were they for, dammit?

The Right Kind of Woman

Looking out over the expanse of the property, watching as a heron dipped down into the choppy water of the Holloway River one brisk March morning, Dre could not have felt better about any of that, any of the money, the time, the stress (on Cara Spencer's part), especially as she watched Tris, Willow, Sam and budding baby Olive, who went by the more gender-neutral epithet of *Oli*, bumble out of the sliding glass doors of the guest abode and meander toward her position on the covered, weatherproof deck that had replaced the old porch. At the tail end of their third trip to Greentown—and their first since Oli's unexpected arrival—they were whittling away the hours of Tristan's all-too-brief Spring Break somewhere infinitely warmer than their snow-encrusted Massachusetts home, not that Dre needed an excuse to welcome them.

"I just can't get over the views!" Sam squeaked with glee as Willow took the steps two-at-a-time and crawled, without apprehension, into Dre's welcoming lap.

Safely embedded in her muslin sling wrap, Oli snored softly as goats whinnied off in the distance. Goats that would be sweetly chomping on grass and feed and hay after Cara Spencer threw it all out for them, before slinging more feed to the chickens and contemplating how much better her life would be if she could only convince her girlfriend/partner (who really cared what title they used) to let her get more Facebook cows, and perhaps a donkey.

"This place is really phenomenal," Tris conceded. "Is there coffee?"

Her eyes were puffy and sleep-deprived, as the eyes of new parents tend to be in those first months of life.

"Inside. I made an extra pot, just in case," Dre laughed. "I anticipated your exhaustion."

The Right Kind of Woman

Burying her hand in her partner's hair as she moved alongside her, Tristan somehow could not have appeared more at peace with her bone-deep weariness. *It's so worth it,* her grin seemed to say, and quietly, she moved through the throng of her closest friends and in through the back door to fill a steeping cup of dark roast before taking a frigid kayak trip down to Sleets Town with Link and Atticus, who were anxious to show her a newly formed brewery, assuming she could *stay* in the kayak this time.

Settling into a chair beside Dre, Sam had trouble wiping the grin from her well-rested face. "Your dad is going to be in heaven here. I mean, it's amazing. Chickens, goats—a river in your backyard. Every time I see it, I'm just blown away."

She knew how much Michael's upcoming trip would mean to Dre, how much it signified for her. Surrounded by her partner's family, it was a welcome change to host the remnants of her own. And she was all too nervous about the two sides coexisting, not that the Holloways could ever be anything less than welcoming.

"It really doesn't get old," Cara Spencer's husky voice called, coming up the back steps and emerging onto the deck, with her own A.B.'s coffee cup blowing steam in the springtime chill.

She was dressed in her farm clothes—time-worn jeans and a heavy flannel shirt buttoned over her MIT sweatshirt, heavy boots encased in mud. Her cheeks were pink and she blew in six different directions. It was the most beautiful sight Dre could ever fathom.

Holding her hand out, she felt her blood tingle just a little as Cara Spencer's palm made contact with hers.

"It really only gets better," she concurred. "Every time I sit back here and look out, I'm amazed it's what I call home."

The Right Kind of Woman

About the Author

Married to the woman of her dreams, mother to two human children and four canine progeny, **Voss Porter** is a tireless advocate for the LGBTQ community in her home state of South Carolina, a passionate storyteller, a little bit of a nerd, and a complete badass. An avid writer from the age of six, she prides herself on her ability to create realistic, modern heroines that deal with realistic, modern problems, while stumbling through life to find love, happiness, and organic groceries.

Voss can reached via email, at vossporter@gmail.com, via website at vossporter.com, on Twitter @vossporter and on Facebook.

Dark Hollows Press

Dark Hollows Press is a publisher of all genres of romantic expression.

We believe our authors are artists and their talent shouldn't be censored, so our authors present high quality stories full of romance, desire, and sometimes graphic moments that are both entertaining and erotic. We have an exclusive group of talented writers and we publish stories that range from historical to fantasy, sci-fi to contemporary.

We invite you to visit us at www.darkhollowspress.com.

Made in the USA
Middletown, DE
21 December 2016